2026 HIGH CALIBER AWARDS

2026 HIGH CALIBER AWARDS

GREG FENNEWALD JOHN HOLT N. JED TODD
ZACH WEEKES RYAN OVERTON L.J. HILSE
MH WOODWORTH RUTH CLARA

Cannon Publishing
https://www.cannonpublishing.us/

CONTENTS

VEXATION

FIRST PLACE AWARD

GREG FENNEWALD

C-21

Ten kilometers east of Mahdyn, Ukraine

"GUNNER, SABOT, TANK." Sergeant Weiss, the Tank Command or TC, ordered in a soothingly calm tone.

"Identified," responded Corporal Augustus with considerably more enthusiasm.

"Fire!"

Augie replied immediately, "On the way!" in his inimitable Lithuanian accent as he squeezed the trigger, unleashing an elongated dart of depleted uranium towards the target at a mile per second. The main gun bucked like a wild bronco and our seventy-ton M1A2 tank rocked back. The main gun breech spat out the aluminum aft cap from the 120mm round; the astringent ammonia odor of the propellant stung my nose.

Three thousand meters away, the turret of a Russian T90 tank catapulted into the air, the latest contestant in the Russian turret toss Olympics propelled by the exploding ammunition in its autoloader carousel. Augie's sabot round had found its mark.

“Target, cease fire. Battle carry sabot.”

That last bit was for me. I’m Private First Class Gertzman, the loader for C-21. I hit the ammo door switch with my right knee, glancing to make sure the main gun breech was clear and ready for another round. The ammunition blast door slid aside to reveal tubes holding 120mm ammunition oriented with the projectile facing towards the rear of the ammo rack, away from the turret interior. I karate chopped the ammunition retaining clip with my right hand and grasped the rim of a sabot round with my left hand, pulling the fifty-pound round out and flipping it end for end in a well-practiced ballet. I guided the projectile’s pointed nose onto the loading tray. My right fist shoved the base of the round into the breech, which ratcheted closed with a solid clank. I raised the arming lever, announcing “Up” into the intercom as I danced back out of the recoil path of the main gun. I did this in slightly less than four seconds, third fastest in the entire regiment. Not bad for country girl from the mountains of Bavaria.

The turret traversed across our sector, searching out more targets but finding none.

“That was a nice shot, Augie.”

“Thanks, Ice.”

“Gertie, pop up and scan our left flank.”

“Roger that, Ice,” I replied as I pushed open my hatch, allowing me to stand on my seat and extend my torso partway out of the turret. I had an M240 7.62 mm machinegun on a skate ring around my hatch but left it locked so I could steady a pair of binoculars to scan to the left and rear of our tank, looking for threats. Well-hidden amongst a thicket of brush was a sandbag bunker housing the remnants of an infantry squad. Tough soldiers, those grunts. They had lost all their vehicles and over half of their platoon, but they still stoically manned their posts and fought hard. Well-led and well-trained, just the way it’s supposed to be in the Teutonic Volunteer Brigade.

Nothing was moving nearby. The noise and violence of modern mechanized warfare had driven the wildlife and civilians away. Plumes of black smoke marked the graves of nearly a dozen Russian tanks and armored personnel carriers. The smell of those fires will haunt my dreams until the end of my days.

"One Vixen Three, this is Hatchet Five Golf, over," the infantry team leader called on the radio.

"One Vixen Three here, send it." Ice replied.

"Can you spare any coax ammo?"

"What say you, Gertie?" Ice asked on the intercom. My chest swelled with pride. Sergeant Weiss had been Master Sergeant Weiss in the U.S. Army and an honor graduate of the Abrams Master Gunner course before volunteering to join the multinational Teutonic Volunteer Brigade. He knew everything there was to know about the tank and our status, but he still deferred to me on ammo. Train your crew well enough and they won't miss you when you're gone. This was why it was so competitive to get onto his crew and hard to stay there. Ice was a natural leader and expert tanker.

"We have four boxes rigged for cross-leveling, Ice."

I kept my eyes scanning my sector but could picture a satisfied grin on Ice's face. He had asked me months ago how to cross-level ammo with other tanks efficiently. The only efficiency for the fifty-pound main gun rounds was a strong back, but machinegun ammo was different. I broke it down and thought it through. I had rigged a harness from paracord to sling four boxes of 7.62x51mm belted ammo over my shoulders, allowing me to carry eight hundred rounds while keeping my hands free for my carbine. We had rehearsed during training exercises, and the paracord harness worked slick.

"I need you to schlep that ammo to the grunts. Give them this too," he instructed, handing me a full can of Copenhagen snuff.

Ammo and dip? Ice must like these grunts. I thought to myself.

"Hicks, shut down the turbine and man the loader's position while Gertie is on a walk about."

Hicks said something unintelligible into the intercom as Augie traversed the turret a tad so Hicks could squirm back into the turret and take my spot. He was from Gloucester, MA and had an accent so thick that even the other Americans could barely understand him. Ice kept him because he was a good driver and an absolute magician fixing and maintaining the tank and just about anything else that needed some attention.

I unhooked the intercom cable from my helmet and clambered down to the ground where I could reach the ammo rig strapped to the outside of the turret sponson box. Load settled on my shoulders; I trudged off towards the infantry bunker with more confidence on my face than I felt in my heart. The hundred-and twenty-meter journey ended uneventfully, and the infantry snagged the ammo cans with thanks and enthusiasm. One soldier was linking the contents of two cans together to make a four-hundred-round belt. Another, with a bloody bandage wrapped around a thigh, was stripping rounds out of the metallic links and filling rifle magazines with the rounds. I handed the can of snuff to the team leader. His eyes grew wide, and he sniffed deeply as he popped the lid of the can, deftly placing a pinch in his cheek. He passed the can around the bunker for any so inclined.

"Are you the one they call Gertie?"

"Yes, sergeant."

"We've heard about you. You're legit. I'll let you buy me a beer once this is all over. Head back to your tank and get ready to kill more orcs."

I gave him a nod and a thumbs up and turned back to C-21, spirits buoyed by the infantry sergeant's compliment and infectious confidence.

I was ninety meters into my return journey when the unmistakable buzz of a covey of drones came from the northeast. I scurried as fast as I could, desperately looking cover. Hicks was shouting something guttural, likely lyrics from a Nordic death metal band, as he cut loose with short bursts from the loader's M240. Ice was banging away with his personally owned Benneli shotgun, scoring some hits based on his enthusiastic shouts. I dove behind the stump of a shattered oak tree and searched desperately for drones, hoping the drone operators wouldn't bother with a single person stumbling about.

I heard drones heading in the same direction followed by small explosions as they deployed grenades against their targets or pulled a kamikaze attack. The deep booms of C-21's active protection system contrasted with the higher cracks of the drone warheads, a deadly symphony building to a crescendo before ebbing into an eerie and uneasy quiet.

Desperate to help my crew, I scrambled back to C-21, heart pounding in my chest. Wheeled drones had broken the right track in two places and fractured a roadwheel arm. C-21 was now an immobile pillbox. Hicks was slumped forward onto the M240, his back ripped open by a drone explosion that took his life. The TC's hatch was closed, giving me hope that Ice and Augie might still be alive. I wrestled Hicks' corpse out of the loader's hatch an onto the bustle rack at the rear of the turret. There is no graceful or respectful way to move deadweight by yourself. I knew Hicks would forgive me.

I climbed through the loader's hatch, careful to not slip on the blood Hicks left behind and saw Ice leaning against the side of the turret, not moving. Shrapnel had shredded the left side of his body. His hands held a tourniquet he was unable to fasten around his thigh as he lost consciousness. Augie had most of his face and neck ripped away by the blast. A drone had somehow managed to lob a grenade into the turret. Everyone I loved was dead. I plopped onto the loader's seat and cried, mourning my friends, connecting the intercom cable to my helmet out of habit. One drone had loitered behind and dropped its grenade on the turret. The grenade landed behind my hatch and exploded, doing minimal damage but the concussion knocked me silly.

My overwhelmed mind went to its safe place, my grandfather's cabin in its idyllic Alpine meadow.

Grandfather seemed impossibly old and had sad, tired blue eyes; eyes that had seen war, suffering, and death. Those eyes had also seen love and triumph and the power of family. The sadness had a depth to it. His white hair was thin and wispy, his wrinkled face a testament to a hard life well-lived. He would watch me struggle with chores without comment until I respectfully asked him how to do it better. He would demonstrate and explain, and I got things done much faster. He was a perceptive man but let me flail and fail before he would help. He was like Ice in many ways. He would catch me daydreaming on the front porch, a thick book balanced on my lap and a pensive look pinching my brows, asking, "What vexes thee, little one?" Those sad blue eyes still conveyed warm love and concern. I smiled at the happy memories.

What vexes thee, little one?

The calculus homework, grandfather. It's just too hard. I floated between dim consciousness and dreamland, recalling how grandfather patiently tutored me in the subjects he could. He stressed to never stop thinking. Break it down and think it through, he would say.

What vexes thee, little one?

It's the girls at school, grandfather. They are so mean...

What vexes thee, little one?

I'm trying to tell you, grandfather. I noted a tone of impatience in his voice. *Was he angry at me? I'm sorry, grandfather!*

"One Vixen Three, this is Lima One, over."

Callsigns! C-21 was One Vixen Three and the regimental tactical operations center was Lima One. I clumsily toggled the lever on the side of my helmet and said "Mmphlr grzzlfiplip." *What the heck was that?*

"Last calling station, say again, over."

I greedily swallowed some tepid water from my hydration bladder and tried again. "This is One Vixen Three, over." I was proud of my transmission despite the energy it took out of me. *Can't embarrass Ice.*

"Welcome back, One Vixen Three. Sitrep, over."

My training came flooding back to me. *Get it together! Represent!*

"This is One Vixen Three Lima, drone attack, everyone is KIA but me. Fuel is yellow, ammo is red, checking systems status now."

I gingerly worked around the bodies of Ice and Augie as I checked the fire control computer and thermal imaging sight. All seemed operational although battery power would run down eventually. Hicks had said we had maybe two hours of run time for the turbine engine before the fuel gave out. Now, how to extract two corpses, each heavier than me? We had trained for this, making use of the chain hoist used to disassemble the main gun breech and the strong nylon straps sewn into our Nomex jumpsuits. I labored mightily, doing my best to ignore the macabre horror of it all.

"One Vixen Three Lima, status, over."

A red haze drifted in front of my eyes. "I'm a little busy hauling the shattered corpses of the only family I had left out of the turret, so unless you are going to back away from PowerPoint and come help me, stay off my back!" I had painfully learned to channel my hostility towards authority, but the events of the day left me in a feral mood.

66th Free Armor Regiment TOC

Twelve kilometers west of C-21

"Give her some time, TACO. Gertie is scrappy and resourceful but alone. She will figure it out. C-21 can report on enemy movements if she can get the thermal sight up," proclaimed Colonel Westerkamp, the Regimental Commander.

The Tactical Operations Center, or TOC, was in a purloined classroom at the local middle school, students and faculty had long since departed for safety further west. A large folding table in the center of the room supported a large map sheet of the area with clear acetate covering it with grease pencil and colored marker symbols all over.

Colonel Westerkamp glared at the map, frowning as if the force of his will could change the increasingly desperate situation. "The Orcs must know that side of our line is destroyed. They still like the old Frunze Academy dictum of reinforcing success. They will push again, and hard. Any useful intel from the puzzle palace?"

Captain Suharta, the tactical officer or TACO from the S3 Operations shop, replied promptly. "Second echelon armor, T-62M's in battalion strength, heading our way about twenty kilometers east of the front line. They are followed by motorized infantry in BTR-80's in an understrength regiment. Intel says the Brigadier in command is a political appointee and not known to be particularly bright or energetic. And, for the record, I prefer Excel to PowerPoint."

"A blind man could see the weakness in our line," the colonel added as he frowned anew and pondered the situation. "Here's what we're going to do," he said as his face lit up with energy and resolve.

"XO, get to the railhead and expedite the unloading of the rest of the regiment. Step on toes and kick asses as needed. Send them forward in no less than company strength to this ridge line to take hasty defensive positions. If the situation warrants, lead everything you have forward in a counterattack."

Lieutenant Colonel Smythe-Jones, the regimental XO, nodded with a raised eyebrow on his patrician face asking an unspoken question.

"I'll get to that Sebastian. Bear with me. Sergeant Major, we need you to go schmooze, bamboozle, or torture the French liaison officer to release the French Foreign Legion infantry battalion to reinforce us. They are spoiling for a fight, are tougher than woodpecker lips, and the mere mention of them makes the Orcs edgy."

Sergeant Major Pagoni, a barrel-chested man that exuded strength and barely constrained violence, smiled broadly, eyes twinkling and bald head reflecting the ceiling lights. Breaking field grade officers to his will was his favorite hobby.

"S3, execute our ops plan. Beg, borrow, or steal some artillery support. I'm taking HQ-60 and HQ-50 forward to reinforce C-21. And yes, Sebastian, I'm sure. We must hold them off long enough for you and the FFL to get into position."

The XO knew better than to argue with the colonel and the Sergeant Major was eagerly anticipating his role in the plan. The colonel left the TOC and jogged to HQ-60, giving Master Sergeant Adebimpe, his gunner and the regimental master gunner, the spinning hand motion to crank up the turbine engine. Settled into the TC's position, the colonel keyed the radio and said, "This is Reaper Six at REDCON one. Gentlemen, shoot to kill." Somehow, the cheesy lines worked for the colonel, his legend growing with each successful battle.

C-21

I had finally gotten both bodies out of the turret and into the bustle rack. I gobbled down a granola bar and more stale water while running through the systems checks and wiping blood and gore off the controls. I hadn't showered in four days before being doused with the blood of my dead crew. Fragrant was an understatement. I used the muzzle reference sensor to update the main gun's boresight, test fired the coaxial M240 machinegun, and checked the fire control computer for errors. The crosswind sensor was down, damaged by the drone warhead that killed Hicks. I left the gunner's primary sight in thermal mode and climbed up into the commander's position. One of the two radios was down because its antenna had been shredded, but the other was obviously working. I wrestled a full can of .50 caliber ammunition up to the M2 machinegun mounted on the TC's cupola. I triggered the radio and reported, "Lima One, this is One Vixen Three Lima, REDCON one."

"This is Reaper Six on the way to reinforce. You are now One Vixen Three Actual. Observe and report your sector. Save some Orcs for us."

My spirits were bolstered by the colonel's swagger and confidence, and help was on the way. I remained in the commander's position, scanning to the east with the thermal sight through the commander's sight extension. My efforts were rewarded with the sight of dismounted infantry in a single file trying to get within RPG range. They didn't use three to five second rushes, bounding overwatch, or any other recognizable dismounted movement technique, just a slow single file with minimal attention to their flanks.

I slipped down into the gunner's seat since I was far more competent with those controls than the one-handed commander's override. I toggled the master arming switch to coax, flipped the sight to ten power magnification, and drew a bead on the ghostly white figures moving against a green background. I mashed the laser rangefinder button and the sight reticle jumped slightly as the fire control computer calculated the aiming point needed for a hit given the distance and relative movement involved. I pulled the trigger and rotated the turret across the target, sending a long burst of thirty rounds into the Orc squad. About half of them fell, dead or mortally wounded. The remainder hit the dirt, crawling desperately for cover. A steady diet of five-round suppressive bursts dispatched two more and kept the last three motionless in the mud.

"One Vixen Three, artillery inbound."

Artillery? Excellent! Then I stopped daydreaming and closed the loaders hatch, armed the main gun with sabot loaded, and locked the commander's hatch in the open protective position. I sat in the commander's position, using the vision blocks to scan close by and the thermal sight for further away. I sent a short burst towards any movement or hot spot I saw. The artillery dropped three-round barrages, stomping the Orc squad out of existence. There must be a friendly drone observing and adjusting the fire.

The infantry bunker was still in the fight, weaving a deadly web with a machinegun and grenade launcher fire. I hoped for more Orcs, craving more vengeance before they got me.

"One Vixen Three, this is Reaper 6," Colonel Westerkamp radioed. "We have you in sight and are observing from a thousand meters back. I'm sending you my lima if I can convince him to walk that far."

That made me chuckle. Corporal Sutton was his loader and the fastest loader in the regiment. He was also a fitness freak. He could be a tank gunner in his own right but preferred to stay on the colonel's tank with its associated prestige.

It only took Sutton eight minutes to make the trek, loudly shouting, "Friendly coming in!" before climbing up to the turret from the rear. He had a face that a dog would love only if a porkchop was tied around his neck, but it was the most beautiful thing I had ever seen as I unlocked the loader's hatch.

"The colonel said you needed a real tanker up here," he said with a rakish grin.

"Then why did he send you?"

"Ha! Good one, Gertie. The colonel did say you are the Actual now, where do you want me?"

"You are a better gunner than me, so you gun and I load." It tweaked my pride a bit to admit that, but it was the right call for the mission.

He rapidly ran through the gunner's and commander's stations, before asking, "How's the ready rack?"

"Three rounds sabot, two rounds HEAT, twelve empty tubes. Six rounds sabot in the semi-ready rack. Let's shuffle."

Sutton helped me move the six rounds over, an annoying task with the need to wrangle thick metal blast doors open and shut. I secured the last round in the ready rack and Sutton asked, "What's in the hull stowage?"

"Four rounds of M829A4 sabot and two rounds of M1028 cannister."

"How the heck did you get your grubby hands on super sabot and cannister?"

"Ice has connections."

Sutton shrugged, then said, "I'm jealous. Let's get those rounds into the ready rack, then charge the batteries."

He rotated the turret to allow access to the hull ammo stowage compartments and kept watch while I wrangled the rounds into the ready rack. He knew it was a one-person job; the inside of the turret was not particularly spacious. The M829A4 was the best American sabot round for the 120mm main gun but in short supply. The M1028 turned the main gun into a giant shotgun with nearly eleven-hundred tungsten ball bearings each ten millimeters wide leaving the muzzle at nearly fifteen-hundred meters per second.

I wiggled into the driver's hole and cranked the turbine to charge the batteries. The thermal sight and hydraulic motors that moved the turret took a lot of energy. Twenty minutes of run time had the batteries topped off. They were only three days old. Ice had connections. "Shutting down, we have fuel for three more charges."

I crawled back into the turret and topped off the coax bin, replacing the rounds I had fired earlier. Sutton looked at me with concern in his eyes and said, "The loader's 240?"

"Yeah, I know," I replied and took a deep breath to calm my nerves. No getting around it, I had to check the M240, it might still be functional. I hoped not. The thought of cleaning Hicks' blood from the gun made me queasy and sad. My hopes were answered by the feed tray cover of the M240 which was bent like a banana.

"Loader's 240 is down, feed tray cover. No spare onboard and it doesn't make sense to move the coax 240 up here."

"Roger that. I think I'll scan from the commander's seat with you up in the loader's hatch with binoculars and keep your night vision handy. The Orcs might try to get tricky tonight."

We scanned our sector diligently and exchanged idle banter to bring some awkward normalcy into this maelstrom. I felt a lot better having Sutton with me. Going into combat alone just plain sucks.

"One Vixen Three, this is Hatchet Five Golf, over."

"Send your traffic, Hatchet." I replied.

"Dismount headed your way with gifts. Don't shoot him."

"Roger, have him stop at thirty meters."

I toggled the intercom. "Sutton, I'm going to dismount and meet him."

I crouched at the rear of the tank, which was in a hull defilade position with very little besides the turret visible at ground level. The dismount had fallen back fifty meters before turning towards the tank and ended up approaching from the rear. He called out loudly several times before answering the challenge question correctly. I lowered my rifle and waved him in. I recognized him vaguely from my ammo drop off earlier. He looked more tired and dirty now, eyes red with fatigue and uniform filthy but his rifle looked like it had just been issued from the arms room. He had a crate of M18 Claymore mines strapped to his back along with a spool of commo wire. He shrugged it off his shoulders and said, "Sarge says we have more than we need, and these might come in handy over here now that your tank is immobilized. He also wants to rig the sound powered telephone. He's convinced the Orcs can home in on our radios even though they frequency hop."

"Awesome, appreciate the help!"

"I can show you how to place them," he said unenthusiastically, hoping to get back to his bunker before the next attack. I felt the same way when I took his squad the ammo cans.

"I know how, but if you help me, we get done faster and back to our posts."

He smiled in grudging agreement. We spread the six mines evenly fifteen meters in front of the tank with about twenty meters in between. That was a lot closer than the book called for but fit our position best. There's no such thing as overkill when it comes to claymore mines. We wired the mines together so they would all detonate at once, unleashing a storm of tungsten ball bearings that would decimate dismounted troops.

Our task complete, the infantryman hurried back to his squad while I threaded the copper wire of the firing circuit to the commander's hatch with plenty of slack. Sutton taped the detonator to the handhold on the ceiling of the turret. Either of us should be able to reach it there. A bungee cord secured the telephone handset to the intercom box on my side of the turret. C-21 did not have the external phone connection on the right rear of the tank like some of the former U.S. Marine tanks had.

"Vixen, this is Reaper 6. Observe and report for now, do not engage. Adjust fire if we get mortars or artillery back, over."

"Reaper 6, Vixen, understood, over," I replied.

"As if the Orcs don't know where we are already," Sutton said.

"True, but would you pick any other two tanks to overwatch us?"

"You have a point there."

"I have to know, how does HQ-60 do a three-person crew?"

Sutton laughed and answered, "Depends who is watching. The colonel has an ego just like everyone else, and he has shot an entire qualification run from the commander's position. Today, he will load. He has a lot more going on than fighting his tank, and his gunner, Berhoffer, is insanely good."

Hearing that the colonel would be loading reassured me for some strange reason. The old man might even break a sweat.

"Contact front!" Sutton exclaimed. "Looks like a pair of wheeled scout vehicles at our eleven o'clock, range thirty-eight-hundred meters. Call them BRDMs."

I looked at the map folded on top of the turret and got a rough grid coordinate, then radioed the contact report to Reaper 6.

"Roger, Vixen. Reaper element will take them out, continue to observe and hop to my push."

The colonel wanted us on his radio frequency to simplify things a bit. He had at least two other frequencies in his ear.

Sutton kept an eye on the BRDMs as they slowly advanced while also searching behind them for the next wave. Orc doctrine had a tank company next, ten tanks on paper but most units on both sides were understrength.

"Scuttlebutt I overheard on the road march up here is a battalion of T62s and a regiment of infantry in BTR-80s. Old equipment, but still dangerous. The Orc general in charge is supposedly a parade ground martinet, a political brown noser."

That fit the stereotype alright, but the Orcs fought hard enough to reduce our section of the line from four tanks and four APCs to one tank and a partial infantry squad in a sandbag bunker.

"Reaper element engaging, out."

HQ-60 and HQ-50 fired at the same time and both BRDMs thirty-five-hundred meters to our front exploded when hit by the HEAT rounds. HEAT was the right choice for the lightly armored BRDMs. The high explosive warheads devastated the vehicles. A sabot round would have passed right through and possibly leave the scouts inside still functional.

The telephone wired to the infantry bunker growled a warbling tone driven by a hand crank. I picked it up and said, "Go for Vixen."

"Observing dismounts in the dry creek, six to ten. The creek is masked from here. You should pick them out at your ten o'clock, six-hundred meters."

Sutton traversed left and searched briefly before announcing, "Tally ho. Perfect coax shot in a minute. Call it in and get permission to engage."

I said into the telephone, "Targets under observation, nice job, out." I then keyed the radio, "Reaper, Vixen, dismounts in squad strength one hundred meters north of TRP N07. Requesting permission to engage, over."

"Smoke them, Vixen, no indirect support available."

Sutton slid down into the gunner's seat, preparing to fire the coax at the Orcs. I stayed up out of my hatch scanning to both sides in case someone was sneaky. Sutton said, "On the way," and fired a textbook burst into the enemy. He followed up with a few short bursts to either finish them off or encourage them to not come any closer. I preferred the former, but either would do right now.

"Target suppressed."

"Roger," then on the radio, "Reaper, Vixen, engaged and suppressed dismounts, continuing to observe, over."

"Roger that Vixen. Expect more guests soon, out."

"Keep loading sabot unless I call for HEAT. Save the super sabot for now." Sutton said. I gave him a thumbs up and opened the ammo rack door to make sure none of the rounds had moved to a different tube on their own. More of a coping mechanism than a trust issue.

Sutton caught sight of the lead platoon of the expected tank company at four-thousand meters and I called it in. Reaper told us to hold fire until he fired. Three M1A2s against three T62s. Great odds on our side, but the other seven tanks in the T62 company would only be a few hundred meters behind, less if their training was shoddy. Sutton was dialed in on his target as it trundled closer, turret swinging left and right as the crew searched for us.

"Reapers, prepare to fire in three, two, one, fire."

Sutton called out "On the way" as he squeezed the trigger. The main gun recoiled then the breech spit out the aft cap. I flew into the reloading ballet instinctively, slamming home another sabot round and raising the arming lever with a report of "Up."

"Target, cease fire," Sutton said after observing for a few moments. The T62 was burning fiercely but the turret was intact. It had a human loader with traditional shell type ammunition, not an autoloader with exposed propellant charges in a carousel like the T72s and newer Russian tanks.

I popped up and looked through binoculars, easily seeing three burning hulks more than two miles away. I started scanning the creek bed where the RPG team had tried to approach. HQ-60 and HQ-50 would easily spot any vehicles before I could, but a lone infantryman with an RPG or armed drone was a serious threat.

Second Guards Tank Army command bunker

Forty-five kilometers east of C-21

"General Rokossov, there are only three Abrams in that sector. Their reinforcements are playing paddy cakes at the railhead. This is our best opportunity yet to launch Operation Borodino. We must act now, for the glory of Mother Russia!"

"Your enthusiasm is commendable. Such passion for duty and the Rodina demands its place in the vanguard," the General replied. Major Yevchenko, the passionate deputy operations officer and suspected GRU mole, stood stock still, struggling to decipher any hidden meaning in the general's blank Slavic face and flat tone of voice.

"I will grant you the privilege of leading the infantry assault. Starshina Rombakh, get the Major a rifle and a ride to the lead air assault helicopter. I wish my duty allowed me to accompany you, Major."

Yevchenko's mouth opened and closed like a fish out of water, but he made no sound. Starshina Rombakh gently ushered him out of the mildewed canvas smell of the command bunker and up to ground level.

General Rokossov sighed and shared a knowing glance with Colonel Stravinski, his Chief of Staff. "That brown nosing chekist bastard is annoying, but not wrong. Launch the operation immediately. Make sure that peacock Colonel with the two T-14 Armata tanks crosses the LD on time."

"I will see it done, sir."

C-21

"Vixen, Reaper, imagery shows the rest of the T-62 battalion is eight clicks out and deployed to attack. Mech infantry will follow. Going to be some hot and heavy work, over."

"Roger Reaper. We will save a few for you, out."

I used the sound powered phone to update the infantry bunker. They were out of anti-armor rockets by now and we agreed they would observe only until dismounted infantry came into machinegun range. Through my binoculars I caught sight of faint black clouds of diesel exhaust. Russian diesel fuel was not renowned for quality and the T-62s were at least fifty years old. I talked Sutton onto them, but the thick forest still obscured the tanks themselves. I estimated the grid coordinates and called in the sighting to Reaper.

The clouds of diesel exhaust stopped moving. "Probably consolidating before they launch their assault," Sutton said. "Better button up, they will use any artillery they have." I pulled my hatch closed and locked it.

"Vixen, Reaper, rocket artillery inbound, hunker down and enjoy the show, over"

"Reaper, Vixen, roger, out."

Overhead, MLRS rockets streaming flaming white exhaust flew east, over the consolidating tanks, releasing hundreds of submunitions onto the tanks and mechanized infantry regiment following too closely. The rockets' bomblets disabled two tanks with engine deck hits and scratched a few more. The aged BTR80s did not fare well, neither did the gaggle of supply trucks carrying fuel and ammunition. Chaos and confusion reigned as commanders lost control of their units. The T62 survivors were effectively cut off from reinforcement and supplies. This was when they normally lost their martial fervor and hightailed it back the way they came. In every battle, the enemy gets a vote. Today, they vote no.

"Contact front!" Sutton shouted. "Many tanks advancing in coherent formation, four-thousand, five-hundred meters and closing." I radioed in the contact report to Reaper.

"We see them, Vixen. Engage at will and good hunting, Reaper out."

Sutton picked a tank in the second line with two antennas marking it as a T62K command tank. "I'm going to transition to other targets real quick. It won't take them long to find us since we can't displace to another position. I'll pop the smoke grenades after we fire two rounds. We must fire as fast as we can for as long as we can."

"I'm with you, let's kill some Orcs."

"I can see why Ice fought so hard to keep you on his tank."

That was a supreme compliment to me. I rubbed at my eyes; the turret was dusty. I raised the main gun arming lever with gusto and reported, "Up."

Sutton waited until the T62K was four-thousand meters away before he said, "On the way." Boom, followed by the reloading dance. Rinse and repeat with metronomic regularity until we had left seven T62s burning fiercely in the distance. The stench of the white phosphorous grenades that cloaked C-21 in thick smoke mixed with the ammonia reek of the main gun rounds, assaulting my nostrils with abandon. A shrieking noise and screech of rending metal made me flinch. A 115mm projectile from a T62 tore through the air just above the turret and hit the M2 .50 caliber machinegun, sending it and its mounting mechanism flying away behind us. Sutton was fast and put an end to the tank that had barely missed us.

Reaper element joined in, decimating T62s wherever they could be found. The new threat drew away some of the return fire intended for C-21. HQ-60 and HQ-50 represented the regiment well, destroying seventeen T62s before the last handful popped their brown smoke grenades and backed away fifty meters before pivoting and roaring off to the East, dark clouds of diesel exhaust marking their progress. One tank stopped after four hundred meters to take a quick shot at Reaper. Berghoffer slammed a sabot through the exposed engine deck and out through the front glacis. We were impressed by the discipline to halt under fire to cover the withdrawal of your comrades and didn't really blame the remainder when they popped smoke, turning suddenly to throw off a sight picture, and firing main gun rounds far over our heads. Maybe a witness would survive and expound on the hearty warrior spirit present in all Russians.

"Down to three super sabot and two cannister. Super sabot loaded."

I opened my hatch and tossed out aft caps piled on the turret floor, then buttoned up again. Sutton updated the fire control computer so it knew it was firing M829A4 now instead of M829A1.

Sutton scanned for fresh targets and said, "Ice said you were real smart and went to University before this."

"Well, nothing cures you of thinking you're smart like studying astrophysics."

"Ha! I'm six months from my journeyman stone mason test, the last test I'll ever take."

Our amiable chatter helped us relax just a little. Sutton had me open my hatch and scan with binoculars. I appreciated the fresh air and the view. The fires of destroyed armored vehicles lit the darkening horizon with flickering shadows. I got my night vision goggles out of the sponson box, seeing a box of twelve-gauge number four buckshot next to the goggles. I took that too and reloaded Ice's Benelli M4 semi-auto shotgun and strapped it down next to my hatch. My rifle was a sixteen-inch barreled AR15 from Ice's collection. Americans and their guns. The semi-auto rifle was a good weapon, but just about worthless against drones. Ice had let me fire a few boxes of shells through his fancy Benelli. I was eager to try my luck on drones and Orcs. Eight rounds of twelve-gauge should leave a mark. Snort.

Our sector of the front was quiet, causing feelings of foreboding. Sutton and I traded positions every thirty minutes, trying to keep sharp. Sutton poured instant coffee into his mouth and worked it into a wad in his cheek, like it was tobacco. My stomach lurched at the sight of it but chugging the last cold Red Bull can from the cooler gave me a burst of energy and a belch that would make Grandmother faint.

The brief respite of quiet was over all too soon. "Contact front, forty-eight-hundred meters. Weird thermal signature, can you make anything of it?"

I clambered over to the TC's position and looked through the sight extension. The thermal sight showed a low-slung tracked vehicle with a huge looking cannon protruding well forward of the front glacis. The cannon swung side to side like a hound sniffing for prey. An identical vehicle slowly rolled into view, covering the lead vehicles. I was puzzled by the unusual shape. Vehicle identification always came easily for me. An idea finally popped into my head.

"Sutton, could those be T14 Armatas?" The Armata was the most advanced tank the Russians had, featuring an unmanned turret with all crew in the hull. Standing orders called for reporting all contacts with advanced Russian tech. The T14 was rarely seen overall and never within two hundred kilometers of the front lines. Something unusual was going on. I radioed the TOC immediately.

"Vixen, Reaper. Do not engage, observe only until Reaper opens fire, over."

"Reaper, Vixen, roger, out."

Sutton tracked the two tanks, commenting on the how low they looked compared to a T62 or T90. "If super sabot doesn't take them out…"

"Why would they send the best tanks they have here?"

"And why are they alone?"

An icy cold hand grabbed my intestines and squeezed. "Are we sure they are alone?"

Sutton cursed colorfully. We had been so focused on tracking the T14 tanks that we lost awareness of the rest of our sector. "Hop into the TC's position and use the CITV while I keep tracking them."

I did as he said and panned the Commander's Independent Thermal Viewer quickly at first, then settled into a disciplined pattern, just like Ice trained me to. Something strange flickered in the distance, ghostly white shapes shimmering and disappearing and reappearing. "I've got something for you to check out when we're done with the T14s. Not a current threat, not sure what it is."

"Roger that, get ready to load, I think Reaper 6 will open fire soon."

I clambered back to my loader's seat. It wasn't a long wait.

"Reaper elements, engage on my mark, three, two, one, mark."

"On the way." Sutton said, sending a super sabot towards the T14, scoring a hit made obvious by the Explosive Reactive Armor detonating. I slammed the next round into the breech, slapped the arming lever up, and called, "Up."

"On the way." The target brewed up this time, hellish orange flames shooting up out of the hatches.

Sutton trained his reticle on the second T14 in time to see it fire the shot that took out HQ-50, the blinding light from the blow off panels launched skyward by exploding ammunition standing in stark contrast to the darkening sky. I loaded the last sabot round and said, "Up, last sabot."

HQ-60 fired a round into the T14's frontal arc a fraction of a second before Sutton fired into its left flank, igniting a debate on which round actually destroyed the last T14.

I loaded the strange looking cannister round. "Up, cannister loaded."

Sutton tapped at the ballistic computer to select cannister from the options. "Let's see what that weird shimmer was."

"Moving," I called out as returned to the TC's position to use the CITV to search the darkness with the surreal green of the thermal sight. The weird swirling lights had not moved and seemed to be three different mounds or clusters.

"Lasing," Sutton said, sending a beam of coherent light to measure how far away the target was. The mound he had lased flashed brilliantly in response, an automatic defensive reaction intended to foil laser guided weapons. The laser really kicked the hornet's nest as all three mounds grew taller, then started moving across our front at a forty-five-degree angle that would bring them within six hundred meters of us.

Sutton toggled his sight to day channel and said, "Look at that! They are using coordinated drone swarms to cover helicopters. Thermal jamming, nets of chaff to mess up radar, reactive to lasers, coordinated lights."

"The helicopters are huge; they look like Mi-26's. Those can carry something like eighty troops." I added.

"You thinking what I'm thinking?" Sutton asked.

"It would be the most epic fire command ever!"

"Then do the honors. We have about fifty seconds."

I moved back to my loader's station and raised the arming lever. With a feral grin I said, "Gunner, cannister, chopper."

"Identified."

"Fire."

"On the way."

Boom, the aft cap clanged to the turret floor, and I shoved the last round home announcing, "Up. Last round"

Six hundred meters away, a cloud of ten-millimeter tungsten balls tore into the coordinated fleet of drones and the Mi-26 cargo helicopter. The tungsten balls were not ballistically efficient and shed their velocity quickly, slowing to barely eleven hundred meters per second by the time they started hitting drones and the chopper. The tungsten projectiles punched right through the aluminum skin of the helicopter and the soldiers inside, wreaking grisly havoc and leaving few survivors, all of whom wished they were already dead when the flames roared through the fuselage.

Sutton traversed the turret slightly, tracking a second Mi-26 as it desperately tried to evade. "On the way." The chopper managed to turn south so the hail of tungsten shot hit the right rear quarter, damaging the tail rotor transmission. It wobbled back and forth a few times before spinning in circles and falling from the sky. The pilot struggled gallantly to control the crash landing, but it was hopeless. Another fireball marking more graves. The third Mi-26 dove sharply for the ground and was lost from view.

The sound powered phone growled. I answered and spoke briefly to the infantry bunker. "Infantry sneaking up the creek bed again, but at least thirty of them this time." Sutton opened the M240 coaxial machinegun's feed tray cover and liberally doused the moving parts with oil.

I opened my hatch and used my night vision goggle to look for the Orcs. Sutton spotted them before me. The infantry bunker held fire until Sutton cut loose. The coax and the fire from the bunker stopped the infantry cold, forcing them to seek cover. I kept my eyes open and called targets to Sutton.

The faint sounds of whistles floated through the air when no one was firing. It seemed to be coming from our direct front, not to our left front where the creek provided some cover and concealment the Orcs had tried to use several times.

"The troops from that third chopper might be organized and coming this way. I think I heard whistles."

"Might be time to bug out, we're not going to hold them for long with just the coax."

I sent a sitrep to Reaper 6, who told me to fall back on foot if it was safe to do so. Reinforcements were on the way, just survive.

We decided to see if there was room for us in the bunker. I picked up the phone. "Hatchet 5 Golf, this is Vixen."

"Golf here."

"Do you have room for two friendly visitors?"

"Absolutely if you bring more linked 7.62mm with you."

"All we can carry. Five minutes."

"Roger, out."

Sutton and I were frantically busy preparing to scuttle the tank so it could not be repaired then used against us. I duct taped a thermite grenade in the open breech. It would burn hot enough to melt and warp steel, making the main gun good only for scrap. Sutton taped a 500-gram block of C4 explosive to the bottom of the thermal imaging sight. He then rigged a common detonator between the thermite grenade and the C4 while I dragged hundreds of rounds out of the coax ammo box and shoved it into nylon assault pouches. Sutton dismounted the coax machinegun and asked, "Ready?"

"Yes," I replied, facing my fear of what would happen next.

Sutton launched the last salvo of smoke grenades; I triggered the claymore mines, all six exploding simultaneously, showering steel BBs in an arc to our front. I popped my hatch and scrambled out of the turret and onto the ground behind the tank's hull. I ditched my AR-15 and magazines for it so I could carry more M240 ammo and Ice's fancy shotgun. Sutton followed out the loader's hatch since the damage of 115mm round that blew off the M2 .50 caliber had completely jammed the commander's hatch.

We heard shouts and screams to the east. Our claymores found targets. The realization of how close the Orcs were lent strength to my lungs and legs as I ran harder than I ever had before. Sutton, the limber gym rat, easily out distanced me and glided like the wind until he was thirty meters ahead. He stopped and dropped into a prone firing position and covered me as I ran by. My lungs were burning and chest heaving when I plopped to the ground to cover Sutton. The cheeky bastard grinned when he trotted past me, looking fresh as a daisy.

I saw movement through my night vision goggles, yelled "Contact rear," and pulled the stock of the shotgun tight against my shoulder. The shotgun was effective to maybe forty-five meters, far less than whatever AK variant the Orcs carried. Sutton must have read my mind and shouted, "Flanking." The Orc squad advanced in single file with minimal attention to their flanks.

I waited until they were forty meters away before firing. The red dot sight made it easy to get back on target. At least three Orcs crumpled to the ground by the time the eighth and final round of 00 buckshot slammed into them. I stood up and started running again, awkwardly trying to reload the shotgun's tube magazine as I went. I gave up after dropping two rounds on the ground.

Sutton fired short bursts from the M240, nailing a few more and driving the rest to cover. I shouted, "Moving," and plodded on towards a thick old oak tree that had been knocked over by artillery fire. Good cover to reload, catch my breath, and link up with Sutton, who jogged up with a little sweat showing. We hunkered behind the tree trunk and reloaded. He took two hundred rounds from my pack. I was grateful for the lighter load.

Shouted commands from the direction of our pursuers drove us to take prone firing positions under the tree trunk. Sutton set his only grenade in easy reach. I wished I had remembered to grab a few.

The Orcs came towards us four abreast. They would run for three seconds, then drop to the ground and cover their comrades as another team of four rose from the ground to run past the first team. Sutton whispered, "I'll shoot rear to front, you do the opposite." He initiated our hasty ambush with a long burst of fifty rounds. I was firing buckshot at the lead team before his burst ended. Two of them crumpled like puppets with their strings cut while the other two dove to cover. Sutton threw his grenade with all his might and yelled, "Run!"

We ran the final thirty meters to the bunker with gusto, shouting out the pass phrase as we neared. We crouched into the bunker and took positions to cover they direction from which we came. The infantry squad was down to three effective fighters. They greedily took the belted ammo I brought them and gifted us a box of grenades in return.

The infantry Sergeant said, "We will withdraw as soon as artillery lands, we've been promised a smoke screen. You two first, then us three. Take a covering position after thirty meters and we will leapfrog."

The artillery arrived a few minutes later and we started our run once the smoke screen built up to full thickness. Sutton and I moved out, heading west with our heads on swivels. After thirty meters, we went prone five meters apart and Sutton shouted, "Set."

The last three infantry trotted past us, one with an arm over the shoulder of his battle buddy and a trail of blood droplets leading back to the bunker. We stayed still, waiting for them to call set once they were in position. The buzz of a small flying drone caught my attention. I soon caught sight of it — one of the cheap Iranian four-rotor jobs that could carry a grenade but were mostly used for reconnaissance. It, and its Orc operator somewhere within two-hundred meters, must have caught the movement and decided to investigate. If it had an IR camera, we would stand out like a beacon. I was determined to take it out before it could summon friends.

I watched it as it slowly followed the blood trail, flying no faster than a walking pace with frequent pauses and pivots. It must not have articulated cameras. Sutton noticed the same and pitched a handful of small stones at it to attract attention. The drone, knocked off course by a stone, came to a stop, pivoting towards Sutton and giving me a perfect opportunity. Rising to a kneeling position, I kept the red dot on the hovering drone and stroked the shotgun's trigger. Buckshot is not the preferred shot size for skeet or bird hunting, but it does quite well against a drone twenty-five meters away. I ran over and fired again into the tangled chassis, shattering the circuit board and battery case.

My momentary triumph was rudely interrupted by Sutton cutting loose with short, rapid bursts at Orcs emerging from the bunker we had abandoned. I thumbed two rounds into the Benneli, bringing it back to a full load of eight. Sutton fired a long forty-round burst, likely the remainder of the linked ammo in the assault pack, and called out, "Moving."

"Covering," I replied, searching the darkness for enemy movement while silently counting to ten. At ten, I fired four rounds towards the bunker and started running after Sutton.

Enemy bullets cracked through the air overhead and to either side. They say you never hear the one that gets you. I certainly did not hear the one that got Sutton.

My heart fell when he said, "I'm hit," and tumbled to the ground. I altered my course and ran to him, trying to assess his wounds. Three rounds hit his back and exited his chest and abdomen. One of his lungs was punctured and he struggled to breathe. I poured a clotting agent on the sucking chest wound, packed it with gauze, and sealed it as best I could with duct tape.

Sutton was able to hold pressure on the gauze I pressed against his abdomen. His breathing was not quite as labored now. He said something too faint to hear. I leaned closer to his mouth. "You're a damn good tanker, Gertie. Proud to be your gunner."

"We did kick some Orc butts."

"I'm done; it won't be long now. Rig my grenades, like Ice showed us."

He was weakening and starting to slur words. "You got it, but stay with me, don't stop fighting," I implored him, holding his hand until the light faded from his eyes and his last breath rattled in his throat. He had three grenades in his web gear. One went under the M240 machinegun lying in the dirt next to him. A functional machinegun was too shiny for an Orc to pass by. The other two grenades joined the three already with me as the cold fury building in my gut erupted into white hot rage. I topped off Ice's shotgun with the last shotgun ammo I had, then lined up my five grenades on the ground in front of me. Enemy fire waxed and waned in intensity, so I laid on my back like I was making snow angels. I pulled the pin on a grenade, careful to keep the spoon pressed against the grenade casing. My arm was mostly straight as I rolled onto my stomach, heaving the grenade as far as possible while staying low to the ground. The remaining four grenades followed the first in quick order. I was in a hurry to pick up the shotgun and meet more Orcs, determined to take out as many of them before they inevitably got me.

I rose to my feet and trudged east, shotgun pivoting left and right, seeking targets, and finding them. A fear-laden voice called out in Russian, earning a vulgar curse and two rounds of buckshot in reply. Three Orcs rushed me from the right. The last six rounds of twelve gauge put them down although I had to club the third in the head with the shotgun stock. Out of ammo and unlikely to scrounge any more, I tossed Ice's Benneli to the ground and pulled my zombie hatchet from my boot. It was marketed as a rescue tool with a hammer face opposite a sixty-millimeter hatchet blade sharp enough to shave with and a pry bar tip at the bottom of the short haft. Brutal in trained hands.

An Orc stumbled out of the darkness in front of me and I pounced, swinging for his head before he could react. I followed his limp body to the ground, desperately yanking at the blade buried in his skull, resolving to try the hammer face next.

A hoarse voice called out, probably the dead guy's friends. I got the hatchet free and crouched, waiting for the Orcs to move. A high-pitched whine in the distance behind me puzzled me for a moment, then I realized what it was — M1A2 tanks roaring across the open country with turbine engines at full throttle. Reinforcements were close, making my spirits soar but not quenching my grim resolve to avenge Sutton and so many others. I clutched the short hatchet in my right hand and my folding knife in my left. Maximum damage in minimum time. With an incredibly vulgar Russian curse, I charged towards the movement rustling the bushes.

I swung the hammer face of the hatchet as hard as I could at the Orc's shoulder, aiming to incapacitate an arm before doing more lethal damaged. He howled in pain and pivoted his injured shoulder away from me. I ducked low and reversed my grip on the hatchet, slamming the blade into his knee, causing him to crumple to the ground. Following him down, my knife stabbed him in the back and kidneys with enthusiasm while my hatchet hacked at his hamstrings. It was messy and involved more stabling and chopping than strictly necessary. I crouched next to the body, looking for the closest threat. I could hear a huge volume of machinegun fire, both the heavy thumping of the M2 .50 caliber guns at the TC's position on top of the turret as well as the sharper report of M240's firing at a higher rate. The volume of fire made me think the tanks were either teamed with infantry fighting vehicles, or loaders were up out of their hatches hosing anything that moved with their pintle-mounted M240's. I smiled at the thought of it.

An Orc that looked barely old enough to shave stumbled into the dead body and looked down into my feral eyes. He shrieked in a high-pitched voice and babbled as he turned and ran. The soldier behind him was made of sterner stuff and raised his weapon at me, a monstrous RG-6 revolver grenade launcher that held six grenades.

Realizing my death was mere moments away, I screamed an inarticulate but passionate war cry and charged. The Russian pulled the trigger when I was four meters away. I was jerked around violently to face west by my left arm. Confused, I looked down at my left arm and saw jagged yellow bones sticking out where my hand and wrist should be. Confused, I looked closer and was squirted in the face by a warm gush of arterial blood. My own blood. Vaguely realizing this was a bad thing, I reacted as we had trained and put a tourniquet just below my left elbow and cranked it tight, shouting in pain. Ice made us practice putting tourniquets on ourselves and others. He usually did it on Friday afternoons at a local pub after a rib sticking meal and generous amounts of beer. Ice claimed having a buzz simulated the mental confusion of being wounded. True or not, I was grateful for his training and high standards. He was the reason I was alive.

Now wondering why I was still alive, I turned to see the soldier with the RG-6 dead on his back from a burst of machinegun fire. Not sure what to do next, I sat there numbly and tried to wrap the stump of my left forearm with duct tape. The searing agony from my nerve endings put a stop to that.

I could hear shouts from behind me, not Russian but French. "En avant! Vive La France!" French Foreign Legion infantry swept East, efficiently crushing the Orc attack, supported by two platoons from Bravo company of the Regiment.

I was loopy from the blood loss and, frankly, I had a heck of a day. My hatchet lay a few meters away and I went to pick it up but fell on my butt when I tried to stand.

A friendly voice said in heavily accented English, "Rest easy, Lioness. Let me tend your wounds." He gently pushed my shoulders down flat and injected morphine in my right shoulder, then started at IV. He wrapped the stump of my arm in gauze and an inflatable sleeve to stabilize the bones. He held a canteen to my lips, and I drank gratefully.

"I am Adjutant chef Henri Beauclerc of the French Foreign Legion. Drone video will make you famous, Lioness."

The kindness in his eyes as he tended to me made me feel warm and safe. I dropped into a deep sleep.

University of Munich

Forty-six years later

"It is with great pleasure that I welcome you here today to celebrate the retirement of Professor Gertzman," the Chancellor of the University of Munich said into the microphone at the podium. "I have been proud to know Professor Gertzman for near thirty years, ever since she received a standing ovation for the defense of her doctoral thesis. I won't bore you with anecdotes of all her accomplishments as the Chair of the Physics Department."

I squirmed in my chair on the dais, as always uncomfortable with praise and notoriety. My daughter reached out from the chair next to me and gently squeezed my right arm, coaxing me into acquiescence.

The Chancellor continued, "I thought it would be far more interesting to hear from people that knew her before that. My wife told me students from my lecturing days called me ether breath and any plan involving me talking less was a good one." The crowd chuckled politely, seemingly glad that this ceremony would not be burdened by the typical starched collars and stiff upper lips so typical in ivory tower academic settings.

The Chancellor yielded the podium to Dr. Harold Nakagawa, my doctoral advisor at MIT. "I knew Elke was a person of unique talents when I saw her sit down at a bench in the integrated circuit lab, remove her prosthetic arm, modify the biofeedback algorithm, and test it out on the spot."

I smiled as a recalled that day. MIT labs always had the best tools and optimizing my prosthesis was practical. Grandmother always said I was practical. "Elke," she would say, "You are practical, bright, and determined but a little plain. Get good marks in school." Grandmother was not the warm and fuzzy type.

Dr. Nakagawa gave way to Chet Jackson, my colleague on the joint NASA/ESA rover mission to the Saturn moon Titan. "The rover was stuck. We studied the telemetry, tried the usual extraction algorithms, pored over it for hours, but nothing was working. Elke said 'When in doubt, throttle out. It might not be the best course of action, but it will end the suspense'. It worked." The laughter and nodding of heads in the crowd indicated many thought that story was quintessential me. I giggled as my daughter said, "No motorcycle lessons for the grandkids, Mom." In our moment of levity, I missed the approach of final speaker at the podium.

"I had the honor of serving with Gertie in the Teutonic Volunteer Brigade during the last year of the Ukraine war." Reaper 6's voice was getting hoarse with age but still had an undercurrent of steel in it.

Memories of the war all those years ago came flooding back in an instant, playing like a movie in my mind's eye. Sights, sounds, and smells, especially the smells were vivid to me now. Only my brothers in arms called me Gertie. Ice, Augie, Hicks, that squared away infantry sergeant — my eyes brimmed with tears.

"The day we deployed into battle, Gertie would tell you she was the third fastest loader in the whole regiment of one hundred and sixteen M1A2 tanks. That was a lie."

Colonel Westerkamp, now pushing ninety years of age but still displaying a natural commanding presence, turned to face me directly.

"Gertie, you were the fastest by a fraction of a second. Master Sergeant Weiss refused to let you leave his crew before going into combat. Sergeant Major Pagoni fudged the scores to keep our dirty little secret. I'm sorry for lying to you, Gertie. But I am absolutely certain you were in the right place at a crucial time."

He took a few steps towards me, and I stood to embrace him, weeping and reminiscing our comrades from all those years ago. The colonel felt frail as I hugged him, I worried I might hurt him by squeezing too hard. Father Time has sympathy for no one.

"The Sergeant Major?" I asked.

"That fat retired bastard has probably pulled a chair up to the buffet table."

We laughed and sobbed in alternating torrents, grieving one breath and comforting the next. "Remember our oath?"

"Of course I do. All survivors of the Regiment are expected to uphold it."

"Indeed."

Reaper 6 exemplified the oath we all took at the end of the war when Russia surrendered. It was a simple oath to say but very hard one to fulfill. Live a life worthy of the sacrifice of our fallen brothers and sisters. Westerkamp parlayed a business fortune into an innovative chemotherapy startup, endowing ninety per cent of his fortune to pediatric cancer charities.

"Private First Class Elke Gertzman, we hold your oath fulfilled." His words somehow made a weight lift off my shoulders. The pronouncement was not his alone to bestow, just his to deliver. All survivors of the Regiment voted. And they have voted no when justified.

LATER THAT EVENING, I reclined in my stargazing lawn chair and watched my youngest grandson, Sutton, set up his new telescope that I had given him for his birthday. Grandma was going to help him see a meteor shower. We were in a meadow next to the family cottage in the Bavarian Alps, the same cottage where my grandfather had looked after me during the summers of my youth. My phone buzzed, which was strange since the cottage was too remote for reliable cell service. A brief glance told me it was a text via satellite from Henri, my dear husband. He was in Marseille teaching orphans of the FFL construction skills by building an apartment building where they would live. "Congratulations and sleep well, my Lioness."

Sutton bounced between the eyepiece and the tablet with the coordinates for the meteor shower with increasing urgency. He didn't want to miss the start of the shower. I thought back on the events of the day, happy memories mixed with sad and felt warmly content. Harvey looked at me with eyes wide and breath panting. He mastered his emotions and said, "Grandmother, I need help!"

I couldn't help but smile wistfully with tears born of equal parts sorrow and happiness brimming in my eyes as I asked, "What vexes thee, little one?"

ELKO TRACT

SECOND PLACE AWARD

JOHN HOLT

I FIRST HEARD about Elko Tract back when I was a sophomore in high school. I wasn't even looking for anything weird that night — I was riding shotgun with my friend P.J. on the way to some "battle of the bands" at a skating rink in Sandston.

The place smelled like stale popcorn and cheap nacho cheese, and half the kids acted like they were about to headline Madison Square Garden, even though they could barely tune their guitars.

P.J. was a few years older than me, a guy I jammed with sometimes. He had a car, a real job at some warehouse near the airport — though I can't remember which one — and that gave him this air of knowing things.

Somewhere along the drive, when the runway lights of the airport flickered in the darkness, he leaned back and said, almost as if the lights themselves had reminded him, "Hey… you ever heard of Elko Tract?"

"It's fucking wild, man," he said, voice low, sharing a story too big for ordinary ears. "During World War II, they built this entire fake town out here. Roads, houses, even a water tower — all to trick enemy bombers. They wanted planes to drop their bombs on this decoy instead of Richmond's factories and neighborhoods. Nobody ever lived there — just streets and structures made to look occupied from above. Everything was just theater, camouflage for the sky."

I don't know why, but the moment he finished, I blurted out, "That's fucking awesome! Let's check it out first — we've got time." P.J. smirked at me, the kind of smirk older people get when they know they're about to drag you somewhere unforgettable.

We turned off the main road and wound through the woods, the trees hunching over the asphalt like silent sentinels, headlights cutting a narrow tunnel through the darkness. Then, without warning, the forest opened up. I swear it felt like we'd driven out of the world and into someone else's dream — a vast expanse of cracked pavement and half-fallen buildings. Not abandoned, not exactly. More like… unfinished. Something meant to exist, but never allowed to live.

We stepped out onto the cracked concrete, the night air sharp and damp, carrying a faint tang of rust and decay. The buildings huddled around us like forgotten stage sets, gray and flaking, windows gaping like dead eyes. Every step I took sounded louder than it should, but the echo seemed swallowed by the emptiness around us.

At the end of one of the fake roads, the water tower rose like a skeletal spike, its rusted frame clawing at the sky. I couldn't stop staring. Even as I tried to convince myself it was just my imagination, that the darkness and the wind were playing tricks, the feeling lingered, stubborn and insistent.

It was there in the small hairs raising on my arms, in the chill that crept under my skin, in the prickling at the back of my neck. The shadows along the edges of the roads seemed to twitch and shift, never fully there, never fully absent. Each one set my teeth on edge, yet I kept moving, forced myself forward. The air felt heavier, as if the tract itself was leaning in, observing, taking stock. I told myself I was being paranoid — hell, anyone would in a place like this — but that didn't make the sensation any less real.

I kept looking at the water tower, its spindly legs black against the dim moonlight. It anchored the unease, a focal point for the unshakable awareness pressing in from all directions. I wanted to turn away, to keep moving, but I couldn't. My eyes stayed locked on it, on the way it loomed at the end of a road that led nowhere, as if it was silently daring me to look away, daring me to acknowledge it.

I told myself it was nerves. Still, I was glad when we got back in the car and headed toward the rink.

For years I didn't think about Elko again. Life happened: school, partying, relationships and bands alike that fizzled out. But the thing about places like that is, they don't let go easy. They wait. By the time I was fronting a halfway-decent goth-industrial outfit, I thought I'd put Elko Tract out of my mind for good. We were good enough that talk had turned to making a DIY music video, and when Matt's girlfriend Alicia — a film student at VCU — offered to shoot it for free, we started tossing around ideas for locations.

And then, before I even realized what I was saying, it slipped out: "Elko Tract." I didn't plan it. I didn't mean it. The name had just jumped from some hidden corner of my memory and landed on my tongue, and as soon as it did, I immediately felt that familiar sinking feeling in my stomach. I wanted to take it back. I wanted to apologize, even though no one had said anything yet.

When I told the guys about Elko, they leaned in like kids hearing a ghost story around a campfire. They wanted the details — what it looked like, where it was, how the hell a whole town could exist and not exist at the same time.

"Wait, hold on," Matt said. "Where exactly is it? And what does it even look like? It sounds fucking awesome!"

So I did reluctantly, careful to stick to the facts — the layout, the structures, the rusted water tower looming at the end of a road — leaving out the unease that had clung to me the first time I'd been there. I kept my voice steady, describing the place like a map, not like a memory soaked in the feeling that had once made my skin crawl. Even as I spoke, I was secretly mystified as to what even made me bring it up in the first place.

I could have kicked myself.

Daryl, our synth player, perked up right away. Said something about how his grandfather once mentioned the place, only back then it wasn't called Elko. Or maybe it was, but his granddad swore there'd been talk after the war of turning it into a real town. Or maybe a shopping mall. He couldn't remember the specifics, just muttered he'd ask his grandfather again if he got the chance.

Buddy — our drummer, the one with the restless knee and the van that smelled faintly of mildew and old smoke — said he could take us out there the next day. We'd pile in like it was any other gig. He grinned as if it were nothing, just another adventure. Preston, our lead guitar, shook his head. He had to work. A sub shop, nothing glamorous, but it was a paycheck. The rest of us liked to rib him for it — Preston with his name tag, slinging sandwiches while the rest of us chased stardom. The rest of us swore we were destined for something better, something bigger. Jobs were for people who'd given up. Our "full-time" was music, which mostly meant staying up too late, drinking too much, and convincing ourselves it counted as practice.

So it was settled. Tomorrow, we'd go.

I caught myself wishing Preston could come with us. Maybe because Preston was sensible. Or maybe because part of me already suspected we'd need somebody like him out there.

What seemed like hours after I laid down to crash that evening, I found it impossible to actually fall asleep. I tossed and turned, staring at the ceiling, but my mind kept wandering back to Elko. I could see the water tower at the end of that cracked, overgrown road, skeletal against the darkness, and no matter how I tried, I couldn't shake the old, creeping feeling that me and P.J. hadn't been truly alone out there on that night so many years ago. The shadows, the empty roads, the ruined buildings — they all seemed to have an awareness that we were there, and I remembered that impossible sensation of eyes on my back, just out of reach, lingering in the woods. My chest tightened, and I kept rolling over, trying to escape a memory I couldn't outrun.

I'm not even sure I really slept that night. Maybe I'd just dozed off for a minute, that half-sleep where your mind hovers somewhere between memory and dream. Then my phone buzzed against the nightstand. I squinted at the screen and froze — 8:03 a.m. Daryl. Just a minute ago I'd been lying there, eyes half-shut, and now it was already 8:03 in the morning. I couldn't believe it — and I certainly didn't believe Daryl of all people was capable of existing this early in the morning.

"Hello?" My voice was gravel.

"Hey," Daryl said. He actually sounded awake.

I sat up, more confused by that than anything. "Jesus, man, what and the fuck are you doing up this early? What's wrong?"

He gave this little awkward chuckle. "So, funny thing. My grandfather was at my folks' place last night. Hell of a coincidence, right? First time I've seen him in months. We got to talking, and I told him about the band, and the video. Told him we were thinking about doing it out at Elko Tract."

That name cleared the fog out of my head fast. My stomach did a slow roll. "You did?"

"Yeah," he said, his voice dipping into that campfire-story register he likes to use. "He gave me the history, same as you — decoy town, fake roads, blah blah blah. But then he told me the other thing. The part I was trying to remember yesterday."

I rubbed my temple, already uneasy. "Okay…"

"After the war," Daryl said, "the county wanted to put that land to use. Roads were already cut, a few of the fake buildings still standing from the decoy project. And this was Jim Crow Virginia — everything separate, everything sorted. So their plan was a state-run asylum. For Black people. They figured they could segregate them real well by stashing them out there — out of sight, out of mind."

I didn't say anything for a few seconds. The phone was warm against my ear. "You're serious?"

"As a heart attack," he said. "They even broke ground. Granddad worked the early crew — grading roads, setting forms, all that. Said it was eerie out there. Like the air hummed. They'd show up some mornings and their equipment would be busted up. Then one morning, they showed up and found out the project was over. It just… stopped. No announcement, no foreman, no trucks. County shut it down and never said why. Whole job gone like it never existed."

"Any idea what happened?" I asked, voice low.

"That's the thing," Daryl said. "Nobody talked. My granddad said it was like they wanted to erase it. By the time integration came along, it was off the record, off the map. But he told me you can't really bury something like that. Not out there. Real creepy."

I swallowed. The creeping weight in his words pressed into me, like I'd inhaled it. "That's… that's fucked up…"

He let out a breath, and for once there wasn't any smugness in it. "Yeah. And listen — when he finished, he got this look. Like he was having a painful memory. Then he told me flat-out: I had to promise him I wouldn't go out there. And that I should talk you guys out of it."

I shifted on the bed, suddenly cold. "I mean, did he say why?"

"Wouldn't say a word more," Daryl said. His voice was low now, careful. "I can't be here all weekend with him visiting and just straight up ignore what he said and head out there with you guys. He was fucking spooked, man. I've never seen him like that. So, count me out."

The room seemed too quiet. My own breath sounded loud in my ears.

Daryl added, "Maybe we should think about finding a different spot for the video."

I stared at the ceiling, the cracked paint suddenly oppressive. My pulse ticked in my throat. "…Yeah. Maybe."

Neither of us spoke after that. Finally, I muttered, "I'll talk to the others."

"Do that," Daryl said softly. "And… just be careful, alright?"

The line clicked dead.

I sat there with the phone in my hand, dread crawling in under my skin like something with too many legs.

Buddy rolled up around eleven, his beat-up van coughing in the driveway like a lifelong smoker. The thing was dented and rusting in places, but it had carried our amps and drums across half the county and back again, so I trusted it more than most people I knew. Matt and Alicia were already inside. She had her camera slung around her neck like a sheriff's badge, fiddling with the lens cap while Buddy tapped the steering wheel.

We lit up before we'd even made it out of the neighborhood. Matt had brought a fat joint, sticky and fragrant, and by the time we hit the third intersection the whole van smelled like a burned forest.

I exhaled, tried to sound casual. "So, heads up — Daryl's not coming with us today," and more pointedly at Buddy, "so we don't have to pick him up."

Buddy, hands on the wheel, shot me a side glance. "Big surprise."

Matt snorted. "What's the excuse this time? Hair appointment?"

"Not this time." I scratched my knee, stalling. "He called me this morning. Said his grandfather was over last night, and they got to talking. You remember how Daryl mentioned his granddad knew something about the place? Well, he told the story again."

That knot in my gut tightened. I'd promised myself not to make it a big deal, so I kept it simple — not the whole truth, just enough.

"After the war, the county planned to build an asylum out there," I said. "They figured they'd use the old decoy roads and foundations. But it was Jim Crow Virginia — meant only for Black patients."

Matt passed the joint to Alicia, eyebrows up. "That's dark."

"Yeah," I said. "Then one day, they just stopped building. No reason. Just packed up and left."

Alicia took a drag, eyes narrowed in thought. "So that's what it was meant to be? An asylum?"

"That's what it was supposed to turn into, at least." I left it there, even though the silence on the other end of the call this morning had weighed more than the words.

Matt grinned at Alicia, "Well, maybe a little spooky vibe's exactly what our video needs."

She smirked faintly, but I turned my face toward the window. The trees along the highway blurred by in streaks of green and gray, and I told myself again it was better this way — to keep it simple. Better not to dwell on the other part.

Something in Daryl's story clung to me, sticky and persistent. I thought about half-built buildings and locked doors that never swung open. About a project stopped dead in its tracks, with no reason given. And as we rode, I swear the air in the van felt colder, like someone had cracked open a window I couldn't see.

We've been driving twenty minutes past the airport when it hit me: I had no idea where the hell we were going. I'd thought, stupidly, that memory would guide me — that something in the old roads would spark, point me back to that hidden fake city. But the years and the fog of a thousand beers and joints had worn the map out of me. Now the pines leaned in too close on either side of the road, every turn-off the same narrow brown mouth into the woods. No signs, no markers. Just empty blacktop stretching under a washed-out September sky.

"You sure you know where you're going?" Buddy asked, trying to keep it light, but his eyes were narrow as he scanned the roadside.

"I thought I did," I muttered. "It's like the goddamned place doesn't want to be found."

Buddy barked a laugh, but it was nervous. "That's the weed talking."

Maybe it was. Maybe it wasn't.

By the time the little store showed up — a squat old building with peeling paint and a Coke sign so faded it looked like a ghost — I felt a sharp relief in my chest. Somebody in there had to know. Buddy pulled the van over. Matt and Alicia stayed inside, Alicia fiddling with her camera while Matt was busy rolling another joint cautiously, using a CD case. Me and Buddy went in.

The screen door wheezed open, and the smell hit me: wood, dust, penny candy, and motor oil. A single fan clacked lazily overhead. Behind the counter stood a woman so old she looked like she'd dried into place. Her back was straight, though, and her eyes were sharp behind the cataract-cloud.

"Morning," she said, voice thin but kind.

"Morning, ma'am," Buddy said, clearing his throat. He leaned on the counter, trying to act sober. "We're trying to get out to the Elko Tract. You know how to get there?"

Her eyebrows lifted a little, like she wasn't used to hearing that name. Then she smiled. "Well now, that's not something I hear much anymore. Young people, wanting to go poking around out there. Of course I know it. Knew it when they were building it, back in the war."

"You remember that?" I asked, a little surprised.

"Oh yes," she said. "Army boys, trucks coming and going. Whole place lit up at night like a carnival. Folks around here thought it was the biggest thing they'd ever seen."

She gave us directions — straightforward, almost cheerful, like she was glad to be asked. But then Buddy leaned in, dropping his voice just a little.

"You ever hear about what they planned after the war? Not the base, but… the asylum?"

Her face stilled. The smile didn't vanish, not right away, but it thinned, soured at the corners. She looked from Buddy to me, weighing whether to go on. Finally, she sighed.

"Mm. You boys must have been talking to someone closer to my age than your own."

"My friend's grandfather," Buddy said quickly. "He told him about it. Said they started work, then just stopped. We were wondering if you remembered why."

The woman's eyes sharpened, cloudy or not. She glanced toward the window, as if making sure no one lingered close enough to overhear. When she spoke again, her voice had dropped.

"I remember. They did start. Roads. Walls. Some of the frame. But the work didn't last. At first folks said it was sabotage — protesters sneaking out at night, undoing what the men built during the day. Equipment broken, tires cut, that sort of thing. But that wasn't why the crews quit. Not really."

She leaned forward a little, voice steady but brittle.

"It was the place itself. Men came back from a shift pale as plaster, saying it never felt empty out there. Like eyes on you no matter which way you turned. Some swore they heard voices in the woods, or tools clanging when no one else was near. A few walked off the job mid-day and didn't bother to pick up their pay. Said they'd rather starve than go back."

I felt the hair rise on my arms.

"So, they blamed it on protesters?" I said softly, half to myself, half to her, not even really asking it as a question.

She gave a small, dry laugh. "That was the story folks clung to. Easier than the other talk. Men said the trees shifted when you weren't looking. That sometimes the shadows felt thicker than they should, even in broad daylight. And at night — well, night was worse. Too many of 'em came back spooked. Eventually there weren't enough willing bodies left to keep the project moving. So the county let it rot."

Her eyes cut back to Buddy, then to me.

"And when segregation ended, there wasn't any point in reviving the idea. But the bones of it are still out there. Empty bones. And bones remember."

For a second, the only sound was the fan clacking overhead.

Buddy cleared his throat. "So, uh… which road did you say we turn off?"

She blinked, like she'd just come back to herself, and rattled off the directions again, quick and simple.

By the time we stepped back outside, sunlight hit me square in the face, but I still couldn't shake the chill she'd left behind.

Buddy and I stepped out into the sunlight, the screech of the screen door shutting behind us echoing in the gravel lot. He gave a half-laugh, half-shiver, elbowing me lightly.

"Man, you sure know how to pick a location. Haunted, half-built asylum, ghost roads… Really sets the mood, huh?"

I laughed too, a little forced, trying to sound casual. "Yeah… it fits our sound," I said, grinning, though my stomach was tight and buzzing. The old woman's words were still crawling along my spine — men quitting, feeling eyes on their backs, the woods moving… I could almost hear the distant scrape of those old foundations in my head, smell the damp pine from that night with P.J. over a decade ago.

Buddy shook his head, chuckling. "Better hope the video shoot doesn't turn into a Blair Witch project."

I laughed again, a little too loud, and then, leaning closer, said in a low voice, "Hey… maybe don't bring up anything that woman said in there. Alicia already knows about the asylum, sure, but the… creepy stuff? Best not freak her out."

He shrugged, his grin easing a little. "Yeah, fair enough. Keep the crew sane." I nodded, though my fingers were still tingling. Inside, I was the one losing it.

We climbed into the van. Matt had a fresh joint lit, passing it to Alicia, who was still fussing with her camera. She looked up, adjusting her strap. "So… you guys find the way?"

Buddy grinned over the dash. "Yeah. An old lady, probably a wife back in World War II just gave us directions. Real nice. Super precise. Sweet woman."

Matt barked a laugh. "Man, I bet she smelled like mothballs and peanut brittle."

Buddy fired up the van, tires crunching over the gravel. Following the old woman's directions, within minutes and after a few turns the road we were on began to narrow, the pines leaning close, almost brushing the windows. The sunlight fractured into bands and shadows, shifting with every bend. And then it all started coming back — the curves of the road, the dips and the stumps, the strange way the woods whispered in the wind.

Every memory from that night with P.J. rose in me: the tight twist of unease in my gut, the feeling of something just beyond the line of sight, the cold crawl of awareness that we were being watched. I could feel it again — the slow, patient weight of the land itself.

Buddy hummed some off-key tune under his breath, trying to shake it off. I stared at the road ahead, gripping the steering wheel like a lifeline.

Then the trees parted.

Elko spread out in the clearing like a secret laid bare. Roads wound into nothing. The water tower jutted up like a sentinel, its rusted steel catching the low sun. Foundations, half-crumbled walls, the geometric emptiness of a town that had never been alive— it hit me like cold water. My stomach flipped, and I cursed under my breath. Whatever had spurred me to remember this place, whatever idiotic spark had made me say we should come back here, I wanted it gone.

My pulse was loud in my ears. The van's engine idled, the only sound besides the faint whisper of wind through empty streets.

Buddy's voice cut through, nervous but trying to be light. "Well… here we are."

Matt leaned forward, eyes wide. "Holy… shit."

Alicia's camera pivoted, lens catching the water tower, the roads, the skeletal remnants of the buildings. She whispered, more to herself than anyone else, "Wow."

And all the while, the land seemed to hum — patient, patient, like it had been waiting for someone to remember it.

I swallowed, tight and dry. There was no laughter left in me, just the long, slow recognition that some things, once remembered, don't forgive. Buddy eased the van to a stop in front of the first structure. It was small, gutted, gray concrete, one story, roofless, a jagged window and a sagging doorway. We climbed out slowly.

Matt held out the joint. I shook my head. Buddy waved it off too. Matt muttered, "You two are killjoys," letting it roll back onto the seat.

Alicia got out and crouched with her camera, snapping pictures of the building in front of us. Her eyes drifted toward the water tower in the distance.

"Creepy," she muttered, raising her camera to frame it. "I definitely want to get a closer look at that."

Matt leaned against the van, squinting at the ruins. "I wonder which buildings are original and which were added later for the asylum plans," he said.

Buddy wandered off toward a taller, two-story gray building, roof intact, windowless. "Check this out!" he called, slapping the wall. "Perfect spot for the video!"

I lingered near the van, unease coiling in my stomach. Matt came over, grinning. "Man, you didn't mention how damn creepy this place is. Perfect for the old-school goth vibe we've got."

I forced a smile. "Yeah… perfect," I said, trying to sound upbeat.

Alicia's voice rang out, pointing toward a small cement structure nearby. "Hey! Come look at this!"

We walked over. It looked like a sealed well, round and capped with concrete.

"Huh. That's weird," Matt said, crouching to inspect it.

Alicia gestured to several more similar structures scattered across the clearing. "There are a few of these," she said. "Looks like wells, but you wouldn't run a psychiatric hospital on well water alone."

"Maybe bomb shelters?" Matt guessed, shrugging. "World War II. Could be storage, hiding spots…"

I shook my head, a little laugh escaping me. "No way… they wouldn't be bomb shelters. This place was built to be bombed. Nobody was supposed to be here. There's no one to hide."

I walked around the cement cap, eyes tracing the shadows. In my head, a darker thought lingered, curling like smoke: Maybe they were sealed to keep something from climbing out. I didn't speak it aloud.

Then it came — a shout from the two-story building Buddy had entered. His voice echoed oddly, bouncing across the hollow walls, fading in strange, warped patterns.

Without thinking, we broke into a jog toward the building, gravel snapping and skittering beneath our sneakers. Shadows stretched long and twitching across the cracked concrete, and the wind hissed through broken walls like a living thing. My pulse hammered in my ears; the hair on my arms prickled. Somehow, I knew again, just as I had all those years ago, that this place had never truly been empty.

As we drew closer, the two-story building seemed to tilt toward us, its gray walls darkening like wet concrete, its windows holding shapes that slipped away when I tried to focus on them.

Buddy burst out of the doorway like a man thrown, not running from something but out of it, eyes wild, face ashen, chest heaving. He stopped in front of us; hair plastered to his forehead with sweat.

"You assholes," he barked, voice high, almost breaking. "You think that's funny? You think that's a joke?"

I blinked at him. "What?"

"Don't fuck with me," he snapped, jabbing a finger back at the door. "I was upstairs. Whole time. I heard you guys down there — whispering, laughing, moving around. Footsteps on the floor, slow, like you were creeping. I heard the stairs creak. You were down there."

Matt spread his hands. "Buddy, we weren't —"

Buddy cut him off, his voice climbing. "I heard you. I don't know how you guys did it. The voices — God, they didn't even sound right. Like they were coming through water, all echo and hiss, like an old tape recorder. Low voices, then high, then back again. Footsteps, too, like someone pacing, then stopping, then pacing again. I stood at the top of the stairs waiting for you to come up. But you didn't. How the hell did you guys make those sounds?"

I swallowed. "We didn't. We were at the well. Not inside."

Buddy stared at us, his face going slack. For a heartbeat he looked like he might laugh, then his jaw clenched. "Then who the hell was down there?" His voice cracked on who. "Because somebody was. I swear to God. And it wasn't just one person either. It was like a whole room of…" He trailed off, scanning the tree line, the doorway behind him.

Alicia took a step back, her eyes darting at the shadows in the windows.

Buddy's voice dropped to a harsh whisper. "If it wasn't you, then somebody else is here." He wiped his palm down his jeans. "More than somebody. And they weren't —" he shuddered. "They didn't sound right."

The doorway behind him gaped like a mouth, silent now.

Buddy's lips pressed into a line, muttering under his breath, "God… what the hell…" His hands fisted at his sides, knuckles pale. "Someone's messing with us."

Matt glanced around, swallowing audibly. "Nobody… nobody's here, dude. Just us." He shook his head, unable to look at any one place for more than a heartbeat.

I could feel it behind me, in front of me, a presence just at the edge of sight. Not a person, not exactly — but attentive, patient, waiting. Every shift of shadow, every tremor in the weeds, felt deliberate, like eyes were scanning, tracking. And I knew, deep in my chest, that it wouldn't let us forget it so easily.

Alicia, oblivious to our rising panic, lifted her camera and tried to break the tension. "Come on," she said brightly, forcing cheer into her voice, "let's go get a closer look at the water tower."

I exhaled slowly, trying to settle my racing heart, but inside, the chill lingered, cold and insistent. Whatever had been in that building with Buddy — or whatever he thought he heard — was still here, patient, unseen, and it had taken notice of us.

Buddy ran a hand over his face, exhaling sharply. "Look," he said, voice tight, trying to keep some control, "we didn't come here to sightsee. We came to check the place out, see if it's good for a video. And we've seen it. So let's get the hell out of here."

Alicia, crouched slightly with her camera slung around her neck, narrowed her eyes at him. "No," she said firmly. "I want to see everything up close. I need to figure out a game plan for the video I'm doing for you guys. Totally free by the way," she emphasized, pressing the word with a pointed smile.

Matt grinned and reached for her shoulder. "Of course, baby. It's cool, right y'all?" he asked, glancing at us with easy charm.

Buddy threw his hands up in exasperation. "Fine. Real quick."

I barely managed to get the words out, my voice tight and forced: "Yeah… I mean, whatever,"

Matt looped his arm around her shoulder as the four of us started down the cracked, overgrown road, the one that cut through the ghost town, leading toward the water tower. The concrete ruins on either side seemed to lean inward as we walked, shadows stretching unnaturally across the road.

Every instinct I had screamed at me. I believed Buddy had heard something — really heard something — inside that two-story building. I forced myself to keep walking, forcing my eyes to stay on the cracked asphalt beneath my feet. The wind whispered through the skeletal structures, brushing leaves against the concrete walls.

Alicia jabbed the camera forward every few steps, snapping pictures, murmuring about angles and composition. Matt leaned casually against her, grinning, but I could see the subtle tenseness in his jaw, the way his eyes flicked toward the shadows.

Buddy stayed slightly ahead, hands braced at his sides, walking with that tight, purposeful stride he always had when he wanted to keep control. But even he wasn't smiling. I could see it in the set of his shoulders, the way he kept glancing over the tops of ruined walls, as if expecting something to move.

The water tower rose slowly before us, massive and rusted, a crooked sentinel over the crumbling town. The road beneath our feet, cracked and overgrown, seemed impossibly long.

My pulse kept time with each step, a drum in my ears, and with every passing second, the feeling grew: we were not alone.

We reached the tower at last, the road giving way to cracked dirt and weeds that clawed up through the asphalt. The water tower rose above us, a skeletal lattice of rusted iron, streaked with orange and black from decades of decay. Shadows pooled at the base, thick and shifting, making the ground look uneven even where it wasn't.

Alicia stepped forward first, camera in hand, and her footsteps stirred the dry grass. She tilted her head, scanning the towering metal. "This is it," she said softly, voice tight with excitement. "This is where we should do the video. It's perfect."

Matt smiled, looping an arm around her shoulder, glancing up at the tower. "Yeah… perfect," he said, trying to sound light, but his eyes flicked nervously to the shadows.

Buddy didn't move immediately. He lingered a few feet back, hands brushing the rusted iron at the tower's base, fingertips tracing the seams. His jaw was tight, and he seemed to be listening to something I couldn't hear, some faint shift in the air.

I hung back as well, letting my eyes wander across the field. The ruins around us were mostly foundation fragments and concrete shells of buildings, but the shadows seemed to crawl. Not the wind, not the sun — but a slow, deliberate movement along the edges of vision. Every so often a shadow would flare against the iron supports, linger, and vanish.

Alicia crouched for a shot, squinting through the lens. "Angles matter," she muttered, almost to herself. "I need a full sense of the space." I nodded, forcing a laugh.

"Full sense of the space," I echoed, but it sounded hollow in the air.

The wind whispered through the lattice of iron, low and sighing, carrying the faint tang of rust and earth. I thought I saw something shift near the base — a dark smear against the shadow — but when I blinked, nothing was there.

Matt shifted beside Alicia, trying to keep her close, but the unease had started to settle over all of us. The air seemed heavier, every breath harder, every step echoing oddly in the stillness.

We lingered like that for a long minute, the tower above us looming, indifferent, rust groaning softly in the wind. I could feel my heart rate picking up, slow at first, then faster, a rhythmic pounding that matched the occasional creak of metal. I kept looking around, sensing eyes I couldn't see, movements that weren't there, the ghosts of the town pressing at the edges of perception.

Alicia adjusted her camera again. "This place is so perfect," she said, voice small, almost swallowed by the wind.

I nodded, words catching in my throat. The shadows at the base of the tower flickered again. Something seemed to lean into the sun, then fold back into itself. My skin crawled, and I realized I hadn't breathed properly in several moments.

Then — faint at first — came a metallic scrape from inside the tower. Not loud, not immediate, but deliberate, a slow echo that crawled along the girders. I froze, listening.

"Ummm… what the fuck was that?" I asked, voice quiet, tight.

Matt glanced up, frowning. "Probably… just the wind," he said, but he didn't sound convinced.

Buddy's hand tensed on the iron. "It… it sounded like it came from inside."

Alicia lowered her camera slightly, biting her lip. "Inside?" she whispered. "How is that possible?"

I didn't answer. My pulse jumped, slow cold crawling up my spine. The wind sighed again, carrying another faint metallic rasp, almost like something brushing along the inside walls.

Then came the first bang — hollow, resonant, vibrating through the dirt under our feet.

Buddy's jaw tightened. "Something is banging from inside," he said, voice low and urgent.

I swallowed, words stuck. The tower loomed above us, rust and shadow and silence punctuated by that hollow sound. Something inside had noticed us. And whatever it was, it was letting us know it.

The silence after that first bang pressed down on us like a lid. My ears strained for the next sound, and the world held its breath with me.

Matt wet his lips. "Okay," he said too quickly, "that was metal shifting. Rust, wind, temperature drop —"

"Wind?" I cut him off, nodding toward the dead grass, stiff as bristles. Not a breath stirred.

Buddy dragged his hand down the tower's flank, fingertips scraping rust. He leaned close like he could hear through the iron. "That wasn't the tower groaning," he muttered. "That was something hitting it from inside."

Alicia hugged the camera against her chest, the lens angled down. Her voice tried for lightness but quavered. "Maybe… maybe something fell inside? A branch, an animal? There's a ladder up there, right? Could've —"

She trailed off because even she didn't believe it.

Another sound rolled through the iron, quieter this time, a drawn-out scrape — like nails dragged along the inside wall. The hair on my arms stiffened. I couldn't stop staring at the base of the tower, at the dark where shadow thickened like liquid.

The kind of dark that doesn't let go once you see it.

Matt finally stepped back, shaking his head. "Look, fuck this. We got enough shots, right? We can call it —"

BANG.

This time louder, angrier. The dirt under our shoes trembled.

Alicia flinched so hard the camera strap nearly snapped off her neck. She gasped, looking at us like we'd have the answer. None of us did.

Buddy's face twisted. "Jesus Christ, you guys hear that — there's something in there." His voice rose with each word, until he was nearly shouting at us, at the tower, at the whole godforsaken town.

"That's not possible." Alicia said sharply, eyes darting up the iron skeleton.

He glared at her, but his chest heaved and he shut his mouth.

We all turned at once when the next volley came — three sharp blows, bam-bam-bam, each one so hard I swore I felt it in my teeth.

The sound clattered up into the sky, echoing back down, swallowed by the bones of the place.

Alicia, hand trembling, raised her camera almost on instinct. Flash burst once, stark white across the rust and shadows, leaving afterimages burned into my vision.

"Fuck this — we're done." Matt barked, grabbing at her arm. But she tore free and snapped another shot.

That's when the banging changed.

Not one. Not three. But a storm — dozens of strikes all at once, overlapping, slamming from every side inside the iron belly. It was chaos and rhythm at the same time, like many fists, or hooves, or something worse, all demanding to be let out.

I staggered back, my pulse thundering. The ground felt alive, trembling under my soles.

"Go," Buddy hissed, not shouting this time but deadly serious. His voice had gone hoarse.

Each echo of gravel under our boots sounded sharper than it should, like someone — or something — was pacing just behind us, keeping step.

The four of us moved fast, then faster, into a panicked trot.

Behind us the banging didn't just continue — it escalated into a furious, targeted assault, a staccato of blows so vehement they sounded less like random impacts and more like deliberate fists testing iron. Each hollow strike carried intent, a message hammered through steel: We know you're here.

The rhythm stuttered and accelerated, as if multiple things inside were pounding in unison, trying to break the cage and claw their way out.

The tower groaned, rust shrieking as if the bolts would tear loose.

We stumbled back through the weeds, half-walking, half-jogging, our nerves frayed to threads, when off to the side of the field we passed one of the cement well caps.

As we moved past it, a noise swelled from inside — not the wind, not the earth settling, but a deep, guttural moaning that rose and twisted until it sounded furious, like something buried alive was bellowing in rage.

It was so loud and raw it rattled in my chest. Matt spun toward it, his face pale, shouting, "What the fuck is that?!" His voice cracked high, panicked, and Alicia screamed, clutching her camera to her chest like a shield. Buddy staggered, eyes darting from the sealed well to the looming tower, where the pounding had multiplied even more — now a whole army of fists slamming, furious, the metal walls shrieking with every blow. The air vibrated with the fury of it, a sound that felt less like noise and more like intent, a warning and a promise. My legs moved before I realized it — a full sprint — and suddenly we were all running, crashing through weeds and gravel, the moaning swelling behind us, the tower booming like a war drum, every strike screaming that we had been seen and marked.

We didn't speak. We just ran, gravel crunching loud under our shoes, shoulders hunched, waiting for the sound of iron bursting open. The van's silhouette appeared through the weeds like salvation, and we sprinted for it as if something unseen was already at our backs.

We slammed the doors almost in unison, a ragged chorus of metal clicks sealing us in. For half a heartbeat, I thought the thin skin of the van might hold back the world outside. Then the tower bellowed another bang — so deep and resonant it shivered through the windows.

Buddy twisted the key. The van coughed and died.

He tried again. Nothing but a whining sputter, then silence.

"Come on…" he muttered through clenched teeth, twisting the key over and over.

The banging continued so loud and angrily it made the van vibrate.

"Buddy, what the hell —" Matt started, voice tight.

"Don't!" Buddy barked, sweat gleaming on his forehead. He tried the key again. The engine groaned and died immediately.

Then came the sound beneath us — the low, guttural moaning from the sealed well in the field. It swelled and throbbed, a sound that didn't belong to anything living, rising in angry pulses with the slams from the tower. The moan vibrated through the dirt, through the van, like it was testing our weight, our presence. Every beat of it seemed patient, waiting, pressing against our ears, pressing against us.

"Buddy, just go!" Matt shouted, his hand gripping Alicia's arm.

"You think I'm not trying?!" Buddy snapped, slamming the wheel.

Alicia's hands shook as she lifted her camera, snapping a shot. The flash lit the van for a heartbeat, bleaching our faces into something raw and unrecognizable. The afterimage burned behind my eyes, red and white, lingering like it had a life of its own.

Buddy twisted the key one last time. The van shuddered violently, the dash flickered — and then, ragged and uneven, the engine roared to life. The moaning from the well didn't stop; it receded just enough to let the van move, but its low, patient pulse still pressed in around us, a reminder that it was still there, still aware. Buddy's hands gripped the wheel tight, and with a harsh sigh, he shifted into gear.

We were moving. Finally moving.

"Go, go, go!" Matt bellowed.

Buddy slammed it into gear, tires shrieking against gravel.

The van lurched forward, the pounding still rattling through the air behind us.

As we tore down the weed-choked road, I couldn't help but glance back once.

The tower still loomed there, framed against the dark sky, vibrating with fury. And I swear I saw the shadows at its base split open, something moving within them — not climbing free, not yet, but waiting.

We didn't speak on the drive back, not really. Matt smoked the joint he'd saved without offering it around, staring out the window like he was watching something only he could see. When we reached my place, we filed inside like ghosts, dropped onto the couches, and just… sat there. No music, no laughter, not even complaints.

After a while they drifted off, one by one, and I was left with a silence that felt heavier than the night itself.

When Preston called later, asking if everyone was still excited about shooting out there, I told him we'd find another spot. I left the rest unsaid. If someone else wanted to explain, that was on them.

Daryl came by a little later with a case of beer, and before long we were absurdly drunk. I was drinking hard, trying to drown out the memory of the day, but the alcohol only made me loop back through it. Every swallow seemed to drag me deeper into the horror we'd just lived. Daryl's curiosity, sharpened by booze, wouldn't let it go — he kept poking, asking how it went, until finally I broke and spilled everything.

Once I started, I couldn't stop, babbling through it all like the words were burning a hole inside me.

At first, he just shook his head with that smug little smirk, told me I'd gotten too deep into the weed. But when I told him to check with the others, the grin faltered. He still didn't buy it completely, but he wasn't laughing as freely now. He muttered that his grandfather must have been right to warn him about Elko, then let out a half-drunk laugh and said he was kinda jealous we got to see ghosts. Said he wished he'd come. That word-ghosts — made my stomach twist. I looked him dead in the eye and told him, "Be glad you didn't."

He must've seen something raw in my face, or heard it in my voice, because for once Daryl went quiet, actually apologized, and didn't try to make a joke out of it again.

It didn't happen all at once — bands never break up clean, not really. It was more like a slow suffocation. Over the next few weeks, the three of us who'd been out there that day kept finding excuses not to meet up. Somebody was sick, somebody's car wouldn't start, somebody's girlfriend needed them.

On paper it looked like life just getting in the way, but underneath it we all knew what was really happening. The truth was, the three of us who'd stood in that field together — who'd heard the banging, the voices, the moaning — couldn't stand being in the same room anymore. Not for long, anyway. We'd look at each other and see the fear we'd felt out there, feel it crawling back up our spines. The silence would stretch too long, or one of us would flinch at a random sound, and suddenly practice was "postponed."

Daryl seemed to get it. I'd told him everything, and even if he didn't fully believe it, he understood enough to let it go. Preston, though — Preston was pissed. To him it looked like we were just lazy, burning out, wasting what little momentum we had. He kept trying to rally us, calling at all hours, hammering on the idea that we had to "get serious." I don't know if any of the others ever told him what happened out there. I know I didn't. Even now, I still can't picture myself saying the words to him.

About a month and a half later, we just… stopped. No big blowout, no screaming match, just this collective shrug of exhaustion. One day we were a band, the next we weren't. Funny thing, in a cruel sort of way — a goth band breaking up because of ghosts. You'd expect overdoses, or jealousy, or the usual sex-and-drugs implosion, but not this. Never this.

A couple of the guys kept playing, joined other little projects here and there. One or two just drifted into jobs, clocking in and out like none of it had ever happened.

Me, I went back to college. Sitting in classrooms felt safer than standing in basements with amps buzzing, waiting for someone to say the wrong word and drag that night back to life. But no matter how far I tried to push it down, I couldn't shake the feeling that the band didn't die — it was killed, smothered by whatever was waiting for us in those fields, banging at the walls, making damn sure we'd never walk in there together again.

About a year later, I ran into Alicia on campus. It struck me right then that I hadn't seen her once since that day, and the realization carried a chill of its own.

The moment our eyes met, I could tell she was thinking the same thing I was — we both knew exactly what memory had surfaced, and neither of us wanted to give it air. We stumbled through small talk for a while, but the silence kept pressing between us until it was heavier than the words we were forcing out.

She told me she and Matt had broken up not long after the band collapsed. I said I'd had enough of music for the time being, that I wasn't chasing it anymore.

She looked at me, eyes dark with something between worry and awe. "I… I finally had those pictures from that day developed," she said, voice low, almost like she was afraid speaking louder would make it real.

I didn't say anything, just waited, feeling the weight of the pause.

She swallowed, fiddling with the hem of her sleeve.

"There's… something in them. Shadows. Shapes. Where they shouldn't be. Around the tower, near the wells… I kept going back to them, trying to tell myself it was just the film, light playing tricks. But the more I looked, the less sense it made. They weren't… random. They were —" She hesitated, swallowed again, and shook her head. "They were… there."

Her hands were trembling, and for a second, I thought she might start crying. "I couldn't keep them," she said finally. "I… I threw them all away. I didn't want to look at them anymore. Didn't want to think about them."

I nodded slowly, understanding perfectly. There was a weight to that day, a memory that refused to lighten, and keeping the pictures would have only made it heavier.

We hugged, awkward and quick, and promised we'd get lunch sometime soon. We both knew it was a lie.

I've done everything I can to convince myself that was the last time I'd ever really think about that place. But the truth is, all I managed was to make it the last time I spoke of it out loud.

The place still lingers, slipping in through the cracks of my thoughts when I'm tired or distracted. I still think about it — more often than I'd ever admit.

Even now, I can't say exactly what we stirred up out there, only that it was real, and it was angry.

And the more I think about it, the less surprised I am. Elko was never meant to be a quiet place. First, it was a decoy, built to take the bombs that should have fallen on real neighborhoods.

Years later, they planned to fill it with the ones they wanted hidden away. Mentally disabled Black men and women, corralled onto land meant to take bombs, built to be erased. Concrete and steel cages, out of sight, out of mind. Fear stacked on fear, thick and unrelenting. Anger seeped into the walls, into the soil, into the still air, lingering long after the planners walked away.

If any place could hold a grudge, it was that one.

If any foundation could remember rage, it was that one.

What we encountered wasn't new. It was born long before we arrived.

And it hadn't forgotten.

WINGS OF GOLD

THIRD PLACE AWARD

N. JED TODD

Oakland, CA. Overpriced Apartment. Summer 2018.

THE DREAM WAS BACK. I was driving through the desert southeast of Baghdad, on the outskirts of Kut. The three trucks in our convoy were taking up position on the outskirts of the city, holding while the main body started to retake the city. Our escorts were Iraqi, and nominally we supported them. In practice, nobody trusted them, so they gave them to the soft boys to baby-sit PSYOP and Civil Affairs, as always. Our patch was soft until it wasn't, till we started taking fire from who knows where. I froze. We were halfway down a little alley, no room to turn around. The Iraqis go left and we went right, herringboned out for security.

Except we were in an alley, not exposed on an open road... He went left into his wall and I went right into ours, and neither of us could go any further forward without backing out first. Shots came from behind, hitting us, hitting the CA guys behind, plinking into the steel plates bolted onto the truck.

Simpson in the turret turned around and returned fire, shots echoing around the cab, smoking hot brass dropping down on us like we were Satan's spit-cup. Olson, he's yelling at me to go forward, Iraqi in the turret ahead is gesturing desperately for us to pull back, and I'm trying to tell both of them that I can't do a damn thing, just sitting there pounding on the steering wheel and crying.

It works about as well as it sounds. Then my door opens up and a shoulder bumps into me and starts pushing. Captain Onkle, Perry, the CA guy, he's pushing me aside, mumbling to gentle me like I'm a scared horse. He'd gotten out of his own truck and come forward to take over. It works. I wriggle past the wheel and the radio well and under Simpson's feet. Perry starts to take my place at the wheel, moves his rifle off his shoulder, and then he crumples, cursing in a whisper. He pulls himself in, lifting his leg with his arms, still swearing in a monotone like he's saying a soldier's rosary.

Door slams shut, and he shifts into reverse, backing up, then forward again, bashing past our Iraqi escorts. There's blood on the steering wheel, on the radio, as Perry keeps his fist pushed down into his lap to stop what bleeding he can. I can't take my eyes off of the Iraqi soldier in the turret ahead. Dream logic, his oversized olive-green flak jacket turns to yellow silk with sweeping sleeves, and his eyes turn red, his face pales until it's just a bone mask leering at me as we pass, as he slides past Perry and disappears into the blood spatter on the corners of the windshield. I can hear him laughing, somehow, louder and louder until it turns into my phone and I'm awake and it's California and the sun coming through dirty windows is morning yellow and not dusty twilight and the stink's not blood and gunpowder and burnt plastic but old clothes and spilled wine. The fear and ashes in my mouth, though, that tastes just the same.

I pick the phone up and swipe and hold it to my ear, waiting senselessly, not saying anything. Finally, a voice comes on, and I'm back in the dream because it's Perry, his voice. Not swearing, this time, and no longer quite so soft, but still holding something back, still trying to gentle me, fifteen years later…

"Charlene? Char? Is that you? I'm trying to reach Charlene Greenbaum, is this…"

I cough, back again. Just a dream, just a wild coincidence. "Yeah, this is me. I mean, yeah, hello Perry, long time no see, no talk, whatever. Funny that, I was just thinking of…" I trailed off, unsure how to finish. Fumbled around for a scrunchy to pull my hair back, a glass of something to wash the taste from my mouth.

"Uh-huh. You were just dreaming, you mean, right? Dreaming of Kut?"

I nod, senselessly. "Yeah. Been awhile, but they've been coming back. No biggie, I'm good."

He cleared his throat. "That's why I called. About you being good…" His voice is happy, promising a secret, like a little kid with a bird's nest behind his back.

"You saw the interview." It was supposed to be a question, but I forgot to raise my voice. It's okay, I wasn't really asking. Everyone had seen the video; damn thing went viral. Half-assed nervous flustered little me ranting about some artificial intelligence gone sentient, held captive on the servers while I tested it. I sounded like a loon and looked it, eye-liner too wide and lips too red, blunt features with caked on make-up, Tammy Faye on a bad hair day but a touch more religious, when I was supposed to be talking tech and selling my employer's new chatbot up on the news. Best press release ever, in terms of getting the word out. But my boss liked good press and not bad, so I was shit-canned as well as a laughing stock. And now my old Army buddies were seeing it and realizing, maybe, just why that little girl looked familiar.

"Shit, Char, everyone saw the interview. So you believe it? You really think AI can be self-aware, think for itself? Have a soul?"

I started to give my rehearsed answer, the one the lawyers

made me repeat back until it was muscle memory, dangling my severance and an NDA to keep me on message. The one about it didn't matter what I thought and Turing Tests and Chinese Rooms and every reasonable ethical requirement has been met. I started, then I stopped. Opened my mouth and nothing came out. Finally I just said what I thought.

"Yeah. Yeah, Perry, I do. Don't know for sure that is what we had there, but I don't *not* know, either. And I think it behooves us to err on the side of caution, when it comes to playing God, to be kinder than required rather than just numbers until proven otherwise. That free will should be free, even if it costs us. That's what I think."

"That's what I wanted to hear, Char. You want a job?"

I did the fish-mouth thing again. Reached behind me and slammed the pillows around till I had a little hard lump I could lean against. Ran my fingers through my hair until I was reminded I had tied it back. Then I came back with all the eloquence I could muster.

"What?"

"A job, Char. You want a job? I'm retired now, and in tech, doing contract work for the government providing bespoke AI solutions to tomorrow's SOF problems. And we need an AI ethicist. One with a clearance, and preferably experience with disinformation and misinformation and social network analysis and PSYOP messaging. Maybe one that knows translation, a linguist. That's a pretty small field. Saw the interview, thought you might be looking for work. You willing to come out to DC? I'm up at Meade now."

"Perry, I'm flattered. But… But I transitioned, remember? Not sure I'm the right face you want on a government contract."

Perry chuckled softly, kindly. "Not a conversation I'm ever going to forget, Char. Nor that fight two years later. But… But that's a part of it, too, to be honest. Your transition." He cleared his throat, uncomfortable now. It wasn't like him, no longer the smooth-talking confident leader with the Jimmy Stewart speeches, just a stumbling embarrassed oaf looking for the right words. Human like the rest of us.

"I got forced out. Last year. I was in command, and the new policy was out. We had a soldier, Santos, and he transitioned. Or she transitioned. Or…"

"And now you're thinking of me and want to apologize?" I wasn't sure exactly what I was feeling then, whether I was supposed to be pissed off, righteous and angry, disappointed it took him so long, or just glad he was coming around. I finally settled on 'hungover', as that part I could be sure of. Left me sounding pretty authentically pissed off, too, so there was that.

"What?" He was genuinely surprised. Guess my pregnant pauses hadn't communicated anything to him. "No, not like that. Or maybe, I don't know, am I supposed to? No, point is, one of my troops transitioned, did it all right, paperwork filled out right and waivers and medical referrals and all the right signatures, then came a tweet from the President and suddenly all that was off the table. Nobody knew what to do, all the policy and legal opinions and the like was one way, Twitter said the other, and Santos in the middle. Screwed for doing exactly what he was told to. We talked about his options, weighed it, and I got him… HER a compassionate release and Honorable Discharge, full benefits."

"And?" Despite everything I was finding myself in sympathy. I tried to remind myself of our fight, of what he said, what I said, but… Words were one thing and acts another. Usually he did the words right, too, but even here he was still acting right. That's got to mean something. I couldn't stay angry.

"Brigade was willing to back me, if unenthusiastically. But above them, First Special Forces Command, they weren't so good. Commander gave me the chance to step out quietly, take reassignment out of command, let me ride out something meaningless until retirement, if I kept my mouth shut. I… I don't know, I got stubborn. There was a pissing contest and as it turns out star beats eagle. Pulled me up on conduct unbecoming and disobeying policy."

The picture of it played out behind my eyes, him on trial. I remembered my own court-martial, the one for cowardice under fire, after we got back. Remembered how Perry stood up for me against my command, stood there tall and proud with the Silver Star shining on his chest, the war-hero pressuring them into letting me off. Remembered what happened after.

Thing is, nobody plans to be a war-hero. You get a chance to be a hero, it means someone somewhere fucked up, and I was that fuck-up, that was why I was in the docks. Out of respect for him and his Star, they let me off with an Other Than Honorable. Out of respect for him and his limp, they made sure I was out, and the 'Other Than' was loud and clear. It was halfway to a relief, a chance to be myself my own way, get back into school, even if I lost benefits. But for him, for Perry… The Army was what he was. His soldiers were his family, what he lived for. He was a true believer. And here he was getting the same treatment.

"You get convicted?"

"I pulled a medical once I got everyone talking, let them give me a med board. He backed off once I was past the point of no return, but… At any rate, it was quicker. Quicker than I anticipated. Originally, I was going to work for a tech company I knew, had an idea for a messaging model, training a machine learning system to do social network analysis and target language messaging. Started, and then word got out any company that hired me would find itself disqualified in bidding. That one I didn't even try to fight."

"Christ, Perry. I'm…"

He cleared his throat. "That's not what I'm calling about, though. That's just the rain falling on the just and unjust alike, no biggie. No, point is, I took what nest egg we had saved up, cleaned out Tabi's college fund, and scraped together enough to set up shop myself in DC. We did well, got a little SBIR, even got acquired. Things are looking up. There was room for a new refinement to the model, some stuff we'll talk about once you're signed, something that rhymes with quantum computing, and now for the next phase we need an AI ethicist. Or an independent review of ethical considerations related to AI. We could get someone on staff to sign off, generate in-house, but then I saw you trending and I thought…"

"You thought you'd offer me a handout? Bail me out again?" I was trying to keep myself sounding cool and disinterested, but it wasn't working. "I don't know anything about your company or the AI you want evaluated." I was stalling, mostly, but he took me up on it.

"You know her more than you think. I call her Little Angel, for that story you read me when I was in recovery. The half-finished one, remember? Trained on a huge amount of counterinsurgency theory and messaging, but also literature and poetry and historical records and the like. First task was to finish the story, complete it. Damned spooky, that."

"Little Angel? You mean Malikah as-Safaraya? It's more like 'King in Yellow'. Or Queen, I guess. I mistranslated. But complete it? You had it write out the King in Yellow? Bone-white mask and the dance, frozen bodies in the center of the city of bronze?"

"Hell yeah. And it made sense; I'll send you a copy. For a given value of sense. I don't ever want to read it again, to be honest, and I just had it in translation."

"Hell of a training set. The part that was left stayed with me for years, it… I don't know, lingers."

"Yeah, it does. First guy we had analyze it, he quit. Said the translation was fine, but he didn't want to work with anything that could write that. There was a reason we never found the full text of the original, he said, a reason they burned it. Disturbing the natural order. Which I'm not disagreeing with, but evil is what we were building, something that can handle thinking twisted. Something to motivate the wrong sort of people, you know? Have to think like a crazy to message one, and there's some things better left for the disembodied to really connect to. Beats giving our own folks bad dreams, outsource the nightmares to the machines. That's her, our little nightmare machine. So, you in?"

I was thinking about it, thinking hard. I took a look around my basement studio apartment, remembered how much the shithole was costing me a month… And how much was left in the bank. Thought about the way the coffeehouse got silent when I walked in, after that interview went viral, became the meme of the week. Did a quick survey of how many resumes I'd sent out this month, and how many I had callbacks on. Thought about my student loans. Thought about my Mom asking me to move back home. Thought about the chance to still do the job I spent a decade of my life working towards, even if it was somewhere I'd never get to talk about. Remembered what'd happened last time I talked about what I did, unclassified though it might be.

"Yeah. Yeah, Perry. I think maybe I might just be interested, come to that." And the taste of ashes and panic was back thick on my tongue, in a way that no amount of hangover could wash away.

NSA Building, Fort Meade, Maryland. Conference room. Fall 2018.

"The flow is a three-step process. First, we do an analysis of the social network we want to influence, determine what is there now, who talks to whom and about what, and what we want that picture to be. That analysis is done in a graph database, which means it stores the data in a way that enables the machine to go deep into the structure, follow the branches and connections with a search time that increases minimally, linear not exponential. That allows us to scale rapidly." Sky was talking, Perry's security guru and lead engineer. She had a windswept bob in a copper red so striking I spent the first few weeks watching her eyebrows obsessively to catch her in a bleach job. Between that and her dimples, she was something like the manic pixie dream girl after ten years and a bitter divorce. For the client meeting she was wearing pin-stripes and a pencil skirt not as flattering as she thought, but she pulled it off. Love will get you far, and she loved what she was doing, loved building something the world had never seen.

She made a little red dot dance around the screen, hopping here and there on a giant tangled spiderweb of profile pictures and connections. Every picture had a little dual flag, Russian and Ukrainian, with how full the flag was of each nation representing their respective degree of positive sentiment, and below that a list of their three top motivations. When she hovered over an area long enough for Perry to adjust focus, that section of the web would enlarge and move to the forefront, shifting the dandelion ball this way and that like a VR roller-coaster. At the moment, the blue and yellow dandelion was being eaten by the larger but sparser red and blue dandelion. The Ukrainian network, the yellow and blue, was half-a-golf ball on top of a red-and-blue tennis ball, with the collision area in a bruised purple and orange mix.

"Once we have an idea what the end-state is, we pass information encoding the current state of the model with what we want it to be." Here she showed two distinct dandelion puffs of approximately equal size, with the Russian ball still visibly sparser, just barely kissing in two places. The robust Ukrainian network was joined at the far left edges by sky blue networks representing European and American networks with business or family ties into Ukraine. The ideal image had the Ukrainian puff all but cuddled into a triple-branched Euro-American bird's nest that faded into transparency at the edge of the screen.

"This is the magic. We take what the network is," a flash to the tennis-ball-consuming-a-golf-ball image, "and what we want it to be," back to the yellow and blue puff held up in the bird's nest, "and we pass that to our optimizer. Then the magic happens. We have a simulated annealing quantum computer that is capable of parsing the two node maps and finding a path from one to the other. It optimizes a path of what nodes to cut off and which to reinforce, what edges need more traffic and what common threads to pull on, how to make the network fragment in the right way. And that is what we've been doing in simulations for you guys now for the past six months, in exercises and retrospective data."

I scanned the table. Three of the guys in uniform and the civilian didn't count at all, they were rubber-stamping someone else's decision. The civ — he might well come to his own conclusion, based on the body language, but it didn't really matter, he was just the guy signing off on the money. Whatever he really thought, his signature only said whether or not the contracting officer's representative, the COR, was authorized to obligate funds. The COR, that was the guy at the table that counted, and that was Sergeant Major Fall. He was the big dog in the room, and he knew it. He sat at the side of whatever office dweeb he'd forced to take the meeting, but his decision was final, eyes obsidian shards above the soft smile.

He was half a foot or more taller than anyone at the table, had an inch and thirty pounds of muscle on Perry even — and Perry was used to shrinking himself enough to make folks feel comfortable. Fall, he didn't do that. He wanted you uncomfortable, wanted the man-spreading felt even if you couldn't see it, wanted to hold your eyes a little too long and make his examination of your body a bit too thorough. But here, even Fall was deferring, albeit to a disembodied voice.

Somewhere in the ether over the table was the voice of the lead for the team working out of the US Embassy in Kyiv, Major Kat Rossi, calling in. It was her push to test Little Angel downrange, provide it in support of our partners and make it a key element of what we were providing. Her demos that sold the Country Team on it, her reports that kept the way cleared for R&D even before it had passed all the required benchmarks — and her twice-weekly carping sessions, 'operator feedback' she called it, that kept Sky and me and sometimes even Perry cursing and coding into the small hours of the morning, reformatting and tweaking parameters and visualizations. We called her the Red Queen because she kept you running faster and faster without ever moving forward. That, and because we fantasized about cutting off her head.

We fantasized, but she actually did it, biting off some poor techie's noggin at least once a month. Bad enough that we kept a closet at the office stocked with tissues and a punching bag ready for damage control afterwards. But for this brief she was sweet as eggnog and twice as cloying, cheer-leading with a smile so wide you could hear it. If I didn't know better, I'd have thought she was someone's grandmother, rather than the guy foreclosing on her farm. She wanted Little Angel, wanted it bad. She'd even muzzle herself for the hour it took for us to sell her command on it, if that was what it took.

"So what does that mean, simulated annealing? And isn't quantum computing expensive and delicate?" The Red Queen was throwing softballs, which was somehow unnatural enough that it was worse than her at her normal vitriol. I fielded the question for Perry while he found that part of the slide-deck.

"Simulated annealing is a more limited form of QC. It only works for certain types of problems — optimization, mostly. Which as it happens is exactly the problem we're working with. It creates a model of the problem, the ground state, then increase the 'heat' in the system until the whole circuit becomes a single quantum circuit in superposition. Then it 'cools' the system back down until it finds a new ground state, the optimized solution you wanted, the best path from start to finish. Does that for every sub-network and fragment, and tells you auto-magically, almost, the best set of messaging and network fragmentation to go from start-state to end-state."

Perry had gotten the right slides up there, with a walk-through of the old Traveling Salesman problem bookended by the particular network optimization we were going for — current state to preferred future state, Russian tennis ball devouring a golf ball to a strong Ukrainian dandelion puff supported by a NATO bird's nest floating past a sparse Russian tree almost denuded of avatar leaves. Perry took it from there.

"The downside is that it only works for some problems. The benefit is that you can have three orders of magnitude more qubits working on it at once — more limited problems, but much bigger ones. And it's cheaper, more robust, repeatable. We aren't a QC company; we just bought the system off-the-shelf. And our algorithms are straight-forward, too. We get a path from one state to another, a list of what needs to be developed, what cut, and in what order. The secret to us as a company is the third phase of the operation, the actual messaging. That is what we offer that no one else does." He paused and caught the eye of every person there, one by one. Then he went on.

"See, we have a generative AI, a chatbot, that generates itself all the right messaging at a speed and scale only possible with AI to accomplish the path the quantum computing solution provided. Little Angel. And because of the training our AI has gotten, she messages in any of seventeen target languages appropriately and at scale, gives us the right themes and messages to inject. A small number of artificial profiles, machine generated and curated, messaging at the right time to the right people, amplifying responses or mitigating as required, carried out over months and years. No one writing messages, no one translating, fire and forget. And where the optimal path bushes out a bit, where we drift from the ideal, it generates traffic to pull us back. If we drift further than that, we resubmit with the current state as the new ground state and generate a new optimization back to our objective."

He let that sink in. "Out of all our simulations using historical data and training sets, thousands of runs, only seven have required retuning, and all but one of those was back on track with no more than forty-three additional steps. Compare that to the normal prospect of just winging it, each individual message approved for each response, and you can see the advantage. It's not just getting to the right spot, it's staying on message and within the approved guidelines, no matter the response. Little Angel isn't cutting through the underbrush one machete chop at a time, lost in the jungle… She has a map and compass, and she cuts with surgical precision."

That had them sold. There was some hemming and hawing, some examples from the simulations and some endorsements of what we'd done to date for the team downrange, but Perry had given them the promises they needed to hear. I gave my spiel about reviewing the output with additional simulations to determine toxicity and the impact of our generated messaging on real-world social networks, and they nodded politely, but the ethics review was a requirement levied from outside. I could have told them I was going to burn doves and feed Little Angel on the smoke and they'd have been just as happy.

As we were finishing up, the suit and the uniforms collecting their papers and finishing their water bottles, gathering up the trash, Major Rossi asked Sky and Perry to hang back a bit to discuss some visualization tweaks for her Ukrainian partners, tune the dashboard. Sergeant Major Fall offered to take me downstairs to my office in the basement, knowing I didn't spend much time here.

"I can take you down to the office while your boss chats.

Unless you think you can find it on your own already. I know it's a maze." He looked at me with disquieting eyes, flat and steady like he was filming, even as the rest of his face and body moved with casual grace.

"I… That is…"

Perry nodded at him, distracted. "Thanks, CJ. I appreciate it. Not hard once you've seen it, but…"

"Hey, no sweat. We all been there. C'mon, Miss Greenbaum. Let's get you walking…" He grabbed up the folders and shoved them into the big banker's zip bag, tossing my unclassified notebook in after it. He stood aside for me to walk past, grabbing a mint Life-Saver from the dish on the desk. There were banal remarks about how easy it was to get lost, some rambling tale about being late for his first meeting with the Colonel. Once we were down an unused staircase and into the basement, the occasional isolated SIGINT soldier our only companions beside shadow and echoes, he corralled me up against a cork message board and leaned in. I gasped, at first, then pressed my lips in a firm line and held my ground.

"Listen, girly. I'm just letting you know what the score is here, so you understand. Perry I trust, and if his company gives him lead on the project, I trust them, too. I know he'd take a bullet for me, or for anyone. For you." With that he tapped me on the left hip once, twice, right where Perry had gotten hit in Kut, years and years ago. Once on my slacks, a second time a little higher, tapping a sweater suddenly way too thin. I felt the heat rise into my cheeks, and involuntarily looked away, blinking furiously, shame flooding through. Hadn't thought he knew, at least not to that level of detail. Hadn't imagined Perry would talk it about it, about me. Not like that. And if I had…

"Sergeant Major, I…"

"Quiet." He paused there, breathing my breath. His was cool, tasting of the Life-Saver. Mine, I knew, was sour with fear, no matter how straight I kept my neck. As planned. Waiting. When he judged me uncomfortable enough, scared enough, he relented, pulled back a few inches. Enough to turn my head and look at him without touching noses.

"You're thinking Perry told me, wondering just how close we are. Just what he thinks of you, that he'd be telling that story to folks you'd never met. Well, you can stop wondering. He didn't. All he said is you were some God-damned Data Witch, a Silicon Valley Ivy League genius that was with him in Iraq the first time. Said you and your 'terp used to read him stories when he was sitting there in the hospital, recovering. Said you read him some crazy-ass play you guys found, haji trash you were translating, the Yellow King or some such."

I winced to hear him say that name, and he stepped back; gave me the bare limits of personal space, satisfied that I was properly intimidated. I breathed a bit, figuring what to say. I could still feel the Perry, imprint of thumb-tacks in my shoulder-blades, and much as I hated it, there was an involuntary flash of gratitude that he'd let me go. Which he knew. Counted on.

He started his spiel again. "He didn't tell me that, you did. In the interview you gave to that magazine, recovery from your fuck-up. You remember that? Said you felt obligated to do the right thing now because you'd done the wrong thing before, in Iraq, and somebody you cared about got shot. Said you couldn't just delay, not do anything, 'cause last time you did it somebody else paid the price. You remember that?"

"I… I remember that. Didn't realize that quote made it into the final story. Look, Sergeant Major, sounds like you and I want…"

"It didn't. Didn't make the cut. And if you're curious, that reporter wouldn't give me anything beyond what was in the story, either. But there was a copy editor that had all the previous versions of the story, the ones with all the shit that didn't make the cut-line. He had gotten into trouble in Tahoe, public intoxication or some such shit, and I pulled some strings with a buddy there that knew a guy who could get them to drop the charges. Guy was willing to give me all the gossip I wanted, after that, first drafts and everything." He took a breath here, tapped the banker's bag on the palm of his other hand.

A door behind him opened, haloing him in blinding fluorescent light for a second. Over his shoulder I saw an indistinct form in the doorway, a cloud of yellow straw strewn about the head, face a pallid mask devoid of features. The woman, whoever she was, took one look at our conversation and stepped back, slam of the door echoing a little down the empty hall.

"I tell you this not because I want you to have warm fuzzy feelings for that stuck-up ass-wad of a reporter, but so you understand what lengths I went to in order to find out who Perry was bringing on. I trust him, and I trust his product. But you, I don't know or trust. All I know is your stamp of approval is standing in between me and getting Little Angel out to my guys on the ground in Kyiv, and they tell me they need it. So you are an obstacle to me, and I learn what I have to about obstacles. Stand in my way and I'll roll right the fuck over you, because I've got folks in harm's way looking for this, and ain't nobody else gonna take a fucking bullet meant for you because you couldn't figure out how to get your fucking ass in gear and drive. You do this one right, we won't have no issues, but you fuck up and I'll show you what I'm doing here, understand?" I closed my eyes for a second, and when I opened them, he was smiling.

"If you're feeling scared here, girly, or wondering what else that reporter told me, don't. I don't go for boys in dresses."

I felt myself go cold, but he had gone too far. This I had dealt with, this threat I knew, prepared for. I raised one eyebrow and lifted a corner of my lips, put just the right sardonic lilt in my voice. "No? Who are you telling that to, Sergeant Major, me or your boner? Because I'm the one with ears."

He took two steps back, breathed in sharply. His hands came down in front of him, almost a boxer's stance. I just smiled, letting my eyes drop to show I saw his hands balling up, and didn't care. He flushed, and then opened his hands and turned away. Chuckled.

"You got balls there, girly, I'll give you that. Okay. I'll take that for you saying you're on board."

I opened my mouth to say something, and he raised his eyebrows. I closed my eyes, breathed, and nodded once, curtly. He smiled. "Good talk, Charlene. Ma'am."

We walked the rest of the way in silence, and I memorized the signs with all the focus I'd ever given to a Soldier of the Month board. Another Sergeant Major sweating me to see if I could take the pressure, and judging me, finding me wanting. Like before, I stopped the twitching, stilled myself. I didn't want to do that walk ever again, never wanted to have that man walk beside me, never wanted to be trapped with him there, not knowing the way out. Gave me a motivation to mapping out the labyrinth, I guess, with the Minotaur there beside me.

ISET Offices, Alexandria, Virginia. November 2018.

Next few months were smooth. I almost never had to talk to the Red Queen myself. The retrodiction was close enough to spotless to be almost suspicious, the present-day stuff less polished but still within easy tolerance. The Sergeant Major went back to his day job, and Perry was so busy tweaking parameters, he barely had juice to answer emails. He made the time, often time-stamped after eleven o'clock at night or before five, but always within twenty-four hours even on the weekends.

I'm ashamed to say I came in twice on the weekend myself, just to see if he took Sundays off. He didn't. Or maybe that *was* off, for him… He answered within hours, and more relaxed tone. If I didn't have to make special arrangements to have someone come in and open the office, I'd have been tempted to shift my schedule to work weekends, just to take something off his plate.

Especially since my analysis wasn't making life any easier for him. I ran the tests over and over, used half a dozen different industry standard network models, one or two of my own design, and every single time things came back the same way… Serious degradation of the anticipated social network within two years, spreading conspiracy theories and network fragmentation, increases in adversary disinformation and reduction in prophylaxis against the same, culminating in a general culling and churn in accounts that led to eight out of ten personas originally exposed to Little Angel's messaging disappearing or dropping most of their social nets for more militant, radicalized or radicalizing limited networks that often enough changed platforms away from forums we had easy access to. Sometimes it was more, sometimes it was less, but it was never anything but a catastrophe for every social network we were modeling. Bright vibrant flowers and puppies and grumpy cats would be washed from the profile-picture network trees by a wave of camouflage and nationalism, streaked here and there with blood and bravado, the only color the ubiquitous blue-and-yellow flags that popped up like old bruises on a battered wife. It was a failure cascade that seemed inevitable in every scenario I could run, a war appearing in the social networks that made all our messaging pointless. And worse than the war was the general sickness and death and paranoia — it was like if World War I was occurring in our feeds, except with the Spanish Flu before the war rather than after. It was the end of the world, or at least the end of our little scripted social network snowglobe. Which meant, to my mind, that our AI had been fed a little too much apocalyptic silliness and started spewing it back to us.

Which would have been fine, time to retune and reconsider, except for one especially chilling detail… The messaging worked. Whatever objectives we set before Little Angel to accomplish, any measure of success we wanted, she got there. Increased friendly versus adversary representation by orders of magnitude, reduced positive reaction to adversary messaging, increased pro-Ukraine sentiments, increased out-of-network support and resonance… It was all a success, just a pruned and radicalized stump of success compared to the previous lush rose-bushes of mixed sentiment and ideology.

Little Angel worked, she just sickened the whole network with her success. Succeeded until the whole network ended up inoculated against adversary messaging, pockets of demoralized Russians posting imprecations into the void, pointlessly. It was toxic, alright, a horribly toxic mix, but damned if it wasn't damn fine fertilizer all the same — Perry had the Agent Orange of generative AI here, so far as I could tell. His AI did just what he told it to do, but in the doing of it would send every network into catastrophic collapse to do it. A cure far worse than any disease we could imagine. And now I had to tell him.

I set up a meeting for the week before Thanksgiving — two weeks to get my ducks in a row and pray for a miracle, pray for something to change. He had an idea, of course, he was up on the general trends and what I was doing, but I hadn't told him that there was no alternative. Hadn't told him I was giving up.

So for two weeks I sat in that cruddy little cube farm in front of some cruddy borrowed workstation, locking the report up in the office safe every night. I stayed there from when it opened in the morning to when the disapproving receptionist finally kicked me out at night, and got used to ignoring the coughing fits that seemed to come over her at a quarter of five each day. I swear, when she came in with laryngitis, she'd just coughed her way to being actually sick.

I felt like a contagion, soiling everything I touched, wanted to wrap myself in a giant tissue and be tossed away. But human booger or no, there were still new carriers for me to infect, new vectors to spread my disease and disorder. It was boom time for killing dreams, and I was in a groove I couldn't seem to quit. Once I had the report written and slides done, I started coming in later and just rehearsing, and then not coming in at all. Wondered if the receptionist worried about me, or just celebrated being able to lock up for lunch again. Either way, home wasn't better… The dreams followed me, and the stress dreams about what I was going to say to Perry blended seamlessly with the old dreams of what I had, or hadn't, done in Kut, leaving me not even wondering what it was that shot me awake in the middle of the night sweating.

Didn't really matter the specifics of *how*, though, since I already knew the *who* — it was something I did to Perry, either now, then, or in the future. A Mobius strip of betrayal and impotent efforts for the guy who'd saved me, then and now.

One particular dream broke through the whiskey sweats. Couldn't say if it was before or after I had the final draft done, but the dream I can't forget. We were back in Kut in the truck, and I was flustered and flailing at the wheel, unable to go forward or back, Perry getting out of his own truck and running under fire to take over, reaching out to yank the door open. But that strange Iraqi with the bone-white mask and the scars on his chest like seashells or wings was in our turret, this time. He poked his featureless face down between his legs and gestured to keep the door closed. I ignored him, the bizarre baring of sharpened teeth in a smile gone wrong, brushed the yellow silk off my helmet. I simply watched through the waving yellow and orange cloth, looked past the bare bone-white legs, sat unmoved as Perry got us out of there, like always.

As he bashed us out of the kill zone and back into the convoy, the creature looked down at me and smiled, stretching one long-fingered hand impossibly far to trail a finger in the pool of blood in Perry's lap. He sketched a line from forehead down my nose across my lips and off my chin, neatly dividing my face in half. Then a second single stroke painted my eyes temple to temple. A third smaller angled stroke across my mouth left the tin-foil taste of another's blood. He smiled. The huge black pupil-less eyes caught me and displayed my image back to me, upside down and reversed. A cross was there across my face, broken footrest on my lips. I hung there upside down in the thing's eyes like the Hanged Man on a Tarot card, and somehow the rocking of the HUMMWV became a pendulum swing in a featureless night, upside down and alone, viewer and viewed all at once, taste of blood and ashes fierce pepper on my tongue.

Even now I can taste it, remember the flavor of Perry's blood. I woke to a power outage and thunder, and never managed to go back to sleep that night, just sitting there on the edge of my hotel bed, staring out at a dark room and empty television, watching the shadows to see if they moved.

After a week of shit like that, the actual meeting was somewhat anticlimactic. Perry made me comfortable as soon as I came in, getting in to the office before I did and having the safe open and report visibly read when I peeked around the corner. He was perched on top of a rickety wobbly office table, bad hip cocked to keep the weight off of it and bad leg stretch out board stiff. The printed slides were scattered across the table, staple torn out and notes scrawled across a few of them. The folder was in his hands open to the alternate modeling, with a red pen grasped in his teeth. He nodded and gestured to take the seat across the table.

"So no hope at all, huh? Back to the drawing board?" For someone that had just had the last three years of his life judged inadequate, not meeting contractual requirements, and probably dangerous, he seemed remarkably chipper. I caught myself wondering if he'd practiced sounding casual in front of a mirror, or if he'd just gotten used to hearing bad news.

"I wouldn't say it is exactly square one, but pretty close. Bottom-line is that Little Angel can't safely be deployed in a real-world trial, not for anything that matters. Not for a warfighter. The damage to the wider social networks and information environment context is simply too great, the fragmentation too intense and too richly supported, to take the risk, ethically speaking."

I took a breath, peeked at him. Stone-faced, but not unfriendly. "Within six months tensions start ratcheting up and friendly and adversary networks start segregating; within a year you start seeing increased radicalization on both sides and decreasing evidence of ameliorating contact in physical space. Eighteen months in there is a complete collapse of economics and social networks, an explosion of disinformation and conspiracy theories, and within twenty-four months networks start dying off. Three years in and it's Mad Max territory, nothing the same and everything broken."

"That bad, huh?"

"That bad. Every time we run it, we get some variation of these effects, some mix of death, disease, and disinformation, and a concomitant collapse of the overall information environment, friendly and adversary alike. No amount of parameter tweaking and measuring of content seems to shift the collapse more than a month or two either way, and of the scenarios we ran only two didn't result in war between Russia and Ukraine. Of those two, one of them resulted in a completely Russian-dominated set of social networks, the other barely better than war. Little Angel is toxic, Perry, I'm sorry."

"But it worked, right? Am I misreading? The overall effect of the generated messaging content is exactly within the guidelines we set, achieving a measurable positive impact exactly correlated with how free we let her play, the sentiment swayed in the right direction every time and corresponding to volume of generated content, yeah?" He tapped the figures in the folder.

"It works, or rather the effects it achieved closely map to the objectives we set for it. BUT, and this is a big but, the reason for the dramatic positive response is a series of catastrophic events that displace and disrupt all social networks. Friendly, neutral, and adversary alike. Those events are exploited more successfully by Little Angel than by the bad guys, but the reason for success is the catastrophic event, not the content."

I paused. Breathed in and out. "And I'm not sure we can count on the Four Horsemen riding to our rescue here, Perry. Conquest, War, Famine, and Death — these aren't our friends. Mind you, every single simulation we've run including two I don't even list, Plague and Pestilence are the background on which the whole gruesome depiction is painted… We just can't seem to shake the simulation away from a global pandemic of statistically impossible proportions, no matter how we tweak and twist. Little Angel wants there to be a plague in the next two years, and everything else is built on that fact."

"So why? What's pulling her there?"

"Don't know. We can't tell. Or, I guess, we don't know *what* but we do know *why.* The problem here is that the toxicity is probably not just a feature of the simulation, it's a response to the training data. See, you're running head-on into physics here… You've got iterated data artificially generated by the system itself feeding your machine. Until you can get around feeding it auto-generated content, you're going to get twisted results. And while we see it coming out in the sim first, it will reappear in target content, too, eventually."

"This is your Second Law of Info-Dynamics stuff, the commentary. It's bullshit. That's not how entropy works, Char. That's exactly opposite. Entropy is increased randomness and reduced form, not increased form and reduced variance. It doesn't make sense."

"Yeah. Okay. So this might be a bit of a Silicon Valley-ism, but it is real, for all of that. Bottom-line, whatever the reason for it, computer systems and algorithms and coding all seems to converge on reducing complexity over time by means of chunking into bigger and bigger units, at larger and greater levels of granularity. Couple of physicists have done paper after paper on it, and the math works. However weird the implications seem. It's like quantum mechanics. Weird and counter-intuitive, but the math works. And those equations explain the model collapse here; explain the way Little Angel starts poisoning stuff."

He grunted for me to continue. I did so, warming to the topic. "First level of assembly language burning pixels for Pong onto a CRT, a whole spaghetti mess of eye-throbbing headache-inducing undifferentiated code. High informational entropy. Next level up, you start making functions in the code that simplify certain actions, allowing you to automate certain features. A little less entropy. Next level up again, you create objects that work together in certain ways, simplifying the level of things you have to keep track of, chunking into bigger and bigger blocks of code that interact in more complex manners — Object Oriented Programming — even less hand-tweaking. Eventually you get something like today, where it's just frame-grabbing real movements onto an environment labeled 'Enchanted Forest Number 7'. You can even have the code itself generate some of the lesser details of the interaction. A lot more complex in outcome than Pong, yet a lot easier to read even if longer. The code is coherent blocks now, patterned. Reduced entropy over time."

He nodded, and I breathed easier. He was getting it. "That chunking, that gathering of features into larger and larger units that interact in more and more intuitive manners, that's the Second Law of Info-Dynamics, however corny the name. Informational Entropy reduced at each stage of development, chunking things to make them simpler and simpler, until eventually what would once have been a whole program is just a single system call with the right syntax and arguments."

"Okay, so that's reduction in complexity, call it entropy or just simplifying shit, whatever you like, but what does this have to do with Little Angel? MAD, right? Model Autophagy Disorder."

"Yeah. Yeah. So MAD… This is still just stuff in pre-print, but it has been passed around the AI community for awhile, and we're convinced, even if it hasn't been published. Model Autophagy Disorder is the even catchier name for something we all know, the way that LLMs and chatbots and generative models of any kind seem to degrade when fed artificial content."

"Artificial. You mean machine generated content, the messaging."

I nodded. "And this is the source of the problem. See, if you accept that informational entropy always decreases, that there is an inevitable move to greater pattern, then when a model starts generating content that it formulates itself and feeds on it, it inevitably becomes simpler and simpler still. The data cannibalization leads to simplified output, and eventually it gets caught in loops and ruts of… Of weirdness, really. Strange generative output that is less and less representative of the real-world. There are even AI ghost stories from it, like Loab, the Ghost Woman that appears in one particular visual model, if you prompt the AI right. Weird freaky image of a sad woman with rosacea, and once she's there, she's stuck — you can't get her out of generated images from that point on. Only solution is to restart the model from a point taken before the negative prompt. Otherwise, big or small, prominent or subtle, you get Loab. It infects the model and draws it after that. What you've got is something similar, with this pandemic as your Loab."

"So, if we figure out at what point we got infected with it, we can restart it and it'll be fine?" He knew the answer, but he wanted me to say it.

I took a deep breath and said it. "No. No, Perry. It wouldn't. The problem is in the design itself, the source of the training data on which the model is built. You generate new content and it might be a different Loab, not pandemic but meteorite, but *something* will haunt it still, just the same. Or different, but still there. You know what I mean."

"So if we went back to the beginning, did the whole training anew, took it from the ground up, started anew with the Kut archive and AQI messaging, all the way back through scraped insurgent traffic… If we stopped it from ever reading the King in Yellow, all that's beside the point, you're saying. What you're saying is even if we started back before that, before any of the training set was there, the design itself was faulty."

"Right. Your content has to be generated for the process to work."

"Yeah. Generated content optimized on a quantum computer, fed into…"

"Exactly. Your network design *has* to generate the content, because the future stuff doesn't exist yet, by definition. It can't help but be generated. Normally you might reconfigure and come back in another few months using only real-world data, trim the data sets and maybe accept a bit wider variance, but for this…"

"Yeah. It's the special sauce. Just didn't know it was tears that gave it the flavor."

I watched him. Finally I said it, knowing how he'd respond. "Perry, let it go this time. I know what the report says, know the ethics here. I wrote it, after all. But fuck the ethics report. I can spin it, massage the details. Fudge it. Bottom-line is just like you said, the messaging works, in the simulation. It does what you said it would do. We know, you and me and Sky and who knows, maybe Little Angel herself knows this won't work over the long term, not the way intended. But that's what they're asking for, paying for. Give it to them. All the caveats on effects you want, tell them truthful, but let them get what they're paying for. Walk away with your contract and your payment, and over the next five years, maybe we figure out some way to avoid feeding it simulated content, figure a way around the entropy chunking. In the meantime, take the money and run. Do the smart thing, not the right one."

He looked at me with those eyes, sad only in my memories. And he smiled, genuine smile, so far as I could tell, if more subdued than usual. "Shit, Char. I can't do that. Gotta dance with the one I brought, after all. That's why I hired you. I knew you couldn't lie to me."

And I felt that now like an accusation, somehow, like bullets I was taking in his place. I couldn't lie to him, but God I wish I could.

NSA Building, Fort Meade, Maryland. Conference Room, Thanksgiving Week, 2018.

Perry set up the meeting to explain the problem to CJ and the Team for Monday, the Monday before Thanksgiving. Which was kind of a giveaway that it was bad news, I thought, but there you go… I'd get to ruin some more holiday dinners; Mom would be proud. Perry briefed it all himself, and he fielded most of the questions, too. Not sure whether that was pride talking or his way of protecting me from the Red Queen's wrath, but I still felt her the whole time.

Which was cool with me. Or if not cool, at least expected. I took it calmly and professionally, and there on the other side of the screen she couldn't feel the conference table shake in time to my knee. CJ, though, the Sergeant Major… He never dropped his gaze from me, not that whole meeting, but never said a word, either. Just sat staring at me. The last few minutes, where they talked recovery options and what it did to the contract, that was a blur. They decided to come back to it after Thanksgiving, finally.

Perry squeezed my shoulder as he got up after, gave me a smile. Then he winked and walked over to the Sergeant Major, engaged him about the Ravens. While he kept CJ pinned I got lost in the corridors and tunnels, until I could burst through the turnstiles to the door and the outside frost-bitten air and ice floes of parking lots to my little rental, and just sit inside it, breathing silence.

Packing that night, I heard the bell ring at about 2130. Figured some poor delivery driver had the wrong address. Opened the door without looking, and froze in the doorway when I saw him. CJ, the Sergeant Major. He pushed his way in and shut the door with his foot. He smiled. He was wearing dark brown slacks and good shoes, a tight tan shirt with the sleeves up and no tie. He leaned against the wall, knowing there was no back exit.

"Sergeant Major, I think you should..." I started strong, except my voice was a hair too high for intimidation. I cleared my throat, and he spoke over me.

"This won't take long, Ms. Greenbaum. Don't worry. I'm not here for you. I'm here for Perry. Sit down, you'll be more comfortable. Over there is fine, I'm not scaring you."

He lied. Or at least he was wrong. I was scared, whatever he claimed. "I'm fine standing. What do you mean 'for Perry'?"

"Look, you and I both know if ISET screws this contract up, can't get delivery, Perry is out. They'll keep him around for awhile, sure, but he's not going anywhere after this. Years of development down the toilet... I don't know how long his contract is, but salesmen don't make what he does, so even if they don't find a reason, he'll get the boot in his ass soon enough, right?"

This was more true. I sat down on the hotel desk. "Perry has more going on than you know, CJ." He winced to hear his name and not the title. I felt a little candle flick of pleasure, small a victory as it might be. "He'll find something. And even if he doesn't, that's the kind of guy he is. He'd rather eat mud honestly than gold leaf dishonest." I couldn't exactly picture why he'd be eating gold leaf, when I said it, but the Sergeant Major got the point.

"Yeah, he would. You're right, there. Perry would take any bullet, no matter how big or small, for anyone, big or small. Even you. Which is why it is incumbent upon us…" Here he stood up from the door, took one step forward before he saw me shrink back, and stopped. Shrunk back to the door himself. "Incumbent on us to protect him from himself. Look, Perry won't sell an inferior product. And he owns Little Angel. But ISET *will* sell crap. If there were a copy of Little Angel available, maybe, one Perry didn't control… Well, then, ISET would have to keep him on to do services, 'cause he's the only fucker that can make it work. Knows it. And I can get them to promise to sign a five-year contract at his present salary or above, so long as they get a three-year contract with us for Little Angel, Corporate Edition."

I thought about it. Thought long and hard about it. The Sergeant Major, say what you will about him, and I will, he knew his job. He waited for me. Knew what I'd say before I did, probably.

"How do I know you're serious? That you really can do it?"

"Phone call with the ISET CFO. Nothing recorded, nothing on paper or electrons, and not the CEO or Operations or BD, no one likely to get subpoenaed. But Harry, he'll do it. Now, if you like. Little Angel works, we all know that. What it does to the environment, shit… I don't believe you, Charlene, is the bottom line, but even if I did, fuck the environment. My guys have a job to do, and this tool will do it. Nothing else can. All you got to do is give us access to the system, your password. I know a cyber guy that can do the rest, can exfiltrate the code-base. You just watch over his shoulder. So you in?"

I didn't say anything, not yes or no, but eventually, after a minute or two, I held out my hand for the phone. He put it in there, gently, and backed away from me all the way to the door, not turning his back, just barely not crossing himself and taking a knee. I let him. I knew just what miracle he was buying here, and knew what we'd desecrate in the doing. But sometimes the devil offers bargains, too.

That night I dreamed of the Iraqi angel again, and Kut, and this time he took a handful of Perry's blood from his lap with both palms and held it to my mouth for me to drink, copper earth and despair coating my tongue and making my teeth slick with it. I woke up screaming, or at least moaning and groaning, and the flight attendant gave me two of those little bottles of tequila when she saw my face. They didn't help. But then again, what would?

I told myself it was me taking a bullet for him the way he had once for me, but I knew better. They kept their word, the company, but Perry quit anyways, took his severance and never answered my calls. Now all those rings go on ringing, turning to klaxons to ringtones and back again, but they don't wake me up, not anymore. And the Little Angel flies free.

I remember the last conversation we had, Perry and me. We went back and forth for twenty minutes about what I'd done and why, what he should do. Finally, we'd both said everything we could and it had become clear that everything I had done had been for nought, that he was going to quit and let himself be screwed out of his product, his code, his nest-egg and his dream. Watch his Little Angel be freed and turned into an Angel of Death for the vultures that had bought him out. He was going to stand on his principles and let them steal his creation out from under him and corrupt it, and nothing I could say was going to change it. Finally, after there was nothing left to say, it ended up just where serious conversations with Perry ever did, in a Bible verse.

"You remember First Corinthians, Char? Chapter 6? 'Do ye not know that the saints shall judge the world? And if the world shall be judged by you, are ye unworthy to judge the smallest things? Know ye not that we shall judge angels?' Char, you're asking me to judge an angel here, something beyond us that makes miracles beyond mortal ken. I'm being a good judge, that's all. Even if someone above me is going to overturn on appeal and give Little Angel a pardon. I gotta do what's right, so at least she knows someone has been an honest judge. Or how else am I worthy?"

I didn't say anything at all. I knew I'd judged the same, but been bribed out of it. Been found wanting myself. And maybe Little Angel would judge me for that, one day. I know Perry did. Knew I did myself. But like a goat separated from the sheep, I leapt willing into the flames, knowing I deserved them. And wondered if maybe, just maybe, one day Perry would reach down his finger to me there in hell, and give me a drop of sweat to drink. Maybe I'd earned it.

———

THE JAGUAR GOD AND THE GOLDEN IDOL

FOURTH PLACE AWARD

ZACH WEEKES

THE ENEMY CAME AT NIGHT, falling upon the Conquistadors as fiercely as the jungle rain. Shadows swayed between the camp's firelights and lunged out from sagging trees. The darkness howled, stretching forth in oblong figures that materialized with jagged weapons raised.

Lord Commander Odilon Alves's company had established their camp on an island they called St. Maria — though surely the wild men that prowled its recesses had other names for it. Under the oppressive storm, the Lord Commander's men had been laying cold and soaking in the mud, coughing and shivering, trying in vain to sleep. When the attack came, they launched up in fright. A cacophony of shouted alarms barked in concert with the black thunderheads above. They reached for their weapons; but the powder for their arquebuses and cannons was wet, and the jungle stalkers were already upon them, slaying the lethargic outer sentries with thrown spears and hacking mattocks before the others could prepare.

Odilon was on his feet, rallying his company, calling out, "To arms!" as he hoisted his own matchlock arquebus. Dense with rainwater, the wood of the weapon provided a hefty, solid beam in his grasp. Presently useless as a firearm, the blocky butt — engraved with a mural depicting a pack of hunting hounds — would serve, as it often had, as an over-long club in the Lord Commander's muscular hands.

Rainwater poured in rivulets from his sleeves. He did not have time to don his shining breastplate and morion, but he leapt up, chanting in the ecclesiastical tongue as he hollered to his men, the fire of battle burning in his core: a familiar warmth against the cold of the rain.

Odilon flashed into action, whirling the arquebus over his head, putting the strength of his broad shoulders in each swing. The enemy leapt into the clearing at the center of the camp. They were lanky, sinuous men, faces dark with sappy paint, white teeth flashing as a hissing war cry escaped their lips.

The enemy tore through his scrambling men: the Nochatl warriors ran the white men through with thin spears and brought cudgels down on the back of their skulls as they stumbled in mud, each blow making a sickening crack that echoed in the clouds. Puddles filled with gore, and the screams of dying men resounded in the night.

Odilon's blood pounded in his ears, and he charged the nearest enemy, swinging the improvised club down on a primitive warrior's head, smashing it to pulp. The body fell to the earth, limbs jiggling like jelly. An iron scent tinged the air, and the Lord Commander took in a deep gust of breath, scanning for another foe.

The Nochatl were an insular tribe of the New World unique to St. Maria Island. They hunted at night, killed outsiders without question, and worshipped the jaguars which stalked the jungle. This much Odilon and his men were able to learn from observing the details of their opposition — the spotted pelts that adorned the Nochatl warriors, the oversized feline fangs they carried as charms, and the iconography of their idols that dotted the jungle paths upon shrines bloodied with offerings to their bestial gods.

Another of the Nochatl came before the Lord Commander, crouched low, spear outthrust, growling like the great cat he meant to emulate in his ferocity. Odilon made a wide sweep with his long gun, batting the spear aside and shattering its flint tip, and on the back swing, he sent the upper side of the butt crashing into the warrior's temple.

The man crumbled, and Odilon stood over the corpse, drew a falchion from his belt, and began a chant: "To me! To me!"

His men needed to concentrate their number and fight together if they were to survive the night. Some of his soldiers, nearer to the center of the camp, saluted him, lances and parts of their metal armor now prepared, and joined his chant, bringing attention to the middle of the action.

They fought together, swiping out with swords and lances to drive back the Nochatl, which leapt upon them with fanatical glee, eager to give their lives for a taste of the invaders' blood. Though his company rallied, Odilon feared it was not enough: a mere dozen clustered around him, heaving with exertion, limbs made heavy in the downpour. All around, bodies lay sprawled at hazard in the muck — few of them were Nochatl.

But the Nochatl quavered before the chanting Old Worlders, who with their united arms of hardened steel crushed brittle spears. Odilon hoped it was enough to cow his foe, to drive them off and make an end of the onslaught, which came in the Nochatl fashion of warfare: sudden, brutal, and quick. The jaguar leapt and sunk his teeth into his prey, dragging the victim off to a gory death; he did not stay and endure a hail of blows from an angry mob.

Crouching and circling the Lord Commander's small squad, the Nochatl warriors held back but did not retreat. They countered the Latin chant with a seething song of their own.

"Now, charge! Break them!" Odilon screamed, and he was

the first out of the formation, sword swishing before him in the sizzling rain.

The Nochatl scattered, avoiding his blows, and they retreated into the trees, disappearing behind the ferns. The momentum of Odilon's charge left him pounding to a stop just before the louring scions of the jungle. Lightning flashed, revealing the heads of the Nochatl as they assembled themselves in the underbrush, ready to pounce. Thunder cracked and shook the dripping boughs.

To either side of him, his men had followed and barreled toward the Nochatl, screaming and swinging their weapons. Odilon was about to turn back and order his men away from the trees to resume a defensive formation, when again the trees before him vibrated — but no lightning flashed, and no second peel of thunder sounded.

The night became still, and yet the trees shivered.

Odilon scanned the shadowy trunks, which then again quivered, now with a renewed racket of wet leaves smacking branches.

An inky shape lumbered into his view. A pair of topaz eyes burned in the darkness, and a long, low growl of thunder sounded not above, but upon the ground.

Odilon took a step back, and the shadow lunged from out of the trees, landing in the mud with a meaty *thump*. An arm black as night and thick as a small tree swung out and caught Odilon's chest, sending him reeling and crashing into a nearby tree stump, against which his head struck, dazing him.

Odilon gasped to regain the wind that fled his lungs, eyes swimming with stars, as he sat up against the trunk. Blinking, he watched through swirling vision as thing that attacked him prowled into the midst of his company, the members of which scrambled back in terror, cursing aloud, assigning the image of the Devil his proper name.

The beast was massive, but swift and agile, its black

haunches rippling with muscle as it advanced upon Odilon's men. Ivory fangs hung from its face, bared menacingly as the fur around its powerful jaws crumpled back in an angry snarl.

Odilon's vision vacillated between a fuzzy blackness and flashes of the creature. It stalked forward on two legs, but its front paws were outheld with claws extended. His mind was bleary, but Odilon thought he saw that the beast, when it reared up and ripped at his terror-stricken fellows, had the chest of a man, and the hips and thighs to match, all melded over with a pelt of faintly silver-spotted black fur on the back and neck. Its head was wholly jaguar, and a swaying tail belied its animal origin, but a man was within the beast.

Odilon willed himself to stand, but his limbs were numb as stone. At the sight of his men dying, carved to pieces beneath the beast's claws, he screamed in rage, but he could not recall if the yell left his lips or remained only in his fading mind. At last, the blackness was too strong to resist, and he closed his eyes, and the void met him.

A WET GASPING noise leaked into the darkness, disturbing an otherwise perfect oblivion. Odilon roused, feeling the weight of his eyelids as he dragged them open. A muddy field met his vision, a camp in ruin, reeking with the piquant scent of fresh rain and death. He groaned and pushed himself from the ground with creaking bones and sore muscles, and he surveyed the carnage.

Bodies lay scattered in the reddened muck — many were dismembered and raked through with claw strokes that left four oblong fissures in paling flesh. Odilon's throat choked, not with sorrow but a swelling a rage that served, at least, to reinvigorate him.

They were all dead — all his comrades, all subordinates for

whom he was responsible, some friends. But Odilon still stood, and he would not waste his breath on sobs. If he yet drew breath, the weighty commission from the Highest authority was yet upon him, and the conquest of St. Maria Island was not yet concluded.

A wheezing cough again caught his attention. He turned to see that he was mistaken. He was not the last one left alive, though he soon would be.

Sprawled on the ground nearby lay Dimas, Odilon's chronicler, who served a clerical function to assist the Lord Commander in his ecclesiastical duties. His rank demanded of him not only to lead his men as a military captain, but also as a spiritual chaplain. Soft-spoken Dimas aided this latter role greatly with his quiet knowledge and genial disposition — the Lord Commander reserved the fiery sermons for himself, but the company's men instinctually went to Dimas for moments of intimate prayer and guidance.

Even Dimas, in the face of the foe, was bound to fight, and so he did, and so he fell. Now, the man lay gasping, hand on a ruined chest, out of which gore leaked from a mangled breastplate.

Odilon knelt beside him.

"Dimas, what did this?"

He glanced at the claw marks that had so easily ripped open the once-shining armor.

Dimas croaked. "The Beast…"

In the crook of his arm, Dimas held something close to his body. He fidgeted and brought it forth with an effort for Odilon to see. It was a golden plate, embossed with an intricate image of the Mother of God. Weakly, Dimas proffered the idol to his commander.

"I will die," the man said, and indeed, his face was as pale as grave linen. "Take this to my family, for me. Promise…"

Dimas sighed and expired. Odilon took the golden plate and clutched it to his chest. It was heavy, solid, assuring.

Odilon fists clenched around the idol.

"I will avenge you." He glanced around. "I will avenge them all."

He closed Dimas's eyes and stood. For some time, Odilon rummaged through the camp, taking inventory of what was left that might still be useful. A quilt of overcast lay over the sky. A humid breeze washed through the jungle ferns at the edge of camp. One side of the camp was open to the beach, on which Odilon's company had moored their boats. Further offshore, their ship was anchored. It lumbered on the gray waters, silent and swaying. His company had come ahead of many other fleets to subdue St. Maria, with the objective to establish the island as a staging ground and in-road for future conquests — but most of the men only followed Odilon in the hope to secure a wealth of ancient gold, hidden in the depths of the New World. Odilon's company was one of the first to come this far, though others landed across the New World in various places as savage as this.

Others of his race were beyond contact, months away by sea, and his home was even farther.

There was no one left aboard the Lord Commander's vessel; his whole company had embarked, and Odilon could not man it on his own — nor would he. He vowed to avenge his brothers, and so that meant he must stay on St. Maria. He did not even consider the rowboats.

In the camp, he found enough water and rations to sustain him for some days, though much of the food was soaked and mushy. There were plenty of weapons, but the blackpowder was too wet. He gathered a meagre store of gear on his person, which included his falchion, some rope, knives, and a compass. He left his cumbersome arquebus stabbed into the ground as memorial in the center of the ravaged camp.

He made a cold meal on the beach, setting himself apart from the bodies of his company, and stared into the murky depths as he forced down as much as he could, despite his reeling appetite.

At last, he made a burial for his men along the trees, burying them with their armor and weapons, relics of their courage that Odilon did not dare loot. Yet, their graves were shallow. If he was to fight on, Odilon had to husband his strength — in later years, proper memorials could be assigned to the worthy bones of his deceased company; he would make sure of it, unless he was meant to join them, only belatedly, in their fate upon St. Maria Island.

He would welcome it.

"Let me die fighting as they have," he said in one his prayers over the dead.

Night neared, and deciding it best not remain in camp, unless the Nochatl returned, Odilon made his way into the jungle, in search of a hidden hollow in which he could take his rest and prepare his lonesome campaign against the foe. He would have to master the jungle and learn the jaguar's ways. He would kill the foe one by one, in ambush after ambush, taking fights only where he knew he could win, for as long as it took, until he died or conquered the island. The Lord God had assigned him to this doom, and he accepted it with the grave solemnity of a faithful warrior. His God would bring him victory or eternal rest — to either of which he would gladly submit.

As he went into the jungle, he carried Dimas's golden idol with him. Its weight became awkward, and the moisture in the air made the metal slick, so that, at one point, it slipped from his fingers and landed with a *thud* in the mud before his feet.

Odilon stopped and frowned down at the idol. It was dark beneath the trees, but the slick metal glinted in the traces of light that yet made way between the vines. He fell on his knees before the idol and considered it, and he thought about the jaguar-man that had laid waste to his men.

Alone in the darkness, his thoughts matched the umbral

nature of the wild land. Perhaps the Nochatl had it right. Their god was tangible, and it demanded tangible things of them: blood and torn flesh. It made no qualms about the savagery of the world and the hearts of men which were obliged to submit before The Beast — for it was the supreme form of their animality. How simple, how pure the idea seemed then before the fading glint of the gold idol — a remnant of a distant god — then sinking into the primordial soil.

Eventually, he picked the idol up and, huddling with it hugged against his chest, he curled between the towering roots of an ancient tree.

He closed his eyes to sleep, but the rustling of the jungle in its nocturnal ritual kept him alert. The air was humid, the bark against his back grating. Yet no man or beast came to disturb his hiding place; and he was alone with his thoughts. Then, as exhaustion melded with vigilance, in dream-like half-visions, his mind fled to things long abstracted by time and space.

———

In Spain, Odilon had grown up as an urchin, who could not name or identify his parents — who they were or where they went were facts faded into mystery. Most of the men he would later command did not know this about him. He had been a large and virile youth, outgrowing many of his peers by the power of a secret blessing for which he, in his childhood, did not yet know the purpose.

He would later discover it.

Naturally, in his situation and with his stature, he found a role as a bruiser for a street gang. When he was a young man, a kindly priest lured him off the streets, as he might a hungry dog to the hearth, and brought Odilon into the House of God. That priest was called Father Alves, and a father he was indeed. The orphan took his benefactor's name accordingly as his own surname, not knowing the name which he was originally intended to carry.

The Lord had something else in mind for him.

Though Odilon proved not entirely witless, learning the ecclesiastical mysteries and language, the cloister was not his destiny; a different fire bubbled in the pit of his stomach, which he then could not name, until it was much later kindled in battle.

The Crown called for men to take the New World, for across the ocean lie glories yet to be grasped, in the conversion of heathen hearts and in the conquest of ancient hoards. Odilon put his name forward as a warrior worthy of the challenge, to board the ships of the Conquistadors, but his Father was not so quick to see him go.

In the twilight wilderness, Odilon then recalled the conversation.

"Remember Saint Matthew," Father said, leaning toward Odilon as they sat side by side in the pews. Before them, the crucified form of the Lord, wreathed in all the golden glory of His angels and saints loomed large. Odilon had been praying, fervently, eyes cast upward upon the radiance promised by those images.

He glanced over at his Father, who clarified what he meant to quote: "He who liveth by the sword shall die by the sword."

Odilon frowned and shook his head. How nearly he toed the line of stubborn folly, but he expounded his feelings in the steady rhetoric he had learned from the clergy. "Is it not so, Father, that that very same Teacher is He who called men, in every nation and in every age, to the business of the sword?"

Father Alves grunted and nodded thoughtfully. "Even so, the verse came from His mouth, and so it shall stand eternally true."

Odilon nodded. "I do not contend that it is untrue, only this: perhaps we should not read it as a curse, but as a warning to the meek. For some men, it might be destiny, and a glory. There are those of His saints that so testify."

He flicked his eyes to the reredos at the end of the chapel, where in the frescoes there were buried among the images of gentle martyrs also the faces of George, Maurice, Sebastian, the Archangel, and other manly worthies that carried a blade in their witness.

Father Alves shook his head. “Many have been wronged by the sword.”

“And many other things put right,” countered Odilon. “By what means did the Lord command Joshua to secure the Promised Land? By kind words? A turned cheek? No, but an unswerving faith and the strength of arms.”

Father sighed. “Your mind lingers on terrible things, my son. How can I get you to hear my wisdom?”

The memory faded, but Odilon’s inner eye lingered on the image of the old cleric. He was a vision of what Dimas could have been, should have been: the slow but penetrating eyes of the learned, the creases of sad but gentle smiles often shone over contrite parishioners, the shoulders hunched from scribing and reading by candlelight.

Odilon loved that man, both the surrogate Father and Dimas, and he wished he could see either of them again. But how could the old priest in his gradual, quiet wisdom understand the fire that burned in a young man’s chest?

Odilon had taken up the call of conquest; no soften-spoken word could deter him. But he carried with him the gift of his Father, and his zeal gave him something that the other Conquistadors often lacked. Many of them proved themselves vulgar men, but Odilon pitied them, for by sympathy he knew what smoldered within them. He had a foot in both realms, that of the saint and the raider, the priest and the soldier. Upon the Spanish ships, he had forged it into one identity: ever in his command was a doomful duality — the call to kill and die, and the call to aspire unto the Kingdom in all their striving.

Both aspects of himself won him respect amongst his

fellows, and he fashioned himself Lord Commander on his own ship, where there was both the soldier's revelry and the templar's solemn chanting in equal measure. His zealous spirit elevated him, and the strength of his flesh commended him.

The Church had redeemed his strength, taking it up from the mud of petty thievery; and Odilon had marched forth with her lessons close to his chest. The Crown had given his strength purpose, putting before him an enemy and fresh lands to conquer.

Now, he had arrived at his destiny, and all the men who had dutifully followed him lay still in the dust. They had lived by the sword and died thereby, their glory secured. But Odilon yet lived, and the agony of his dreams was that he was not then feasting with them in the company of the valorous dead, where gathered around the roaring hearths were the swordsmen of all nations and ages whom he had so sharply cited against his caring Father.

Father had said that the verse would stand eternally true, so then why did God keep Odilon alive? For what purpose?

Lingering on these thoughts, and muttering near-incoherent prayers, Odilon's weary body eventually dragged his mind into sleep.

When he awoke in the balmy dawn, Odilon fastened the idol of the Blessed Lady to his side with some rope so that he could carry it like a satchel. He wandered in the jungle that day, foraging what fruits he knew were safe and hunting.

Eventually, he found a stream of clear water, hunched beside it, and set about making a fire to cook the meat of a small lemur he had killed with a thrown spear he had cut out of a branch. As he began striking the flint over dry leaves, he heard a splashing noise in the nearby water. He rose and took up his falchion in a flash and hid in some nearby ferns.

A woman arose from the stream and padded with bare feet onto the muddy bank on which the fire barely smoldered. Odilon watched with breath caught in his throat. The woman was bare from the waist up but had a skirt of slimy fronds that hung about her legs. In a similar fashion, her dark hair hung like rain-wet vines over her shoulders and chest. Her gray eyes shimmered like the water from which she emerged as she scanned the forest.

The woman circled the beginnings of Odilon's fire, examining it curiously, and then she milled about the impromptu camp. Odilon held himself still, stifling his breathing, watching the strange woman as her circuit of the camp became gradually wider.

At last, she passed before the shrubbery in which he hid, and Odilon leapt out when her back was turned, wrapping an arm around her neck. He made to subdue her, and it should have been easy considering his size advantage, but she fought back with surprising strength.

She instantly tensed in his arms and flailed outward, and he lost his grasp on her still-wet body. Thinking quickly, Odilon reached out a boot and hooked his toe around the front of her shin, tripping her. She rolled in the dirt, recovering with agility, but before she could stand fully, the tip of Odilon's sword was pressed under her chin — but he did not drive it home.

She sat up, scanning upward along the length of steel that held her life at stake, and then to man responsible, and she gasped, her face brightening.

Odilon thought it was a strange reaction, but he pressed on with his purpose. This could be a woman of the Nochatl, who might bring word of his continued presence in their jungle to her tribesmen.

He shouted, "Nochatl! Are you Nochatl? What is your tribe?"

He knew the words would be meaningless to her if the woman truly was native to the island, but he relied on his tone to deliver his effect; and if she was Nochatl, she would naturally understand his intent.

One side her lips turned up in a wry grin, and she held up her hands languidly in a gesture of playful surrender. Then, she opened her mouth and spoke in a flowing, melodious voice.

"Come thou, man of the sea, lower thy weapon. I have come to aid thee, not harm thee."

Odilon's mouth fell agape. "How is it that you speak in a tongue I understand?"

"I know many tongues," she said, "some even men have forgotten, for I have swam in many waters that flow upon the earth."

Still astonished, Odilon asked, "Who are you?"

"Thou mayst call me Caulli."

Recovering somewhat from the surprise of this unexpected turn of fate, Odilon removed his blade from the woman's throat and allowed her to stand.

He said, "I have never killed a woman before, but I will not hesitate if you prove to be my foe."

Caulli stood, and Odilon kept his falchion pointed outward, fixed upon the woman; and his eyes were similarly transfixed. Now standing and in full view, she was alluring, with a lithe, shapely body clad in almond-colored skin. Odilon's eyes wandered over her brazen appearance, heart racing, but he maintained his guarded posture.

She stepped closer, paying little heed to his weapon, and looked up at him. The smell of a rolling stream of rainwater in springtime filled Odilon's senses, reminding him of home.

"What shall I call thee?" she asked, scanning his powerful stature with an enigmatic smile.

Odilon shivered but held his ground.

"I am Lord Commander Odilon Alves," he answered

proudly, "and would know if you are my enemy or not. Are you Nochatl?"

"Nochatl…" Caulli tried the word with a musing tone. "That is what thou callest the dark men that occupy this dark island."

Odilon nodded and adjusted his grip on his sword.

Caulli continued: "I am not of them, though I know of them, for they tried to capture me when I arrived in their midst, forgetting the reverence their kind owe to my person."

A cool, dangerous edge suddenly colored her tone.

Odilon shook his head. "I know nothing of that, but I am sworn to defeat them. If you are not my foe, depart from me. You are but a distraction and temptation."

With effort, he kept his eyes locked on hers.

Caulli emitted a shimmering laugh. It was a lovely sound, which carried no malice — a surprise. After a pause, an amused twist played upon her lips.

"Thou art stranded here — alone," she said. "But thou needst not die here. I can deliver thee from here, and I would like to."

She eyed him over once more, and Odilon made a low growl of warning in his throat.

"What keepeth thee here, I wonder?" she said, unphased. "What sane man would stay here to die? Come with me! I know the flow of the rivers and may carry thee upon them swiftly, far from here, to any luscious land abound, even perhaps to thine home…"

"No!" Odilon snapped. "I have sworn to avenge my fallen brothers. To this purpose I am bound until I die, or The Beast is brought low, whichever is first. I will not leave."

"Then, wherefore dost thou linger beside this lovely stream? Thine enemy awaiteth elsewhere."

Odilon huffed and lowered his sword a degree. "I do not know where they hide! I would hunt them, track them, learn their ways until I could strike the fatal blow to their monstrous god, which goes about in the flesh of man and beast combined."

Caulli fell silent, and her starry eyes became distant as she considered this. When she spoke next, her tone was no longer playful and flirtatious, but solemn and bold.

"I know the one of which thou speakst. I know also the location of their temple, from which the Jaguar God ariseth. I arrived there, as I went within the rivers of this land, and I met the Nochatl in their lair. Poxlom and his ilk made to capture me as a prize, but as swift as the running water, I escaped their clutches."

Her eyes fell on Odilon with intensity — she now considered him something other than a plaything.

"Perhaps the Stars have sent a destroyer to punish Nochatl for the iniquities visited upon their messenger, and thou art the agent of the doom thereby set."

Odilon squinted at her. "Poxlom?"

"Poxlom is he who leadeth the Nochatl in their worship. It is he who taketh on the form of the jungle cats. He is a black giant, ancient as the earth. It is he that killed thy fellows. It is he that thou hast sworn vengeance upon."

"Then I shall kill him," Odilon said. "Yet, I would know also what manner of creature you are. You say strange and dreadful things, like no woman I know. What are you?"

Caulli shook her head, her dripping hair playing upon her shoulders like snakes drooping down from tree branches.

"Do not heed that detail yet. We are speaking of Poxlom. Other matters may become clearer to thee in time." She paused for a moment of consideration. "Thou sayest thou shalt kill Poxlom. How?"

Odilon shrugged. "However I may, in which ever way best presents itself. I shall ambush him in the jungle or assassinate him in his temple. And if steel is not enough to end him, I will call upon the power of my God, and whatever result pleases Him, I shall accept."

His hand lingered over the golden idol on his hip.

Caulli glanced at the shining plate fearfully and whispered, "I see. It is so."

"So…" Odilon prompted. "If that is all you have to say, let me be about it. Tell me where his temple is or leave me alone."

"I shall show thee the way," Caulli said. "I shall bring thee to his temple and thou mayest battle him alone."

A thrill of fearful excitement washed through Odilon.

"How so?" he asked. "I would gladly challenge him before his tribesmen, to make proof of his defeat before all heathen eyes. Does he understand the honor of the duel?"

Caulli shook her head. "Not as thou wouldst understand it, but the thrill of the hunt shall move his heart. Thou shalt face him beneath the shadowy boughs, in his most terrible aspect, with which thou art already dreadfully familiar. It shall be in his domain, if he would accept thy challenge."

"So be it," Odilon said. "Lead me there."

ODILON MARCHED with his blade pointed generally in the direction of Caulli's back as she walked in front of him. He kept a close eye on her but internally chastised himself whenever his eyes fell to her swaying hips.

Caulli led him upon a winding path which retraced many of the steps he had already taken. They passed through the place where he had fashioned the spear and slain the lemur, which then lay behind him, beside the stream, likely now to feed some fortunate scavenger.

If what Caulli had told him was true, following her promised a swift and decisive end to the Lord Commander's mission on St. Maria — whether that end meant death or victory, Odilon was eager to meet it and put the spirits of his fallen brothers at ease, one way or another. His vow weighed upon him like invisible stones: the longer he left it unresolved the more vain it seemed of him to have ever spoken it aloud. He must see it done or die.

They passed the roots of the great tree within which he had spent the previous night. At last, they came upon Odilon's disheveled camp. Caulli explained that he had wandered off in the opposite direction of the temple when he departed the camp, before he had his guide to direct him properly.

To this, Odilon grunted an acknowledgement as he made his way toward the tree line along which he had buried his comrades.

Their shallow graves had been opened, and their bodies were missing.

"What is the meaning of this?" he growled, standing above the overturned soil, using the tip of his boot to sift through the dirt, frantically looking for any trace of the dead.

There was none.

Caulli came up beside him and said, "The Nochatl. They must have returned and stole the corpses of thy friends. I assume that is what thou art looking for."

"Why?" Odilon asked through gritted teeth.

"They use blood and corpse-flesh in their rituals, and their meals," answered Caulli serenely. "I have seen it."

Odilon kicked the overturned dirt with a snarl. "A desecration! An abomination!"

His throat choked, and he went limp as the paroxysm of anger passed; and he fell on his knees before the open graves.

"I led them here," he said, gasping. "I would lead them to glory…"

He paused, heaving against the tears which threatened to overwhelm him.

After a long silence, he turned to Caulli, who stood behind and beside him, looking down at him with an unreadable expression.

"And now," Odilon said, "I would put the dead at peace,

knowing their ignominious ends have been answered, and yet…" He trailed off and swallowed. "I have left them to a worse fate than a shallow and restless grave. The Nochatl would submit them to devilry which would cause their souls to revolt."

He stood and scanned the trees beyond. "The Lord as my witness, I will not permit this to stand. I will kill them all, if I must — may the Almighty guide my hand as His judge."

Caulli only smiled at him.

Odilon fingered the golden idol at his side. "Come, swiftly! Lead me there without delay! This cannot end soon enough."

He trudged off into the trees, leaving Caulli to bound ahead of him and resume her lead.

Night fell as the two of them wound their way deeper into the jungle. Caulli padded swiftly down winding paths, which became increasingly furrowed with moss-clad crags and titanic roots from which arm-thick vines hung. Odilon marched after her, grim and untiring. Now, there was no sunlight shining through the distant canopy, and the chorus of the things that came alive at night filled the shadows overhead. But, ahead of Odilon and his guide, a fuzzy orange glow emanated from the heart of the jungle, and a deep, thrumming rhythm pounded between the trees.

They neared the light, and at its source, buried in the tangled wood, a ziggurat came into view, its bulk rising beneath the endless ceiling in layers of black stone. A tall and narrow ingress gaped upon the face of the infernal monument, from which firelight throbbed, coming in concert with the pounding of drums from within.

Caulli stopped before the entrance and glanced back at Odilon.

"Here it is, the dark heart of Poxlom's domain. We shall go in, and thou shalt see for thyself the horrors thou hast only yet imagined."

Odilon followed her toward the pyramid, which crouched in

the jungle like a seared skull, its entrance like jaws splayed wide to an unnatural extent.

Within, oily fires blazed in broad stone braziers, which stood low to the ground, flanking an inner lane. The lane led through the center of the temple, and Odilon and Caulli stood on one end. Across its length the throne of the Jaguar God loomed opposite them. A white chair, comprised of bone and spinal columns, sat atop a plinth of obsidian marble, its jagged construction overlooking the flickering fires and the writhing figures that moved within the hall of the ziggurat. On the chair, a black figure hunched, but from a distance, Odilon could not then perceive more than this.

The spectacle before the throne consumed Odilon's attention. Around the fires that lined the fringes of the hall, Nochatl warriors, clad in jaguar pelts, moved in a swaying dance, while others pounded frantically on animal skin drums. Another portion of them, wearing headdresses made of fanged skulls, used blunt stone knives to carve into pale bodies that littered the floor. Periodically, these flesh-carvers would rise with a hunk of meat and fling the viscera into the fires, which caused the flames to subside and simmer with a flickering hunger. Glancing around the place, Odilon identified the pale bodies as those of his men, now stripped of their clothes and armor. Along the fringes of the hall, metal implements of war lay piled up along the moist walls like the spoils of conqueror's hoard.

At the end of the hall, a portion of the priests carried bleeding shanks in upraised hands as they chanted and ascended the throne's stairs. There, they rung out the flesh, spilling blood into vases that stood before the dark figure on the throne.

An overwhelming stench of blood and smoke assaulted Odilon's senses. His stomach heaved, and he faltered, and his eyes fell upon the nearest pyre to the entrance. Dimas stared back at him, his eyes and jaws flung open in a rictus stare. His head lulled on the floor, between the dancers' stamping feet — separately, his body sizzled in the nearby flames.

Odilon grasped his falchion and let out a howl, and he lunged forward, stabbing the blade through the back the nearest Nochatl who danced before Dimas's burning corpse. The dancer gasped and went stiff, eyes and mouth wide in surprise. Slowly, he slid off the sword and fell to the floor, where his stiff face slapped into a shallow puddle of blood.

The Nochatl ceased their chanting in favor of a cacophony of howling alarm. Odilon lunged at another with his sword, but the warrior scrambled away. Jaw clenched, teeth grinding, in haze of blinding rage, Odilon marched forward, swinging his weapon wildly, crying out in Latin, "Lava quod est sordium!"

Caught in the depths of their revelry, Odilon's sudden entrance and furious assault surprised the Nochatl, and they whirled about the hall in confusion; but some found their spears and clubs and faced the invader.

Above them all, the black giant on the bone throne stood and bellowed a word. The hall fell silent; the Nochatl froze, shocked out of their panic, replaced with a deeper dread. Only the fires danced yet in the temple, and Odilon stood in the midst of the foe, surrounded, blade outheld and whirling in every direction. But, at the command of the black giant, he too paused and looked up.

The man — if he could even be called such — stood on the top stair of the throne dais, and he pointed at Odilon and emitted an awful laugh. His skin was not just black, like the peoples of Africa, it was obsidian as the stone of the ziggurat. Only two glinting eyes shone upon his countenance, and when his smile cracked, ivory fangs glinted in the firelight. Even from a distance, Odilon could tell that this giant was, indeed, gigantic: hulking with muscle, standing well over the priests that cowered at his feet, their offering ritual interrupted.

The giant spoke. Only then did Odilon notice that Caulli was beside him. She stood, unphased by the carnage, and she translated the giant's eldritch tongue, which rolled forth in booming syllables.

She said, "He is Poxlom, and he hath called his warriors to cease. He wisheth to meet the man that would defy him. Step forward, brave Odilon."

Odilon squared his shoulders and marched toward the throne, the Nochatl parting before him. Caulli followed just behind him.

They stood at the foot of the stairs, staring up at Poxlom and his shadowy might, which loomed as sure as stone, a black and bloody idol in living flesh.

Poxlom crossed his arms and looked down upon Odilon with a haughty laugh. His eyes flicked to Caulli and burned with lust, and a smirk crossed his dark features.

Caulli addressed Poxlom in his own language and indicated Odilon.

Poxlom's gaze then fell upon the invader again, and he spoke, while Caulli translated in Odilon's ear: "Even the pale messengers from the seas, which come with staves of thunder and metal as hard as the face of the moon, cannot best the beast in his domain. Here things untamed rule, and they need not steel from the Stars. Blood feedeth them, the flesh of the slain is their strength — theirs is the ancient might of the earth, not the alien things of the void in which the distant Stars swim.

"But there is some strength in the Pale Ones, the invaders, so I see in the man before me. That is good. Thy flesh shall fill my belly, thy blood shall soak my throat, and a new strength shall come to me."

Poxlom laughed.

Standing before Poxlom's bulk, hearing his boast echo within the hall, Odilon remembered the doubts that filled his soul on the first night he went away from his ravaged camp with the golden idol. Here was a god in flesh. Was his faith in a God eternal and sublime enough to defeat the titan that stood before him? Odilon knew the fear of the Israelite scouts who first entered Canaan — he knew what inspired them to doubt and deliver an evil report of the giants that roamed the Promised Land.

But he knew the end of their story, and he decided, he would not be one of the faithless — he would be one of the conquering faithful. This is the vision that drove him from the Old World and into the darksome New World. The souls of his fallen men watched down upon him, expectantly.

Odilon grasped the golden idol on his hip, and in one hand raised it above his head. It shone above the Nochatl, who all gazed upon it in greedy wonder. Poxlom's eyes widened at its luster.

"Translate my words," Odilon said to Caulli.

She nodded and obeyed as Odilon delivered his challenge to Poxlom: "My God's blood is upon me, and it is stronger than any soul of earth. You have destroyed His messengers and desecrated their souls, but one yet remains undefiled! I challenge you, Poxlom, in the name of my God. Fight me yourself, and we shall see which champion the heavens favor!"

Poxlom bellowed, and Odilon heard his words through Caulli's mouth.

"Thy god is a foreign god, far from his country! Who here can defeat me? Comest thou with this river nymph" — he glanced at Caulli — "that filleth thy head with false promises, slippery as a fish in the waters in which she swimmeth, and bethink thee to defeat me, the beast, lord of the untamed things?"

He laughed again. "No! But to prove my boast, I shall accept thy challenge, Pale One."

Poxlom scanned the hall, glancing over the Nochatl held stiff in terror. "These wretches, they shake in fear before the fire and thunder of the Pale Ones from afar. They fear yet further starry legions from the sea. In defeating thee, lowly man, I shall prove to them that Poxlom's dominion is secure!"

Poxlom waved a hand at Odilon. "We shall go into the jungle

and hunt — I shall hunt thee, and thou shalt hunt me, and may the supreme predator win."

The black giant let out a roar which shook the temple.

Snarling at Odilon, he concluded: "I shall let thee leave my temple now, and thou shalt have a day to contemplate thy folly. I shall come into the jungle when the night falleth again next and stalk my prey, and I shall take that pretty plate of gold as a prize to adorn my throne — along with thy skull."

Still grasping the golden idol, Odilon shook it above his head. "It shall never be yours!" he shouted and Caulli translated. "It shall grace a fine home in the sunny place from whence it has come!"

Poxlom snorted in derision, and the twisted face of the giant disgusted Odilon. At first, he had made the challenge to resolve question of his lonesome trial. Which god was supreme? Was his oath vain or righteous? He would answer the question with end of Poxlom's life or his own. But now, he hated Poxlom and would be glad to kill him.

Caulli put a hand on Odilon's arm and whispered urgently to him. "Thou must go. He shall not accept my interference in this trial. Thou must face it alone. I will remain here. Fear not, I will be quite safe."

She departed his side and melded into the crowd of Nochatl.

Odilon turned and marched out of the hall, the golden idol glinting in the crook of his arm, which held Poxlom's gaze until it disappeared from view.

Poxlom resumed his seat on the bone throne and, in an elated meditation, imagined the prizes that would come to him. He thought of caressing that golden plate with a bloody claw. He imagined stamping the life out of the defiant white man, who showed much vigor — his blood would be delicious, invigorating. He respected the man's fearlessness. It would only make his defeat that much sweeter. Poxlom tired of the cringing, obsequious men that surrounded him. He welcomed the challenge of the Pale Ones, while the tribe under his thumb simpered before him, begging him to take away the threat.

Fools.

His strength was meant to be exalted upon the earth, and the Pale Ones provided the opportunity.

Finally, he imagined Caulli submitting to him. Presently, she went to the pool of the temple which trickled beside his throne in a stony grotto. She swam and lounged, unhurriedly, feigning ignorance of how her wet body demanded Poxlom's attention. It was annoying, because she knew that Poxlom knew that he could not grab her now — she would meld into the water and disappear, like last time she wandered into his temple.

Poxlom did not know what pact she had made with the white man, but surely it was contingent on the trial of the hunt. If the white man won, he would have her admiration. If Poxlom won, he would prove his superiority, and then she would be his.

Poxlom considered all this inevitable, and so the annoyance of her coquettish behavior was a little irritation.

The day passed with the Nochatl proceeding in their rituals. They burnt the flesh of the invaders and ate it until they retched, and even then, they carried on chanting and dancing, goaded on in their revelry by their fanatic priests.

Poxlom paid little heed to the spectacle and did not move from his chair until night fell again. He then arose and snapped his fingers to gain the attention of assembly of priests who lay sprawled before his throne, heaving from their exertions.

At his command, the medicine men leapt up fearfully, their worshipful terror of Poxlom overriding the protest of their exhaustion. They ascended the steps, and Poxlom pointed at the vases of blood gathered about his chair.

The priests, in teams of two, hoisted the vases up to Poxlom, who took the vessels one-by-one in his meaty hands, raised the vessels to the sky, and tipped them, pouring the thick liquid over his head. As the blood washed over his face and shoulders, he shivered in ecstasy. With each wave of dark fluid that washed over his skin, a silky black pelt was left in place of his flesh. His face, dripping with viscera, elongated beneath the deluge, and dagger-like fangs grew in his expanding mouth. His limbs stretched forth, claws sprouted from his hands, and his back hunched, though he became no shorter. As the blood washed over his backside, a swaying tail of black fur grew there.

Vigor swelled throughout Poxlom, and his mind became mired in bloodlust; and now his body had the power to satiate his thirst without end. His thoughts contained no words, only images of leaping and slashing, biting and tearing, stalking and killing.

He roared and slashed out at the priests around him, decapitating one, while the others fell down the stairs in the urgency of their retreat.

The Jaguar God bounded out of his temple.

The hunt began.

Odilon had made his preparations. He had returned to his camp as the sun was rising. The arquebus that he had embedded in the dirt remained standing where he had left it.

He slept a short while and ate, then set about making traps and preparing his weapons. He dipped his falchion in the latrine pit, covering the whole of its blade in muck — it would hide its luster and carry a foul poison. He did the same with his knives, and the stakes he prepared for traps.

He went to the old tree under which he slept the night before last, and around its premise, he dug pits and pulled back branches to trigger his traps.

In the evening, as the jungle darkened, he prepared his most deadly trick. He had found a small portion of gunpowder that the rain had not ruined. There was a cannon in the camp that was yet in good condition, left untouched by the Nochatl, as they feared its alien design and purpose.

When it was night, he found a patch of mud, and stripping himself all clothes, he rolled on the earth, covering every part of himself, so that he was as dark as the jungle soil. Finally, he unstrapped the golden idol from his side and dipped it in a waterfall, making its surface shine. He climbed the tree, and in its central crook, he lodged the idol so that it alone would sparkle in the night.

Presently, he assumed his position in the tree, beside the idol, pressing himself against the trunk to blend in with the bark.

He sucked in a great breath and bellowed, "Poxlom! I am here!"

His voice echoed in the jungle.

Odilon did not have long to wait until he heard the rustling of branches at the edges of the clearing. The silver spots of the Jaguar God shimmered faintly in the darkness, as one shadow deeper than the rest moved between the trees. Odilon watched as the beast smelled the ground and pawed gingerly at patches of leaves and strangely bent saplings. The Jaguar God sniffed at the traps Odilon had prepared and, avoiding them, continued to stalk further toward the tree.

Odilon snapped a branch where he held a twig behind the golden idol in the tree. Yellow eyes shot up and fixed upon his position.

The Jaguar God made a low growl and prowled about the base of the tree, licking his whiskers. When the gold plate did not move, the beast leapt up, digging his claws into the bark of the tree, until he was level with the crook in which the idol stood.

Odilon held his breath, pressing his limbs against the trunk until they were sore with strain. The Jaguar God's breath gusted over him as the great cat sniffed at the idol and reached out with a paw to swipe it.

Claws raked over bark and metal, and the golden idol tumbled from the tree.

At the same moment, Odilon took his falchion in both hands and pointed the blade downward. He lunged out from his hiding place and fell upon the beast, blade first. The sword plunged into the cat's shoulder. Poxlom yelped and fell from the tree with his ambusher latched upon him. The two landed entangled in the mud with a bone-shaking crash.

Poxlom flailed, but Odilon rolled away from the flurry of swinging claws and steadied himself. His sword remained in his hand, and across from him, the Jaguar God hunched, snarling as blood ran down his shoulder.

Odilon held the end of a rope in his other hand, which connected to a point above him, in the tree. He had leapt down with the rope tight in his grasp. Now, he tugged it. A mechanism flicked, a spark of fire lit the darkness where the golden idol had been, and there was a faint sizzling sound.

Poxlom had eyes only for Odilon, who stood his ground and waved his sword, calling out, "Come on! Come get me!"

The Jaguar God pounced. In a flash, the monster was upon him, crushing jaws locked like a vice around Odilon's collar. He screamed and fell to the ground under the weight of the beast.

The scent of death leaked from the cat's jaws, now so near to Odilon's nostrils. One of the beast's yellow eyes was in his face, burning with malice.

Below the pounding of blood in his ears, the sizzling sound of Odilon's salvation was distant. A thousand frantic prayers ran through his mind.

Poxlom bit down further, and Odilon's collar bone creaked as it bent. One of the cat's front paws pinned his sword arm to the ground. Odilon groped for a knife on his belt. When it was in hand, he rammed its blade into the beast's flank.

The Jaguar God winced but his fangs only dug deeper.

At last, here was the answer Odilon sought. His God was silent, and there was only the god of the flesh, which he had chosen to oppose.

Now, his death would confirm the truth.

BOOM!

Poxlom flew off Odilon, his jaws taking a chunk of skin with him.

Wincing, gasping, Odilon rolled to his side. He saw the tree, its boughs now cloaked in a cloud of acrid smoke. Within the smoke, there was a clump of leaves and mud in which Odilon had hidden the cannon. The rope he had pulled triggered a makeshift lever that dragged a match and set it against the fuse. The crude mechanism had been likely to fail — but it was a risk Odilon had to take to use the deadliest weapon in his arsenal against the beast. He only had to ensure that Poxlom remained in the right spot for long enough.

It worked, only just.

Odilon muttered a prayer, sparing a chuckle of disbelief at the timing of his God's intervention. Then he stood and faced his foe.

Nearby, the Jaguar God stumbled in the mud, missing a leg, blood soaking his pelt. The giant cat whined and slumped to the ground with a gurgling sigh.

Odilon advanced, chest heaving as he stood above the beast, who then looked up at him with pitiful eyes.

"You are no god — nothing but an animal," Odilon said before he thrust his blade beneath the jaguar's chin, driving it into the creature's brain.

The Jaguar God fell still.

Odilon returned to the temple with the pelt of the Jaguar God draped over his shoulders. The Nochatl fell before him in worship. Caulli met him beside the bone throne, smiling knowingly.

He set the golden idol on the seat of the throne. It shone out over the abased Nochatl.

Odilon turned to face them and called out, Caulli translating, their voices resounding in tandem: "Behold! My God has conquered! This shall be a hallowed place, where the dead remain undefiled, where no man shall feast on the blood of man again."

The Nochatl quivered in fearful affirmation.

Odilon slumped against the throne, feeling his exhaustion and pain. But he sighed with relief. It was done. St. Maria would no longer be a place of horrors. He would remain here, until more of his race came to join him. Until then, he would rule the Nochatl in the worship of their new Eternal God.

Caulli placed a hand on his arm and said, "I can heal that. Come now, rest and be clean."

She walked to the pool beside the throne. Before she slipped into the water, she glanced over her shoulder with a smile, saying, "Come."

Odilon dropped the jaguar pelt from his shoulders and followed her into the water.

In a quiet Spanish monastery, Father Alves knelt before the reredos, his morning prayers flowing in wispy syllables. Outside the high windows, birds chattered and fluttered between the branches of trees swaying in the summer breeze. The inside of the chapel was cool and quiet, filled with a holy silence suddenly shattered by the unlatching of a door and the tread of feet down the aisle.

The footsteps fell silent behind the Father.

"Father?" A timid voice ventured.

Alves sighed and groaned as he rose from his knees. He turned to see the mousy face of a young lad from town. The youth clutched a broad, flat package and a packet of papers against his chest, his eyes wide and fearful that he should invite the ire of the Holy Church for disturbing the devotions of her keepers.

Alves smiled gently. "It's all right, son. What is it? A confession?"

The boy shook his head. "I've been paid to deliver something to you." He held out the package and the papers.

"A gift, then? From whom?" Alves asked. "What does the letter say?"

The boy looked down and hesitated. Alves's smile broadened. Of course, a cheap runner had likely read what was meant to be confidential; but the Father was a kindly shepherd.

"I won't be upset. Tell me." Alves stepped forward and laid a palm on the boy's shoulder.

Haltingly, the boy finally let out, "It's from the New World. A man from the docks, coming back on the conquerors' ships, gave it to me. He said it's addressed to you."

Alves's brow furled. "The New World?"

"Yes, it's about someone with your name, one Lord Commander. There's a long story written there. I couldn't really make it out…"

The boy prattled on for a few sentences longer, but Alves's mind drifted away. "Could it be? He left years ago. I figured…"

"Give it to me," he interrupted the runner.

The boy handed over the papers, and Alves grasped them up, scanning rapidly over the first few pages, with a long gasp. "So, a confession after all…"

Glancing back up at the boy, his eyes flicked to the flat

package in the lad's arms, and prompted the messenger: "And that? Does it go together?"

The boy nodded and proffered the package. The priest took it and quickly made the sign of the cross over the messenger. "Thank you, son. Go with God."

The boy bowed and swiftly retreated.

Morning prayers completely abandoned, Father Alves found a discreet corner in which to read. But he first ripped open the brown paper enveloping the package. He found an ornate plate hidden within, the center of which was embossed with a familiar scene of the Holy Mother of God. Unsure what yet to do with this, Father Alves set it aside and turned to the letter.

He read it over and over; the tight and scratchy script was familiar to him. Odilon yet lived! Apparently, not only did Odilon live, he thought enough about Father Alves and Mother Church to address them in writing; but it was the manner in which he now lived that concerned the confessional tone of the letter. The nature of it was not immediately plain. Was it a confession of doubt, or that of the manner in which his son overcame his doubt? Or of other, baser indulgences?

Father Alves had heard of worse indignities performed by the Lord's appointed warriors overseas, but none so subtle and wonderous as Odilon's tale, for in it was a foreboding that addressed not only the mundane sins of the flesh, but something more.

What had Odilon found? That there was demoniac worship abroad was not news to the Church, but for one such idol to take on flesh and singular form…

Had their zealous aspersions upon the alien world beyond the ocean taken on the weight of prophecy?

In no way did Odilon condemn the Church or her mission, but he sought a father's private counsel, for he was then in a world only thence projected in words and stories, and embattled in the material reality of it, he plunged as a spearpoint into theretofore unbroken flesh.

A strange smile, accompanied by a sacred sorrow heavy in his breast, crept onto the Father's face. So, it was that Odilon, his son, had been appointed to terrible deeds. That much was plain.

Father Alves clutched the letter and glanced over at the golden idol, the role it had played in Odilon's adventure now clear to him, and also its purpose for being delivered to him now. At the end of his confession, Odilon had humbly asked the Father to bring the gold plate to one Senor Dimas Moreira with the news that his son of the same name had died in the New World. As for the matter of his demise, the truth was in Odilon's own tale; he asked Father Alves to share as much or as little detail as discretion deemed prudent or his conscience allowed.

Before getting up, Alves craned his face to the emblazoned ceiling and said, "Lord, have mercy on our souls."

KNIGHT BEAT: GRAVE DIGGER

HONORABLE MENTION

RYAN OVERTON

THEY SAY "VIRGINIA IS FOR LOVERS". Whichever pencil-pushing desk jockey came up with that slogan should be shot. Because if you're in my field, you know who Virginia is really for. The Undead.

"Looks like you drew the short straw, Tornincasa." Commissioner Mortimer said with a sarcastic smile. "You've just been assigned to one of the most haunted states in the union. Welcome to The Revenant Division of Virginia."

The surrealness of becoming a death cop still hasn't worn off, even after over a month of working here. When your boss's office has the head of Chessie mounted to her back wall, it's hard to find normalcy after that. The only concession to this assignment is its awesome armory.

"Shooter ready?" the indoor range attendant shouted as he raised his timer.

I let out a slow, steady breath as I readied my service pistol. The UDN-38 felt incredibly comfortable in my grip. The reduced size of the .38-caliber caseless ammo made the grip incredibly compact and ergonomic. But the integrated suppressor did make it a bit front-heavy. I gave a nod to the attendant, ready to begin.

The loud buzz snapped me to full alertness as my targets came alive. The pained moans and sickening squelch of dead flesh alerted me to the three reanimated cadavers crawling to their feet. The range lights began to flicker and dim, a natural side effect of the zombie's unnatural rebirth. When these poor sods offered to donate their bodies to science, I'm sure none of them thought it would be this.

"Sorry guys." I whispered, mostly to make myself feel better about this disgusting training exercise. "It's only business."

I was able to tame the UDN-38's recoil, the small, fast round being surprisingly nearly silent. The round burrowed deep into the zombie's sternum, the pain barely registering on his face.

I continued into my Mozambique Drill, firing a second round into the zombie's chest. The second shot wasn't enough either, though the intense bleeding was slowing it down substantially. It looked at me with what seemed like fear mixed into its mindless hunger for life. I wanted so badly to look away, but I knew I needed my eyes open for the final shot.

With one more pull of the trigger, I fired a round into his head. The small, fast round smashed through his skull, sending bone splinters and brain matter into the air behind him. With its brain thoroughly ventilated, the poor bastard was returned to his eternal rest.

I repeated the drill on the remaining two zombies, two shots to the chest followed by a lethal head shot. The final cadaver crumpled to the ground only about a yard and a half from me. The hot, stinking gore contrasted with the cold rush of ectoplasm leaving their bodies. No matter how many times I did this drill, it never got easier.

"7.2 seconds." The attendant announced as he stopped the timer. "That's 0.2 seconds better than last time, Kathy."

"Thanks, Joe." I said, feigning nonchalance about the whole thing.

"Corporal Tornincasa." A voice buzzed over my radio,

"Please report to Commissioner Mortimer's office for assignment."

"On my way." I said hesitantly back before holstering my UDN.

"Don't worry, Kath." Joe assured me. "Whatever it is, you and Miroslav got this."

I gave a solemn nod to Joe before walking out of the armory.

I walked the dim halls of the Division, the lights flickering from either negligence or residual ectoplasm drifting through the air. The harsh concrete walls kept the below-ground armory and technical offices at a brisk, chilling temperature. Every time I walked through here, I started to wonder if this is what the dead felt like.

I finally made it up to the ground floor. Some warmth returned to my body as I weaved between my fellow Revenant Officers. Their navy-blue uniforms reflected my own. A silver and black badge in the shape of a star with a splayed raven set in the center was our badge of office.

It was a bit odd passing by so many women on my way to the office. Revenant Division was a majority female force. I remember it being explained during orientation that since our partner Revenants are predominantly male, them being bonded with female officers made them more compliant and protective. Seemed like faulty logic to me, but I can't argue with the results.

Finally, I made it to the commissioner's office. I took a steadying breath before pushing the door open.

The office was small and cold, though it made up for it with its extravagant decorations. The walls were covered with pictures of previous successful operations of The Revenant Division of Virginia. Officers from decades past posed with the bodies of dead Cryptids and Undead like big game hunters of old.

Even some trophies, like the decapitated head of Chessie, the Loch Ness Monster of Chesapeake, hanging on the back wall.

The serpent's head was about the size of a football, with a mouth full of needle-thin teeth. It seemed to stare at me as I walked in, grinning to itself like it knew a joke and had no intention of letting me in on it.

Mortimer herself sat at her desk on the far side of the room, staring with her cold, dark eyes as I approached. Her sunken face and raven hair made her look like she was a walking corpse herself. 'Course, I would never say that to her face.

Then there was my partner.

I struggled to look at his face. When people say a person has looks that can kill, they probably mean a face like Miroslav's. His skin was deathly pale, contrasting with his yellowed teeth. His hard, Slavic features were covered by a thick, tangled beard. Yet it was his eyes that freaked me out the most. Those yellow disks set in blackened sclera gave air to a primal cunning and savagery I had seen in no living man.

"Kathy!" Miroslav boomed in his deep, disturbingly jolly voice. "How was your target training my friend?"

I gave a shaky thumbs up to the Revenant, always thrown off by his jovial attitude towards life. For someone who was a Winged Hussar in life, I always expected him to be a lot more somber, like the other Revenants.

"You two can talk on your own time." Mortimer barked with her gruff, raspy voice. "I have an important problem that needs solving and fast."

Mortimer opened a drawer and pulled out a case file before chucking it in my lap as soon as I sat down. I opened it, finding a picture of an open plot of land with several holes dug into it. Another picture of a parking lot with even more holes dug into it. As I looked deeper at the parking lot, I started to recognize the surrounding building. This was the Williamsburg House of Mercy on the William & Mary College Campus.

"Just got this report in this morning." Mortimer clarified.

"Campus security said all this happened overnight, and the nighttime guards were all found dead."

My stomach dropped at that. Knowing whoever dug these holes was willing to kill those guards meant they were digging for something important.

"Any idea what these goons were digging for?" I asked.

"The boys in the office say a bunch of Spanish Flu victims were buried there in unmarked graves back in the 20s." Mortimer explained bluntly. "We're still finding bodies to this day."

Mirolsav stroked his messy beard, deep in thought, before asking, "Who would want bones of the sick?"

"We can't confirm a suspect yet." Mortimer muttered as she looked at a picture on the far wall. "But given the nature of the crime, I have a hunch."

On the wall, mounted like a trophy on a plaque, was a scrap of black cloth. It was a part of an armband, with a white diagram of The Vitruvian Man on it. The diagram was inside a gear, with a blue and purple lightning bolt behind it. I knew that symbol anywhere. The symbol of the death cult that awoke me to the undead. The Hermetic Order of Victor Frankenstein.

"We're not sure what they want with these bones, but whatever it is, it can't be good." Mortimer remarked. "Arm up for combat against humans and Simulacrums, and get to work. Sergeant Kirchner and Revenant Abdallah will be on standby."

I closed the file and got to my feet. Miroslav seemed excited at the prospect of a brutal fight with Simulacrums.

"Is good that I sharpened blade extra sharp last night." He said, a wicked, bloodthirsty grin on his face.

Mortimer rose from her desk and glared at us with a stare that could freeze lava.

"Do or die, R-3." She barked the motto of our Division.

Both Miroslav and I snapped to attention before offering a salute to the Commissioner. "Do or die, ma'am."

THE DRIVE DOWN to William and Mary was thankfully uneventful. Mostly because we kept getting stuck in student traffic. Leave it to me to choose the exact moment everyone and his roommate decided to break for lunch.

"I still say we should have gone by horse." Miroslav joked beside me.

At least the scenery was nice. The buildings borrowed a lot of cues from nearby Colonial Williamsburg, keeping with the retro, old-school appearance. The students ran the gamut from energetic and jubilant to exhausted and stressed out as we passed them by.

As I pulled our cruiser over to the curb, I looked over to see the warning tape across the entrance to the parking lot. Even here, I could see the deep, messy holes peppered across the pavement.

"Stay here and look… normal." I said to Miroslav as I stepped out of the car.

Miroslav simply offered a bored sigh as he reached into his jacket for a travel-sized bottle of wine. I looked at him, dejected, but unable to stop him from drinking on the job.

"What?" he asked with a knowing grin. "You are the one driving, my friend."

I shook my head before shutting the door, adjusting my overcoat in the cold autumn breeze, and walking over to the crime scene. I walked casually, trying to look like I belonged there. Regular police were already on the scene, forensic specialists scurrying around like ants at work, searching for any evidence of who did this.

I counted eight holes across the small parking area, along with a handful of bloody smears along the ground, with chalk outlines marking where the night guards were killed.

"Hey!" a stern voice yelled at me. "The hell are you doin' here?"

I looked over and found an older detective stomping over towards me. His khaki coat covered his uniform, and a shoulder holster was just barely visible under his armpit. His brown hair was thin and prematurely graying, even his miserable excuse for a mustache. I could tell there was no point in beating around the bush with him, so I cut to the chase.

"Kathy Tornincasa, Special Investigations." I said, flipping open my badge holder.

He narrowed his eyes at my badge, clearly unhappy to see it.

"Why's some government spook out here?" He asked bluntly.

I couldn't blame him for distrusting me. Hell, I would have said the same if I were in his shoes. But, given the severity of this case, I couldn't let him stop me.

"Just in the neighborhood." I snipped back. "Now are you going to tell me what you've found or not?"

The Detective narrowed his eyes at me before thankfully relenting.

"What we can tell, bunch of goons snuck on campus last night with shovels and picks, dug up this place like a squirrel before winter, and fucked off into the night."

"And the bodies?" I asked, gesturing to the blood smears.

"Killed trying to stop the suspects." The Detective growled. "Poor bastards. Forensics say three were beaten to death with shovels, and a fourth was strangled to death. Grabbed him so hard his neck broke."

I sympathized with the detective. The grizzly scene playing out in my head would turn the stomach of even the most hard-boiled beat cop. But with the final mention of the guard's broken neck, I drew closer to confirming my suspicions.

"Those goons leave anything behind?" I asked coldly.

"Not a whole lot worth mentioning." The Detective said, glancing over his shoulder. "Except for one thing."

I followed him over to one of the blood smears. The blood had obviously already dried, forming a thin dark red crust over the pavement. But only a few feet next to it, I saw something else that drew my eyes. Similar smears of a dark burgundy color.

"We reckon this is the suspect's blood." The Detective said. "Forensics have already taken a sample. Those fucks won't get away with this."

I recognized the unnaturally dark fluid anywhere. It wasn't blood, it was Vitae. An alchemical fluid used to animate The Order's Simulacrums.

Simulacrums were different from other undead. Rather than being restless spirits deciding to take a walk, or corpses imbued with magic by a necromancer, Simulacrums were test-tube babies. Through a combination of Weird-Science, alchemy, and no shortage of grave robbing, a Simu can be stitched up and given rudimentary intelligence by its creator.

"Any surviving witnesses?" I asked.

"None that have come forward yet." The detective said with a sneer. "With how busy the place can be, I'll bet dollars to doughnuts someone saw this brawl go down."

As the detective finished his rant, I felt a familiar prickling on the back of my neck. It's difficult to describe, but it's something of a sixth sense I have. I could feel someone watching me.

When I looked over my shoulder, I could see a modestly dressed young man leaning nervously against a light pole. He had a guilty look on his face, like he had something to say. I knew that look anywhere.

"Thank you for your time, Detective." I said to him with a nod. "Whoever they are, they'll pay."

I started walking over to the young man, trying to look as unthreatening as I could. He seemed like an innocent enough kid, but I could just tell he had something he needed to say.

"You need something, sonny?" I asked him, trying my best to smile naturally.

The young man flinched with surprise when he noticed me approaching him.

"Yeah. Yes, Ma'am. I think I have some information." He stammered out before launching into a breathless explanation.

"I'm Jim Towers. I'm a medical student here. I just got done with my Human Anatomy class this morning with Mr. Kellogg. He's a great teacher. Bit eccentric, but he knows what he's…"

"Easy there, Towers." I said, trying to calm the kid's nerves for his sanity as well as mine. "Take a breath, and cut to the chase."

Towers thankfully did as I asked, taking a shaky breath before continuing.

"Sorry. Sorry. Okay, so during our lesson today, Professor Kellogg referenced this illegal dig. He was really unbothered by it. Hell, he used it as an excuse to change the lesson to the history of the Spanish Flu Epidemic. I don't want to be a snitch, but the way he talked about it was just so suspicious."

"It's okay, Towers." I said, processing what he was saying. "Thank you for coming forward with this. It takes a lot of guts to report people you respect. Do you know where your professor is right now?"

Towers snapped his arm up, gesturing down the road.

"He should be in Adair Hall, room 326. His next class should be ending soon."

"Sounds good." I say to him as I turn to go back to my car. "Thanks again for…"

"Please don't do anything brash." Towers blurts out, interrupting me. "He's such a nice guy, and I could be reading way too deep into this. But, I just feel that…"

"Towers!" I said more sternly this time, thoroughly fed up with his rambling. "Relax. I'm not going to throw your prof in the slammer if he didn't do anything."

"Thank you." Towers mumbled breathlessly.

With that, I slid back into the cruiser, greeted by Miroslav's predatory gaze.

"Good news, Rotski. We have Vitae." I told him. "Looks like we can put your tracking skills to use."

"Is good." Miroslav chuckled. "Good to know I did not sharpen blade for no reason."

Miroslav reached into the back seat and pulled out his main weapon. While he had his own service pistol, a monstrous .44 magnum, he and many other Revenants preferred using melee weapons. In his case, a *Szabla*, a Polish Cavalry Saber.

The thin, curved blade was encased in a velvet-covered wood scabbard. The brass hand guard and wooden grip had no modern accommodations, looking exactly like it would in the 17th Century.

"Come," He demanded. "We fight them."

"Not here, you pycho!" I shouted back. "Not where the students can see you!"

Miroslav gave a derisive grunt before lowering his sword.

"Good." I said with a sigh. "Now, I got a hot tip from a student that one of the profs is acting weird. Prof Kellogg."

"What does cereal man want with bones?" Miroslav joked, playing at his own ignorance.

I just rolled my eyes and continued.

"Kid said that the prof seemed a bit too enthusiastic about the digging last night. It's not much, but it's a start."

THE PARKING LOT of Adair Hall was thankfully sparsely populated. The old brick building carried an air of utilitarian simplicity, but still managed to have an old sort of charm to it.

Miroslav and I stepped out of the cruiser. The Revenant put a pair of sunglasses over his eyes, hiding his black sclera and making himself look like a normal human, at least from a distance. Before we could walk in, Miroslav stopped, his nostrils flaring as he sniffed at the air.

"There is scent of Vitae on air."

"What?" I asked. "Here? How fresh is it?"

"It is faint." Miroslav clarified, clicking his tongue as he tried to taste the alchemical residue on the air. "Is few hours old. Must have faded from last night."

I grit my teeth. If there were Simulacrum here, this would get really bloody, really fast. I already had my UDN-38 on me in a concealed shoulder holster under my jacket, a .45 ACP G-21 on my belt holster, and a silver Karambit folded on the back of my belt. Even then, I knew we would need some more stopping power against Simulacrums. Miroslav and I exchanged a wordless look. The Revenant smirked with a nod before opening the back seat and attaching his sword to his belt.

"Alright." I said with a steady sigh. "Let's go."

Miroslav and I simply walked into the building. I had my badge at the ready in case anyone asked. The undead naturally disrupt video cameras, so thankfully, as long as I stayed close to him, there would be no concrete proof we were here.

Walking through the quiet halls, I felt a sudden chill through my bones. That same chill of dread I always got when I questioned what I was doing.

"Am I doing the right thing?"

"Are we ready to fight Simulacrum?"

"What if the Prof is innocent and we're on a wild goose chase?"

I pushed all those thoughts down under my mask of duty. It was my duty as a Revenant Officer to keep the dead from harming the living. This was all just part of the job.

"You okay, Kathy?" Miroslav asked me, a rare tone of concern in his voice.

"I'm fine, Slav." I grumbled back.

Miroslav's snarky grin returned as he patted a pocket on his jacket. "Does someone need some liquid courage?"

"Hard pass." I said, not wanting to taste his decaying backwash.

Finally, we made it to room 326. When I glanced through the door window, it looked like the students had left a while ago. The many tables were left empty, and the projector screen on the far side of the room was dark. The only person there was an older gentleman sitting at the professor's desk.

"Wait here." I ordered Miroslav as I pushed the door open.

As I walked in, I got a better look at the prof. He was an older man, probably in his mid-forties. His short, blond hair was graying at the sides. His face was hard like weathered stone. Even his mustache looked sharp. A white coat was draped around his scrawny body. A garish purple and red tie that even the sleaziest car salesman would avoid hung from his neck. He glanced up from his laptop as I approached, eyeing me over with beady brown eyes.

"Can I help you, miss?" The professor asked me as I approached.

"You Professor Kellogg?" I asked, trying to sound non-threatening.

"That I am, young lady." He responded; his raspy voice became more apparent.

"A pleasure, sir." I assured him. "I'm Tornincasa, one of the new campus security officers. I'm just trying to get familiar with all the profs around here."

"Ah." He muttered curiously. "An unfortunate day to start."

"You can say that again." I said, feigning nervousness. "I'm hoping I can stay on the day shift."

"Yes. Yes. A crying shame, that." Kellogg said, stroking his mustache in thought. "There are so many great mysteries under this ground. Such a shame that life had to be lost in search of knowledge."

I tried my best to read his face. Though, given how unmoved it was, I couldn't tell anything about his emotional state.

"You seem to know an awful lot about this case, Prof." I said, trying to be neutral.

Kellogg's eyes narrowed at me. "Are you accusing me of something, ma'am?"

"No sir." I assured him. "I'm just trying to help the police get to the bottom of this case. Every bit of information helps."

Kellogg's expression lightened a bit before launching into a passionate tirade.

"Well, my assumption is that these diggers were after the bones of old Influenza victims. You would call it the Spanish Flu. Terrible epidemic. We're still finding skeletons buried here."

"Why would someone want these bones?" I asked, trying to drag a confession out of him.

"Well, naturally, there is historical value to them." Kellogg continued. "You could sell them to a museum or a medical institute for a bundle. The remains of the virus would still be in the remains, so it would, in a sense, be like uncovering fossils."

"Seems like a lot of effort to go through for a nest egg." I responded. "Why not dig for something more practical, like arrowheads?"

Kellogg winced, though his hard face displayed no emotion.

"Beats me, Ms. Tornincasa." He responded. "That's their business to know, and your business to figure out. Now, I've told you all I know, so please leave me to my work."

I frowned as he ushered me to leave. My suspicion of the old prof had grown more. He was hiding something, but I needed to be subtle if I was going to get to the bottom of this.

"Thank you for your time, sir. Have a nice day."

I slowly stepped back out the classroom, only to realize Miroslav wasn't there.

"Miroslav." I called quietly. "Where the hell did you go?"

I slowly skulked through the halls of the building in search of my undead partner. I walked past a maze of classrooms and science labs looking for him. Checking every corner and listening closely for any sign of him.

Eventually, I found him, sniffing at the air coming from a janitor's closet.

"Miroslav, what the hell are you…" I started, but he shushed me before I could finish berating him.

The revenant wordlessly pointed to his nose, then to the door. I didn't need any sign language skills to know what Miroslav was getting at. I nodded, drew my UDS, and prepared to breach.

Miroslav slowly drew his sword, the quiet hiss of silver-plated steel seeming to ring through the hall as the revenant took a breaching stance on the opposite side of the door.

I reached into my pocket, pulled out my skeleton key, and slowly unlocked the door. I quickly threw open the door and stepped back, allowing Miroslav to rush in, bellowing a war cry as he swung his saber through the air. I followed behind, prepared to fire on anything that moved.

"No!" a pathetic, small voice screamed. "Please, don't hurt me anymore!"

Once the lights came on, I finally got a good look at the inside of the closet. It seemed as standard as you might expect a janitor's closet would be, except for the nearly naked man with his hands and legs zip-tied on the floor. His face was twisted with terror, and his neck was bruised, revealing he had been strangled recently.

"He smells of Vitae." Miroslav bellowed, gesturing at the man's throat with his sword. "This whole room reeks of the unnatural."

"What the fuck?!" the man shouted. "I didn't do nothin'. I was just coming to grab my mop when this big naked fucker pulled me in here, choked me out, and swiped my clothes."

"We're terribly sorry, sir." I said, trying to calm down our new witness. "Slav, cut him loose."

Miroslav gave me a disappointed look before slicing away the zip ties around the janitor's wrists and ankles.

"Now, if you don't mind, sir." I asked. "Could you tell us what this person looked like?"

"He was this big, pale, mean motherfucker." The janitor described, trying to fit in as much vulgarity as he could. "The fucking freak was completely naked, didn't even have hair or eyebrows or nothin'. He didn't even have a cock; I tried to kick him in the jewels and he didn't even flinch. He was covered with scars all over the place, but those are probably going to be hard to see with him wearing my uniform."

"Thank you, sir." I said, trying to come up with a suitable lie for the janitor. "The person who attacked you is a known criminal and murderer. My partner and I are trying to find him after he broke out of jail last night. Do you happen to know where this man is now?"

"Right behind you."

I immediately whirled around at the strange voice, my pistol at the ready. Before I could see anything, a huge jug of cleaning chemicals came sailing towards my face. Miroslav sliced it in midair out of reflex, spraying us both with a thick, blue-grey sludge. I felt fine, but based on the sound of sizzling meat and pained howls of Miroslav, he wasn't.

My vision finally focused on the man outside the door. He was dressed in tight-fitting, blue coveralls, the fabric failing to conceal his tightly corded muscles. A simple black baseball cap covered his bland face, though his yellowed eyes shimmered with mischievous glee.

"Glad to see someone took my bait." The simulacrum chortled as he quickly stepped into the closet and closed the door.

I would have had more room to fight in a phone booth compared to this closet. And with Miroslav howling in pain, and the janitor screaming in terror behind me, I couldn't hear myself think. Regardless, I unfolded my Karambit and prepared to fight.

The Simu immediately opened with an inhumanly fast jab to my face. I dodged back, hitting my head on one of the shelves. I tried to hook his wrist with my knife, but he pulled his arm back and used his other hand to grab my uniform.

Miroslav finally recovered from his pain and took a cleaving swing with his *Szabla*, trying to lop off the Simus' head. He and I both ducked in synch as the blade thankfully sailed over both of us.

"Hold still, *kurwa*!" The Revenant demanded.

The Simu delivered a powerful back kick to Miroslav's side in return. The powerful blow would have shattered the ribs of a mortal man, but The Revenant was thankfully built tougher.

Before he could give me the same treatment, I hooked the blade of my knife under the wrist of the Simu's grasping hand and sliced. The thin skin tore like wet tissue paper, ripping through muscle down to the bone. Thick, burgundy Vitae oozed onto my blade like syrup. The silver blade stung the undead's flesh, halting its supernatural healing factor.

Before I could do a follow-up slice on its throat, the Simu hissed with pain, slamming the side of its head into my face. Blood gushed as the creature broke my nose and rattled my teeth in my head.

I cried out with pain, but that was quickly silenced as the Simu grabbed my neck and started to throttle me against the shelves. The world began spinning as the fucker bashed my head against the shelves.

At that moment, I remembered I had my pistol in my off hand. I fired a point-blank shot into the Simus' thigh. The silent snap of the UDS was drowned out by the pained wail of the Simulacrum. It took a hand off my throat and used it to cover its fresh, weeping bullet wound, but I wasn't free yet.

"I'll crush you with just one hand!" The Simu shouted as he continued to choke me, his mischievous look turning to one of murderous rage.

"Like hell you will!" Miroslav retorted before stabbing his curved blade up under the Simu's armpit and through its shoulder.

He managed to wedge the blade right into the Simu's shoulder joint. With a quick twist, the arm popped from its socket with a disgusting, wet snap. The Simus arm dropped from my neck and went limp at its side as it roared in pain. With another grunt of effort, Miroslav sliced his blade forward, cleaving the arm completely off.

The Simus cries became more pathetic and fearful as its arm fell to the tiled floor. It almost seemed human in its pain. But I couldn't think like that. This was an undead monstrosity, and it was my job to put it down.

Miroslav drew a slash across the Simu's back before stabbing it through its lung. The Simus cries became bloody gurgles as its Vitae oozed from its mouth.

With my own bloody roar, I hooked my Karambit onto its neck and sliced it open, arteries and all. I followed up with a quick stab under its chin, forcing its head up like a bottle cap, tearing its throat open even more. Vitae poured out of the Simu's throat like a waterfall of purple sludge. The Simulacrum gurgled out its last bloody breath before falling limp, hanging from our blades like a pig on a spit.

With the fight over, I could finally breathe. Or at least breathe as well as I could with my broken nose.

Simulacrum weren't like other undead; its body wouldn't rapidly decompose or fade away like a vampire or a ghost, making Simulacrum bodies a lot more difficult to hide. Though we at the Revenant Division had alternatives.

I pulled out a green pill about as big as my thumb from a pouch. Thankfully it didn't get smashed in the fight. I jammed the pill into its open throat. I nearly gagged as I pushed the pill through the gunk and let it sink into the Simu's stomach. The Alchemical Unbinder would take effect any second, decomposing the Simulacrum's alchemical bonds and dissolving it into a featureless pile of clear slime. If no one cleaned it up, it would get pulled apart by any carrion animals and insects in the area.

"What the fuck!" the janitor screamed as he stared on in horror. "What the fuck is wrong with you people! You killed him!"

"Easy there, buddy." I said, trying to calm him down as I pulled out my amnesia spray.

Before the janitor could continue, I gave him a quick spritz of the spray. The blue vapor forced itself into his nose and mouth, drowning out his fear with a fatigued drowsiness.

"Now, here's what you saw." I said with as much authority I could muster with a nose full of blood. "You were locked in here by a group of students. You were stripped, beaten, and were about to be killed. Thankfully, for you, they got bored of your suffering and decided to leave you here to die. Blink twice if you understand."

The janitor slowly blinked twice like the most out of it stoner. At least I knew the suggestions had taken root.

"Good. Now get some rest. Your saviors are going to be walking through that door any minute now."

With that, the janitor went out like a light.

"You have such a way with words, Kathy." Miroslav painfully chuckled as he took a swig from his wine bottle.

"Not in the mood, Rotski." I jabbed back, holding my broken nose. "That confirms there are Simus on campus. Now we need to find who's in charge of them."

I holstered my weapons as we both walked out of the closet, heading back to our car. I needed to get my nose set and call for backup. It may have only been 7:41, but I could tell this was going to be a long day.

NIGHT FELL a lot faster than I was hoping for. Even after resetting my nose and taking a healing accelerant, it still hurt like hell. At least I wouldn't have to talk through a nose full of blood.

Miroslav recovered from his burns, too. That jug was full of Alchemical Quicksilver, harmless to living things, but to an undead, it's like getting splashed with acid. Thankfully, we were able to get that gunk cleaned off him, and his natural undead healing took care of the rest. It's always a little freaky to see a man you know is dead recover from these massive wounds. But it did raise the question of why the Simu had anti-undead chemicals.

We waited in our cruiser, holding a little stakeout in the staff parking lot. We were parked towards the back of the parking lot. Out of sight, out of mind.

Admittedly, the story I fed to the janitor did stir up some shit on campus. Daytime security was questioning students about who ganked the janitor, only to find no one would confess. Thankfully, this meant that the night cleaning staff were too afraid to stay the night. No chance of being seen by bystanders.

On the other hand, the teaching staff were taking their sweet time leaving. The slow trickle of cars left campus one by one, except for one. A little grey Volkswagen Golf GTI, with plates that belonged to Professor Kellogg.

"Well, seems like someone's doing overtime." I said after running the plates.

"Is best we pay him visit, yes?" Miroslav asked me, partly unsheathing his sword for emphasis.

"If it comes to that, yes." I replied, gesturing with my radio. "But I want to wait for our backup to arrive."

After getting my nose broken, I called in Sergeant Kirchner to help with patrolling the campus for Simulacrums. She reported no sign of any more Simus, but I wasn't convinced. After what we saw in the closet, they could be hiding anywhere.

Before I could continue that thought, I saw Kirchner's

cruiser, R-2, come around the bend. She pulled up next to us, and both she and her Revenant partner stepped out.

Now, I'm not one to mince words here, so I'll just be upfront about this. Jeannie Kirchner was pretty… like "turn a gay guy straight" levels of pretty. From her short, chestnut hair to those beaming blue eyes. A gorgeous, fit figure and radiant, tan skin that any woman would kill for. I tell you, with ladies like Kirchner, pretending to be straight to my parents is going to be an uphill battle for me.

Her uniform hugged her body in all the right ways, though I could make out the slight swell of a stab-proof vest underneath. Her UDS-38 was holstered at her belt, along with an MP7 SMG slung on her shoulder. With the suppressor and adjustable stock, it was ideal for fighting in tight corridors.

Of course, where there was beauty, there was also a beast. Revenant Abdallah was the Revenant of a Moroccan soldier who fought alongside the old US Marines back in 1777. His uniform was mostly standard, with the addition of a *keffiyeh* and a scarf covering his grotesque face. His amber skin was not as deathly pale as Miroslav's, but he still had the same blackened eyes as all Revenants.

Unlike Miroslav, Abdallah didn't carry a sidearm at all. A long, sharply curved *Nimcha* hung at his left hip. The mini scimitar had no modernizations, just like Miroslav's saber. The wooden pommel of the sword was carved into the shape of a horse's head.

On his right hip, he had a *Koummya* dagger. The more straightened blade was ideal for stabbing, rather than the slashing and hacking blade of the *Nimcha*. The thin handle always looked like it would snap at even the slightest resistance, but it thankfully never did.

When both Kirchner and Abdallah were here, I felt a whole lot more confident in our chances.

"You are blushing." Miroslav teased behind me.

"Shut up, Rotski!" I said defensively, holding my cheek. "It's just cold out tonight."

I stepped out of our cruiser before Miroslav could make me feel any more embarrassed.

"Nice to see you again, Kathy." Kirchner said in that light, friendly voice I love so much.

"You too, Jean." I replied, trying to sound as cool and nonchalant as I could. "Glad to see you came prepared as always."

Jean pulled her MP7 around, holding it at low ready.

"Better overarmed than under dirt." She said with a cocky grin.

Meanwhile, Miroslav and Abdallah were greeting each other in their own way.

"How it has been, *Ciapak*?" Miroslav bellowed, saying the Polish slur against Arabs as simply as the most harmless nickname.

"A whole lot better than you, *Abid*." Abdallah retorted, pleasantly calling Miroslav a slave.

The two Revenants both chuckled at their crass greetings before grabbing each other by the forearm and shaking. It always amazed me how well those two got along. I guess death has a way of tearing down barriers, even between historical enemies.

"Right." Jean said, walking towards the entrance. "No reason to keep them waiting."

The four of us moved up to the door quietly. Jean crept in first, sweeping the hall with her MP7. Abdallah backed her up, his silver-plated blades drawn in case a Simu charged into melee with us. I drew both my pistols, my UDM-38 and my G-21. While I should have been using an MP7 or some other SMG like Jean, I preferred my dual wielding approach. Finally came Miroslav, covering the rear, his saber in one hand, and a massive .44 magnum in the other.

The utilitarian halls of Adair Hall felt colder as we crept

through, our flashlights illuminating our way. I couldn't help but feel like we were being watched the whole time. Every shadow, every closed door, every dark corner could be hiding a Simulacrum ready to strike. I kept at least one pistol trained on our three and nine O'clock positions, waiting for even the slightest hint of movement.

We skulked up the stairs and made our way to Kellogg's classroom. After a few minutes, we got there to find that the lights were off. I peeked in to find no sign of the prof anywhere.

"Where the hell did he go?" I asked myself.

"Shit." Jean cursed quietly. "Alright, think, where would a Frankenstein cultist be hanging out at this hour?"

"Let's check the science labs." I suggested. "Maybe he's trying to cook up some more Quicksilver."

Miroslav shuddered as he rubbed his chest.

We quickly scampered towards where I saw the science labs, moving a bit quicker than we were originally. Still no signs of Simulacrums as we moved through the hall, but as we rounded a corner, we saw a pale glow of light from under the science lab's door.

"I think we found our professor." Jean remarked as she crept up to the door.

I moved up next to Jean, Miroslav, and Abdullah, moving into breaching position behind us. I tried my best to hear through the thick, wooden door, straining to hear what was going on in there.

"…And with just a little Lazarus added to this sample, you'll see something spectacular."

The voice obviously belonged to Professor Kellogg. Whatever he was doing, I could tell it wasn't good. But after he did whatever he was doing, I heard a different voice that surprised me.

"That's amazing, sir!" Towers said with a tone of youthful wonder. "Look, they're all reactivating!"

"What the fuck was that kid doing here?" I wondered as I peeked through the door's window.

I could see two figures dressed in HAZMAT suits. The table they were at was covered with chemicals, medical tools, and a microscope. Six lab tables were set out in a V-pattern, with them at the head of the room. Shelves and wheeled carts lined the walls, with a supply closet at the front right-hand side of the room.

On the far wall, I could see a projector screen, showing a concerning display. It showed dozens of viruses, the spider-like microbes floating grey and dead on a white background. Some of them were glowing purple, shaking in place as they flailed their spindly legs, returning to life like zombies. Whatever they were doing, I couldn't let it happen.

"Breaching!" I shouted as I kicked open the door.

I rushed forward; both my pistols leveled at the two suited scientists. Jean moved up next to me, covering my right flank. Miroslav and Abdullah charged in behind us, their blades singing through the air as they prepared to fight.

"Hands up! Freeze where you are!" I demanded. "We've got you cornered! I'm placing you both under arrest! Resist, and you will be shot!"

The two figures raised their hands, turning to face us. Through the plastic face shields, I could make out the stony face of Professor Kellogg, as well as the young, scared face of Jim Towers.

"Nice of you to join us, Ms. Tornincasa. Or should I say, Officer?" Kellogg said with a grin.

"You knew I was with Revenant Division from the start, didn't you?" I asked.

"Of course I did, you fool girl." He snapped at me. "I had my protégé here sus you out the moment you got here." He said, smiling down towards his assistant. "Excellent work, Towers."

Towers didn't seem overly thrilled about being praised. The

poor bastard was shaking in his boots as he stared down the barrel of my G-21.

"You know that he ratted on you?" I asked without thinking.

"Ratted?" Kellogg chuckled. "No. No, Ms. Tornincasa, you see, I wanted you to find out about my little experiment."

Just then, an explosion of movement came from behind us. The shadowy silhouettes and eye shine of six Simulacrums scampered up the hall from behind us, blocking the door. Four more emerged from the supply closet on the far side of the lab. They were armed with whatever was at hand. Picks, crowbars, and shovels mostly, but a few were armed with drum-fed G-17s. They were dressed in basic field workers' clothes, staring at us with looks of violent savagery.

"You see, I needed a test subject for my experiment." Kellogg snickered wickedly. "And you brought three more with you."

"Engage contacts!" I shouted as I fired two shots at two Simus in front of me.

The Simus staggered back as my silver rounds were buried in their chests. The Simus behind them shoved aside their wounded comrades as they sprayed into us with their switched G-17s. I threw myself to the deck as pistol rounds sprayed everywhere.

It looked like Kellogg and Towers had the same idea as they scrambled for cover under the hail of gunfire.

"*Jezus, Maria*!" Miroslav bellowed as he leaped into the fray, saber swinging and magnum blazing.

He effortlessly cleaved off the arm of the nearest Simu as it was bringing a crowbar up to block. The Simu cried out in pain as its arm clattered to the ground, before it was silenced as Miroslav blew its head off with his .44 Magnum.

"*Allahu Akbar*!" Abdulla shouted as he whirled into battle like a hurricane of blades.

His *Nimchu* hacked through a Simus shovel, snapping it in half like a candlestick. Before the Simu recovered, Abdulla followed up with a spinning slash to its throat with his *Koummya* before decapitating it with a final swing of his scimitar.

Thankfully, in the time it took for that to happen, the two gunners ran dry on ammo. Those switched Glocks fire fast, and these Simus didn't think to conserve ammo.

"Suppressing!" Jean shouted as she returned the favor, blazing away with her MP7.

The Simus ducked behind cover, though one of the gunners was too slow, getting three silver 4.6 mil rounds stitched across his neck. The three rounds tore bloody chunks out of the gunner's neck like piranha bites. His head slumped to one side as he fell to the ground, dead.

With the Simus too afraid to poke their heads up, I crawled to a flanking position on the left side of the room.

"Eat lead you fucks!" I shouted as I pumped two rounds into one of the shovel users.

The silent double snap of my twin pistols was completely drowned out by Jean's torrent of fire. I almost didn't hear the Simu shriek in pain as my shots took him in the hip and bicep, respectively.

He didn't take too kindly to that, considering he responded by hurling his shovel at me like a javelin. I rolled back just in time for it to miss my face, but it still tore a big gash through my uniform and into my shoulder.

I covered the wound, trying to recover from the pain, but before I could, I saw the Simu crawl over to me like an ape. He threw himself at me, raising his arms like a gorilla trying to smash my head. I had only one shot to escape. I kicked off the nearest table, sending myself sliding across the tile floor. Not a second too soon, as the Simu smashed the tiles where my head was a second before.

"Checkmate, Frankenstein!" I shouted before returning him to the grave with a shot to the head from my G-21.

"Shit!" Jean cursed as her MP7 ran dry. "Reloading!"

Without a hail of gunfire forcing them behind cover, the two remaining Simus came charging out. The one with the pickax rushed towards Jean, swinging at her as she fumbled with her spare mag.

I tried to gun him down, but the one with the G-17 finished reloading.

"Eat lead, copper!" he yelled at me, copying my insult.

I shirked out in pain as the Simu gunner tore three shots into my leg. The burning hot rounds seared into my thigh and shin like tiny fireplace pokers. Thankfully, the fucker still had no recoil control, sending most of his shots cracking into tiles around me.

I was able to scramble back on my elbows into cover behind one of the tables. My right leg still hurt, but adrenaline is a hell of a painkiller. I was able to keep my cool long enough to hear the gunner rushing my position, ready to finish me off.

The second I saw his foot poke around the edge of the table, I immediately snapped a shot at it. His foot exploded into bony splinters as my .45 blew it off at the ankle. The Simu stumbled, landing flat on his face as Vitae gushed from his foot stump.

"Prefire, fuck-wit! You heard of it?" I yelled in his face before ventilating his skull with another .45.

With my problem dealt with, I needed to save Jean. As I looked over, I saw Jean narrowly dodging around the Simus pickax, her Karambit clutched in her off hand. Jean managed to land an occasional slash at the Simu, but nothing hard enough to put it down.

I knew it was reckless, but I had no choice. I raised my UDS and snapped off a shot into the Simu's back. Obviously, a single silver .38 wouldn't be enough to drop the Simulacrum, but it bought Jean enough time to grab him by the shirt and bury her knife up to the hilt in his temple. The Simu immediately went limp, occasionally twitching as he died.

In the mayhem, I completely lost track of our Revenants.

Thankfully, they were still kicking ass without us. Two more of the Simus had been hacked to bloody chunks, leaving just two standing.

A Simu cracked Miroslav across the face with the edge of his shovel, slicing his flesh down to his jaw and cracking a few teeth. He stumbled back, holding his face as I heard a sizzling sound. The edge of the Simus shovel was coated with Quicksilver.

Miroslav's cocky smile quickly turned to a sneer of berserk rage. He howled as he sliced his saber deep into the Simu's shoulder, the blade catching halfway into the sternum. Miroslav followed this by smashing the barrel of his magnum into the Simu's mouth, shattering his teeth before exploding his head from the inside. Gore rained around him before he kicked the limp corpse off his sword.

Abdulla wasn't doing much better. The last Simu stabbed him in the side with his pickax, the Quicksilver sending searing pain through the Revenant's side.

"You can't draw blood from a stone, *kahba*!" Abdulla joked through the pain as he sliced off the Simu's main hand with his dagger.

The Simu dropped his pick before Abdulla did three follow-up slashes, drawing a Z-shaped pattern from leg to neck. The first slash carved open his thigh. The second disemboweled him, before the final slash cleaved off the Simu's head.

"Last contact down!" Abdulla shouted, confirming that the last of the Simulacrums were dead.

I stumbled to my feet, the pain of being shot slowly returning as my adrenaline faded. Jean and I slowly closed on Kellogg and Towers, surrounding them from both sides.

"Alright, enough fucking around!" I yelled at them. "Hands up or I'll shoot your asses too!"

"Don't shoot! I surrender!" Towers screamed as he popped

up from behind the table. The little fucker startled me, and I almost blew his head off.

Kellogg was slower to reveal himself, glancing at his assistant with annoyance.

"A marvelous display of martial prowess Ms…"

"Can the pleasantries, doc!" I yelled at him, my voice getting sore from yelling through the fight. "You're under arrest for reanimating the dead, resisting arrest, assault and battery, and a fuckton of other things!"

"Fine. Fine. You've caught me." Kellogg said, defeated.

"Kathy, you keep them covered. I'm going to confiscate any evidence." Jean ordered as she looked over the table.

Thankfully, nothing important had been hit in the gunfight. The top of the microscope had been blown off, but the sample in the tray was in a contained Petri dish. There were plenty of beakers and test tubes full of God-knows-what, along with a plastic zip-lock bag with a dark bone inside.

"What's this?" Jean asked as she looked over a black and white notebook.

She opened it, seeing a bunch of diagrams and equations. I was able to see a few out of the corner of my eye. If I had to read them myself, it would have made my head spin.

"Shit." Jean swore. "It's written in an obscure German dialect. I'll try to translate."

Jean began rapidly mumbling to herself in German, trying to decipher the mad doctor's writing.

"When… resurrected… flu strand… will result in… death… and… resurrection…? These fuckers were trying to make a Necro Flu."

"So, add creation of bio-weapons to the list of charges." I barked as I shoved my gun even further in Kellogg's smug face.

"It is treatable." Kellogg said, shrugging nonchalantly. "My colleagues are working on a treatment as we speak. It was to be a very… lucrative exchange after we infected the Governor."

"Oh! That makes it so much better!" I yelled at him. "Now get moving! We're bringing you in!"

"Fine. I know when I've been beat." He said as he slowly walked around the table.

Then he smirked as he looked me square in the eye and said, "Are you sure you don't want to search us first!"

Before I could do anything, Kellogg shoved his hand in my face and sprayed this thick, green gel from under his suit sleeve into my eyes.

"Ah! Fuck!" I cursed as I fired at where I thought he was, only to hear my bullet clack harmlessly against the back wall.

"Grab the sample and let's go!" Kellogg shouted as I heard Jean struggling and firing her SMG in a panic.

I rubbed the gunk off with my sleeve, only to be shoved into the table behind me by Kellogg. Towers had the bag with the bone and the sealed microscope dish tucked tight to his side like a football as he and the prof booked it for the exit.

"Slav, grab 'em!" I ordered, trying to get steady on my wounded leg.

Miroslav smirked as he and Abdulla guarded the doorway, ready to cut the two cultists down. Before they could, Kellogg sprayed both of them with a familiar blue-grey slime from his other wrist. The Quicksilver seared both of the Revenants, causing them to lose their grip as they grabbed for them.

"Shit! They're getting away!" I yelled as I tried to speed limp out the door. "After them!"

I followed the two cultists through the dark halls, hobbling along behind them and snapping off shots. They were too far ahead of me and gaining ground fast. Every time I managed to snap a shot at them, they ducked around a corner. Chasing them down the stairs wasn't easy either, since I wound up tumbling down a flight.

I chased them to the rear entrance. Naturally, they made it out before I got there, rushing to their waiting Volkswagen. I threw myself through the doors just in time to see them start pulling away.

"Halt!" I shouted desperately as I fired at their windows and their tires.

My .38 rounds cracked harmlessly against their windshield; they must have had it modded with bulletproof glass. While I tried to shoot the tires, the pain in my leg and the speed they were going at threw off my aim. All I managed was Swiss cheeseing their passenger side doors. Regardless, the two cultists peeled out of the parking lot and out onto the street.

"Kathy, are you alright?" Miroslav shouted as he and the other two finally caught up.

"I can be alright later." I croaked as I hobbled over to R-3.

I threw open the door and sparked the engine to life.

"I'll drive! Rotski, you shoot!"

Miroslav grunted his acknowledgement, slamming a speed loader into the cylinder of his magnum as he ran to the passenger door.

"We'll try to cut him off at the pass!" Jean shouted as she and Abdulla ran to their cruiser. "Good luck, Kathy."

"I don't need luck. I have ammo." I muttered to myself as I flipped on our siren and peeled out after Kellogg.

We raced down the vacant street, siren blaring into the night. We zipped passed the various campus buildings and made it onto the highway leading to Colonial Williamsburg.

As we blazed down the road, Miroslav reached into the glove box and pulled out our supply of healing accelerants. I took one immediately. I knew it would take hours for the bullet wounds to heal, but at least it would dull the pain.

"You're sure I can't…?"

"Not now, Rotski!" I barked at him before he could offer me a swig of his wine

Finally, after seven minutes of chasing, we began catching up to the Volkswagen. Once we got onto a straightway, Miroslav rolled down his window and leaned out.

"Hold still, *kurwa*!" Miroslav shouted as he tried to line up a shot with his magnum.

There was a thunderous boom as Miroslav fired off his first shot, blasting open the rear window. The Volkswagen swerved as broken glass showered the driver, but the prof was able to regain control.

Miroslav fired off a second round, this one aimed at the rear passenger side tire. The .44 blasted through the passenger side brake lights, though it couldn't get through the car's internals.

"I can't get a shot!" Miroslav shouted.

"Hang on!" I shouted.

I swerved into the oncoming traffic lane, trying to give my partner a better shooting angle. Thankfully, with his third shot, Miroslav was able to blow out the driver-side rear tire. Kellogg's car was thrown into a skid, sending it fish-tailing as the prof tried to retake control.

"Brace!" I shouted as I prepared for a pit maneuver.

Our cruiser drifted to the side and slammed into the Volkswagen's back. Miroslav cursed in Polish as he ducked back inside our car. I'll admit I got a bit too close to slamming him into the car with that stunt. The sudden crash sent the car spinning out of control and brought it to a screeching halt in a ditch.

Everything hurt. I did my best to recover from the crash, but all the pain and exhaustion was catching up to me. I clutched my thigh as I pushed myself out the door. Miroslav moved to cover the passenger side door, his massive magnum still smoking.

"Last chance, fucker!" I shouted as I drew my UDS-38 and took aim at the driver's side door.

Towers stumbled out of the door, one hand raised, the other trying to pull off his facemask. I was about to shoot him, before he spilled the contents of his stomach on the side of the road.

Kellogg was much slower and calmer to get out, holding one hand up defensively as he looked at me.

"Good thing this isn't on my insurance." He joked, gesturing to his wrecked car.

I quickly fired a warning shot over his shoulder. Even though the shot was nearly silent, it still got the point across. "I've had enough of your shit! Hands on the hood! Now!"

Kellogg scowled at me as he slowly straightened up.

"Yes, as you wish, Officer." Kellogg said slowly, as I noticed the glint of a pistol through his door window.

I struggled to call it a firearm of any sort. It had the vague shape of a pistol, sure, but it was bulky and had all sorts of glowing fuses and reflective surfaces. It looked like it belonged in a steampunk convention, like most Weird-Science inventions.

I didn't give him a chance. I shot him twice in the chest before he could bring his gun to bear. The prof grunted in pain as the rounds tore through his suit, but I was surprised when no blood gushed through. He had a ballistic vest under his suit.

"To the task!" Kellogg roared like a battle cry as he leveled his handgun at me.

The barrel radiated bright blue for a moment before a lightning bolt arced out at me. It blasted through the cruiser's window, striking me full in the chest. I fell flat on my back, body spasming and surrounded by shattered glass.

Miroslav fired off a shot, but it deflected off the roof of the car. As Kellogg brought his lightning gun around to fire on my partner, I knew I had only one chance to save him. Just like the Mozambique Drill demanded, if two shots to the chest didn't stop him, go for the head.

I used what strength I had left to raise my UDS-38 and snapped off a shot. There was a sudden pause as the round crunched through Kellogg's skull. Time seemed to slow as I waited to see if my final shot had any effect. At first, I thought the bullet just deflected off his skull. But, after what felt like an hour of silence, my accuracy was rewarded with a waterfall of blood and brain matter cascading down the side of the professor's head. The lightning gun dropped from Kellogg's hand as he collapsed to the ground like a falling tree.

I allowed my arm to flop to the ground beside me. Everything already hurt, but now it hurt even worse after being zapped. I just gazed up at the stars as I heard Miroslav shove Towers against the car and handcuff him. I could hear Jean pulling up in her cruiser, but I couldn't bring myself to care.

I just… wanted some rest…

My return to consciousness was a slow and arduous fight. When I opened my eyes again, I was greeted with the dim, hazy glow of ceiling lights. My bed of asphalt and broken glass was thankfully replaced with a halfway comfy mattress. I could tell that I was in the Revenant Division infirmary, and that the only thing keeping me modest was a surgical gown and some bandaging around my thigh.

"Kathy!" an all too familiar voice called beside me. "Is good you are awake, my friend." Miroslav looked down at me from my bedside, his psychotic grin almost comforting in this circumstance.

"What… what the hell happened?"

"You fell unconscious after Kellogg zapped you with a lightning pistol." Jean said as she stepped up next to Miroslav.

"I meant after that." I said, a bit snappier than I meant.

"Well, after that, we took Towers into custody," she said. "Thankfully, the Necro Flu sample didn't break during the chase, so we managed to bag that too."

"Thank Christ." I said, breathing a sigh of relief. "So, everything's been settled?"

"For the time being." Jean said, looking down at me with her sweet smile. "But Towers has been spilling his guts with all the forbidden alchemy his master had been teaching him. The Order of Frankenstein is planning something big."

"Is no big deal." Miroslav assured me, slamming his fists together. "We fight them."

For a moment, I allowed myself to smile. Maybe it was the painkillers, but Miroslav's excitement was infectious.

"Well, you get better soon, Kathy." Jean said as she stood up and walked to the door.

Before she left, she gave me a playful wink. "If for nothing else, get better so I don't have to do your paperwork for this case."

As she left, Miroslav looked down at me. His wry smile returned as he opened his coat and revealed a fresh bottle of wine.

I'm telling you. After the day I had, wine never tasted so good.

MISS IMPERIUM

HONORABLE MENTION

L.J. HILSE

"I'M NOT ENTERING a beauty pageant. Get that through your heads right now!" Rajeen rejected the suggestion her companions had just made. The three of them sat around the table in their spartan hideaway eating their evening meal.

Merle and Nedra exchanged looks. Nedra picked up on Merle's proposal. "Rajeen, you are without a doubt the prettiest of us. You're the only one with a shot at getting past the district competition. Look at you. You're the tallest. You've got a bustline that the two of us together can't match. Your gorgeous hair's down to your waist —"

"Anyone can dye their hair red," Rajeen interrupted. She pulled off the short, black wig she'd worn for their day of running small cons and picking pockets.

"Sure," Merle agreed. "But yours is all natural which is unusual. That will catch the judges' attention. You've got a friendly personality. The person who does this has to mingle with the others and be sociable."

"Plus, there's a talent portion. We all know you have the best singing voice of the three of us and you play that old instrument of Uncle's beautifully," concluded Nedra.

They sat looking at each other. Although the oldest of them at twenty-two, Merle was also the shortest. She had chin-length light brown hair, brown eyes, and delicate features. With the right clothing — she could still pass as a young teenager. Nedra at twenty, went the other way. She could project an older, more mature woman. Almost as tall as Rajeen, Nedra's shoulder-length hair was much darker and her features more rounded.

Rajeen shook her head. "But I'm a nobody — we're all nobodies. I don't think I'll get very far. These things are probably rigged anyway. If you're serious about this, you'll have to have the best bribes for the judges."

"Will you at least try? For Uncle? For us?" Merle held up her left thumb showing the small scar on the ball. Nedra did the same.

Swallowing her misgivings, Rajeen nodded and held up her thumb as well. They pressed them together and recited their vow from years ago. "Through thick and thin, through feast and famine, through orbits high and low, we'll stand together for long as there's air to breathe."

The vow they made as idealistic teenagers always brought up complicated memories.

Bellamy Benton had raised his orphaned nieces, Merle and Nedra, along with a foundling he brought home when the girls were very young. He named the baby Rajeen and told the girls to think of her as a sister. They'd been inseparable ever since.

As they got older, Uncle, as they all called him, taught them how to survive in the tunnels, caverns, and concourses of Imperial City. They learned how to change their appearance, run a con, pick a pocket, stay off all official registries, and avoid security drones. When Merle and Nedra got old enough, Uncle offered them the opportunity to join the Underground. They found the name hilarious as only rich Martians lived in the domed part of the city. The rest lived… underground. Of course, the Underground didn't do much to oppose the Imperial

Order besides commit minor acts of sabotage and circulate rude songs. The sisters carried the message wafers members used to maintain secure communications. He'd been reluctant to involve Rajeen and kept putting off her requests to become involved.

Then, two years ago, Imperial City Security detained and imprisoned Uncle Bellamy. They still didn't know if he'd been arrested because of some con he was running or for all the anti-Imperial protest songs he wrote for the Underground. Every few months, they took turns risking a prison inquiry through a public data terminal to make sure he was still alive. The Imperial Prison system wasn't known for its hospitality. The fact that his status still showed active after two years gave them hope.

"Speaking of air," said Nedra, "it's about time to siphon more out of the municipal system. Getting a bit stale down here." Their hideout in a walled off section of a sub-basement of the city's air scrubber plant gave them easy access to two of life's necessities: breathable air and potable water. The plant had kilometers of pipes transporting both.

In addition to music, Uncle Bellamy possessed a gift for mechanical work. He'd briefly been employed in the plant during his youth until the management double checked identity creds and realized his were forged. Before that happened, he'd built the false wall in the lowest level of the plant that created their cramped hiding space.

Living in the capital of Emperor Maximus II should have meant access to the best schools, jobs, healthcare, and parks. But to qualify for those, you had to join the Imperial Party. Uncle Bellamy never had.

Nedra walked to the far end of their long, rectangular room and used a telescopic pole to nudge open the makeshift vent on the side of a tube. Fresh, cool air treated with a light floral scent flowed into their space. She stood there for several minutes enjoying the breeze on her face before closing the vent and returning to the table. Too long and the outflow would be picked up by system monitors as a leak to be investigated.

The three finished eating their meal of protein kabobs. Merle opened a packet of dried fruit they shared for a treat.

"I had a good day today." Nedra broke the contemplative silence. "While you two ran the melon drop, I lifted five transit buttons and three different female ident cards." Nedra reached into a secret pocket inside her jacket and pulled out her booty. She spread the idents on the table. "How much did you get for the rare antique vase the mark supposedly caused you to break?"

Merle smiled. "He coughed up five hundred Imperial credits. Rajeen put on an excellent performance crying over her great-grandmother's special vase shipped all the way from Earth."

"That's a good score. We're going need every credit for top class forgeries for Rajeen for the pageant."

"We're also going to need beautiful clothing — not just for her, but for her manager and stylist as well." She pointed to herself and then Nedra. "Is there anyone we trust to make those garments? Or do we buy retail?"

Rajeen spoke up. "This is going to cost an awful lot. Are you sure this is the best way to free Uncle? I mean, we could pay for a prison break with the money we're talking about!"

Merle shook her head. "Even if it worked, they'd hunt him the rest of his life. If you win the pageant, you get to ask his Imperial Majesty for a special request." She said their ruler's title with mocking reverence. "As best I can tell from the public news sources, the requests are honored — as long as you don't get crazy. Most contest winners ask for a bigger living space or Imperial College tuition. I found one reference to a pardon, so you would be able to ask for that."

Nedra added, "When you win, the prize money will more than cover our expenses."

Rajeen looked doubtful. "You're putting a lot on my shoulders. Like I said, you better have some good bribe money too."

Merle and Nedra returned to their planning.

THROUGH THEIR NETWORK OF CONTACTS, they found a personal appearance salon in a decent, but not rich part of town. Merle and Nedra dropped Rajeen off there the next day. Their instructions to the owner were to give Rajeen the works from head to toes.

Nedra, wearing a blonde wig and the nicest outfit she had, headed off to scout luxury clothing stores in the high-end precincts, the kind that scanned your body for a perfect fit.

Merle, trying to look as poor as possible, went to see Hopper, the best forger and fence they knew.

Data stick secured in an inner pocket, Merle used one of the stolen transit buttons to take a round-about route to Hopper's decrepit-looking storefront. She entered a business that deliberately looked uninviting. Shelves lining the walls held used and refurbished electronic equipment. Everything from handheld readers to holo projectors to larger processing units with full screens lay crowded together in no particular system.

Merle browsed for a moment, double checking that no one had stopped on the street outside. Then she approached the bored-looking man at the counter, who had also been watching the street, and gave the code phrase.

"Hi, I'm here to see Hopper about a battery pack for my aunt."

The man activated a hidden control and the door into a back room slid open. He motioned with his head.

Merle went into the small storeroom and the door closed. She waited while hidden cameras examined her. Another door retracted and Merle descended a metal staircase to Hopper's workshop.

She worked to control her nerves and project calm. Visits to

Hopper, though necessary, were unpredictable. It depended on his mood. She waited while he ran some type of scan, making sure she wasn't wearing a transmitter to rat him out to the "vests," as they called local law enforcement.

Hopper sat at a sparkling clean metal table manipulating several computers through their holo screens. The overhead lights reflecting off his bald head reminded Merle of images of ancient light bulbs she'd seen. She pegged his age at about fifty. Exceedingly pale skin gave a false impression of weakness. Eventually, he relaxed back into his chair and nodded for her to speak.

"We need new creds. Running a scam and we need to look at least middle-class well off."

"Cards only or with interwebs backup?" he asked in a detached voice.

"Both."

"Costs a lot more. You've never asked for the backup before." He sounded slightly more interested.

"It's a long con."

He named a price.

Merle winced.

"What if I give you half of that upfront and we cut you in for a percent of our take. That could potentially net you more."

"Ten percent."

"Three."

"Seven."

Merle shook her head. "We have a lot of expenses to set this one up. We're taking a lot of risk. Five is the best I can do."

He studied her for a moment. She kept her face open and sincere. It was one of her best skills.

Finally, he nodded. "Let's get on with it."

She handed over the data stick and the cards Nedra had lifted yesterday and they got to work.

NEDRA ENTERED the Parisian Paradise store on Imperial Way and paused to study the layout. Various mannequins on rotating stands displayed the store's current fashions. She pulled out her comm and started making voice notes, just loud enough to be heard by the sales associates.

"Acceptable quality fabrics. Construction methods look adequate. Not sure about the taste level, but we could probably work with it." She continued wandering and peering as close as she could get to the clothing.

She thought they'd never take the bait, but finally an older woman approached her. "May I ask what it is you are doing? Is there something we can help you with?"

Nedra looked up with a practiced expression of surprise. "Oh, well I'm not supposed to say until her manager decides. I'm just gathering information."

The woman peered at her, puzzled. "What are you referring to?"

Nedra looked around theatrically then whispered, "The Pageant."

When the woman still looked puzzled.

Nedra clarified. "The Martian Imperial Pageant. You know, for the title of Miss Imperium."

"Oh," the woman finally caught on.

"I'm scouting sources for the pageant clothing for our client. We've never seen such a natural beauty. With the right clothing, she's going to mesmerize the judges. She's, well, really I've said too much already. I won't take any more of your time."

"Wait," the woman said. "We'd be very interested in working with you and your client. We have some special fabrics and designs that we don't have out on the sales floor. Come have a seat in the holo-salon and let me show you."

Nedra made a show of checking the time on her comm. "I am a little ahead of schedule. Sure."

"Come right this way."

MERLE FINISHED with Hopper who promised her new idents by the end of business the next day. The online backtrail took a little longer but would be in place within the week.

As she walked two kilometers to a different transit entrance, she thought about the next major goal. They absolutely had to find a temporary base of operations that wasn't near their crib in the air treatment plant. Merle didn't want to ask anyone in the Underground for help on this scheme. She was pretty sure they would shut the whole thing down as too risky. It put Rajeen in a very public spotlight.

But she'd always adored an old saying of Uncle Bellamy's. "Fortune favors the bold," he often told her, especially after one of his crazy cons paid off.

Back in the transit tube, she settled into a seat and took a quick glance around the compartment. Nobody seemed interested in her. She pulled out her comm and scrolled through newsbytes while keeping her ears open to the conversations around her.

One discussion in particular grabbed her attention. Two women were talking about their upcoming trip to Earth. If Merle followed them home, maybe she could find a place for their pageant operation to squat for a few weeks.

She stayed on well past her planned stop. Six terminals later, the women exited the tube. Merle strolled along behind them. She hung back and cursed softly when they headed to the shuttle cart stand. If she followed in a cart, it would be too obvious.

With a grumpy sigh, she headed back into the tube system.

She entered a compartment and the doors closed before she realized who else was on board.

Newly minted Martian Planetary Security Detective Brock Perez slouched back in his transit tube seat. His first few days on this crime-control task force had been as boring as vacuum. His target hadn't done anything noteworthy, and Brock was confident it wasn't because he'd been made.

The guy had perked up when the young woman, or girl, hard to tell her age, got on the tube. He'd stood up and gone to her with open arms. She'd been startled but accepted the hug. Then they'd sat together chatting. Getting caught up? Or was it some type of coded conversation?

Detective Perez tuned in his listening device more precisely by shifting his position on the seat and leaning his head up against the tube wall beside him. The small earpiece did the rest.

His clothing blended in well with all the other worker drones in their plain coveralls. Knowing he'd be assigned to the task force, he started growing out his buzz-cut brown hair weeks ago. He'd let his beard grow to cover a scar on his chin. That, along with his brown eyes and light brown skin, made him blend into the background. Having one of those unremarkable faces made him a good candidate for undercover work. He often wished he weren't quite so forgettable… especially with the few interesting women he'd met.

As the conversation went on, his initial excitement died down. All their talk centered on a death in his target's family and entreaties to get back in this woman's good graces. So much for hoping she was someone higher up in the criminal organization meeting with a foot soldier. After two days on this assignment, Brock had concluded that this guy didn't have the brains to be anything but a muscular messenger.

Brock wasn't sure why he did it. He rarely played hunches. But when the woman got off and switched tube runs, he followed her instead of staying on his target. The guy was probably headed to his usual bar anyway. Brock could pick him up there later. The woman seemed much more interesting.

NEDRA WONDERED what was keeping Merle. They were to meet at the salon. She couldn't wait to get somewhere private so she could tell them about her score.

She was about to go into the salon alone when Merle came around the corner from the tube station. Her sister moved on autopilot and was about to pass Nedra without noticing her.

Nedra sighed and shot out a hand to grab Merle's arm. Hopefully, whatever had happened wasn't too bad.

"Hey," she greeted Merle. "Whatever it is, let's not spook Rajeen."

Merle nodded vaguely and let Nedra guide her into the salon.

They signed in with the reception-bot. Soon the sliding doors opened and the owner of Illume, Fina Delton, came to greet them. The short, dusky-skinned woman smiled at them.

"My staff and I have had such a fun day! You brought us a diamond in the rough and we are presenting you with a polished gem." She waved the doors open again and Rajeen walked toward them with a shy smile.

Nedra looked at Rajeen in astonishment. She glanced over at Merle and saw the same look of awe on her face. Turning back to Fina, she said, "Amazing — just amazing! You have indeed made her shine. She is stunning!"

Trimmed to her shoulders, Rajeen's red-gold hair hung in a silken shimmer. Her skin glowed with a natural look, even though Nedra could see skillfully applied eye enhancers and lip color. They had given her a manicure and treated her nails with the latest color-change tech.

"Good, you are suitably impressed!" Fina preened. "You put the right clothing on this young woman and you are — without a doubt — looking at the next Miss Imperium. Now, come in back. Let's go over our suggestions for make-up, hair products, and the nail tech."

"Do I really look like I could win?" asked Rajeen as they herded her through the doors.

"Honey, we'll have to put a bag over your head to get you home," Nedra told her. "The way you look now could start a riot."

THEY DIDN'T COVER her up, but they did make her wear a wig and wash off the makeup before they all left the salon to take different routes back to their hideout. Since she'd had an easy day, Rajeen volunteered to pick up food on the way.

As she paid the noodle vendor, she got that uncomfortable feeling that make her back twitch. Uncle had trained them all to pay attention to those vague sensations. They often meant the subconscious had picked up on some small bit of data. She stood chatting to the food vendor an extra minute to fit in a couple more scans of the area. The people on the concourse looked like the usual workers heading for home.

After thanking the vendor again, she doubled back and entered the neighborhood Pantheon temple. She didn't have a strong affinity for any of the ancient Roman gods that Maximus the First had instituted as a state religion. Instead, she chose the shrine that gave her the best view of the entrance.

She knelt on the patterned mat in front of the holographic projection of Venus. You could interact with these holograms.

Whisper your prayers. Hear soothing, encouraging words in return. Leave small or large offerings.

Moving her lips without saying anything out loud, she kept her head bowed, but her eyes on the wide opening from the concourse. No one followed her in. Gradually she relaxed. Pulling out the smallest credit chip she had, she dropped it in the slot at the base of the hologram's plinth and left.

There were still lots of people passing by, but no one loitering. After a few more stops to window shop, she decided it was safe to head to their refuge.

WHEN THEY WERE all seated around the table, Nedra told them about her success at the clothing store. "The manager took the bait. They're willing to provide free clothing for Rajeen provided we tell everyone where we got her garments."

"That's amazing!" Rajeen looked over at Merle and prodded her. "Don't you think so, Merle?"

Merle picked at her container of noodles. "Huh. What? Oh, the free clothing. That's nice."

"Come on, spit it out. What's going on? You've barely talked since we met at the salon," demanded Nedra.

Merle gave them each a forlorn look. "Tommy Parker."

Nedra groaned. "Not him again!"

"Can't the guy take a hint!" asked Rajeen.

Sighing, Merle shook her head. "We bumped into each other on the transit line. He misses me. Asked me to give him another chance. Wants to prove he's changed. He looked so sad. His grandmother died a few days ago."

Nedra put a hand on Merle's shoulder. "We don't have time for this right now. You've got to keep your head in the game!"

"I know," muttered Merle. "But I've been missing him too.

Maybe we can just be friends. I just wish he wasn't such a good kisser. He melts me right down to my toes."

"Yeah, but if I recall correctly, he wanted to be kissing lots of different girls," groused Rajeen.

"I've got a list of things to keep you so busy you won't have time to think about — melting," Nedra told her. "Tomorrow the two of us, as manager and stylist, go shopping for clothes and then the next day we'll take Rajeen to the Parisian Paradise boutique. Plus, I need to get the application submitted for the District Nine pageant. Now, thoughts on temporary housing?"

Merle perked up a little. She told them about the women on the tube. "But I couldn't follow them home."

"There must be some way to find out about empty apartments," mused Rajeen.

Nedra finished chewing some noodles and looked at Merle thoughtfully. "Say, um, did Tommy ever mention if his grandmother lived alone?"

"I think so, why do you —" Merle paused. "You're not thinking what I think you're thinking, are you?"

"Well, if she's dead, she doesn't need her apartment, now does she?" Nedra defended herself.

"I would have to tell Tommy what we're up to. Did you think of that? The management must know old lady Parker died. They probably have a waiting list."

"We need it six weeks, tops. You don't need to tell him about Uncle. He can just think we're trying to win the prize money. The whole pageant process goes pretty quickly once the district competitions are done. If Tommy could stall the management… he just needs to convince them her apartment's full of painful memories and the family needs time to process their grief before cleaning it out. We could pay for a month or two of rent, so it wouldn't cost his family anything."

Merle thought it over. "I guess it wouldn't hurt to ask."

"For that kind of favor, Tommy might expect more than

friendship," observed Rajeen. "Are you sure you want to do that?"

"Well, if it helps get Uncle out of prison, it's worth it. Right?"

"Oh, absolutely," agreed Rajeen with a smirk. "And if you have to put up with great kissing — and what comes after — for a few weeks, you'll just have to grit your teeth and bear it!"

Much to Merle's chagrin, Nedra and Rajeen burst out laughing.

A DAY after all three women attended the funeral and wake for Tommy's grandmother, Tommy took them to visit his gram's place. They got off the elevator and Tommy led them through the maze of corridors toward the vacant apartment. He had his arm around Merle's shoulders while Nedra and Rajeen walked behind them.

Only a little taller than Merle, Tommy had a strong, stocky build and dark coloring. While sad about his grandmother, he was thrilled to be dating Merle again.

He worked for a little organization known as the Concourse Kings. They didn't consider themselves a gang. They ran a business that provided the populace with things the Imperial order disapproved of. They ran gambling halls, sold protection, and could provide a variety of illicit substances for the right price. A few decades ago, several of these enterprises had divided Imperial City into territories. It cut down on bloodshed and made it harder for Martian Public Security to gain leverage on them.

Tommy glanced back at Rajeen, who wore a wig and had no makeup on. "Tell me again why Rajeen's the one entering the pageant and not you? You know you got the looks, babe."

"Thanks, Tommy, but I'm too short. Rajeen's the best choice of the three of us."

"Agree to disagree, Sugardrop." He squeezed her shoulder as they went round a turn in the hallway.

Nedra held back and turned to Rajeen to mime gagging. Rajeen stifled a laugh.

They caught up to the others as Tommy placed his palm on the security pad to the apartment. The door slid open and they entered.

"We'll have to update the palm pad with the three of you before I leave. Feel free to look around. I told my ma I would pack things up, so we should do some of that. Otherwise, she'll be over here nagging me."

"We'll help," Merle promised. "We just needed an address for the pageant application and a place to store all the nice clothing and accessories. On pageant nights, we'll sleep here."

The three women surveyed the space. The apartment had a compact sitting room with two built-in seating banks with cushions and retractable footrests. A large entertainment screen occupied the wall to their right. Straight ahead sat a table and four chairs. Beyond that a tiny galley-style kitchen had chilling and heating appliances. A short hallway branched off the seating area to the bathroom and beyond that, the bedroom.

Nedra headed that way. "Let's take a look at those closets."

The bedroom contained a full-sized bed with built-in storage on the wall around the headboard. Across from the bed, the closet took up the entire wall.

Nedra touched the retract sensor and the closet doors slid open.

Divided into thirds, the stuffed closet contained a section of drawers, an area of open shelves full of folded items and footwear, and a space for hanging garments.

Shaking her head, Nedra sighed. "Not nearly as much space as I hoped for." She turned to Tommy. "Can we clear this out now? We've got clothing scheduled for delivery in a few days."

"Sure. I've got compression packs in the living room. Fill

those and then I'll get them to my mom's place. Just remember to handle stuff with care, after all everything here was my gram's."

Merle assured Tommy they would be respectful. "We'll take turns packing while you get each of us logged into the door security. Besides you don't want to see your gram's underwear, do you?" She giggled and gave him a kiss.

With all three of them working, they cleared the closet in half an hour and piled the small, but heavy compression packs in the living room. When they were done, they stood in the hall and double checked that their palm prints opened the door. Back down on the street, Rajeen and Nedra headed off on their own, leaving Merle to enjoy Tommy's attentions alone.

Once they were out of earshot, Nedra spoke the thoughts they were both having. "I never did understand what she saw in him. I just hope when this is all done, she can disengage without moping around for months like last time."

BROCK WATCHED as Parker and the women emerged from the housing unit. He'd gotten a verbal reprimand for leaving his target the other day. Telling his supervisor he was following some hunches and hadn't even stuck with the first female didn't go over so well. If he did it again, there would be an official censure on his department file. Brock couldn't help but wonder what he might have found if HQ hadn't called him to task the other day.

He looked forward to telling his boss how these women had showed up again. And they kept changing their appearance with wigs. That had to be significant. He labeled them Tall, Medium and Shortie in his mind. As they split up, he stuck with Parker and Shortie.

He still couldn't fathom how they all connected. Parker's

grandmother had lived in this building. Perhaps the women were simply friends who came to help him. But as he found them together again, he gained confidence that there was more here to unravel. Convincing his supervisor to give him some latitude wasn't going to be easy.

The implanted tracking tech offered reassurance that HQ could find him quickly in case of trouble. On the other hand, they also knew when he got creative, like the other day, and started wandering about strange slums trying to figure out where the women had disappeared to. He wondered what it would be like to not have chips implanted in his body that —

The supervisor's voice in his earbud interrupted these guilty thoughts.

"Perez, status report."

He leaned into the collar of his coverall where the built-in mic was attached. "Parker and all three females from the other day were in the building where Parker's relative lived. All have exited. I'm following Parker, who is with the female he met on the tube. They appear to be headed for the transit line."

"Status update accepted. Stay on target. HQ out."

The next week passed in a boring haze. Brock was more than ready for a couple of beers while watching the hover races when his shift ended. He'd been on his way to his favorite bar near the community center when he spotted them again. There, down the concourse, walked the trio of women. At least he thought it was the same three. Now Tall one a redhead instead of a brunette.

He was on his own time. It wasn't a suspicious part of town. He just happened to be going the same direction. It looked like they were head to his bar when they stopped short and entered the community center.

An electronic sign above the doors clued him in. "District Nine Miss Imperium Pageant." That explained the excited groups of people pouring in. Nothing suspicious about entering a beauty pageant, he guessed. He stood debating the bar or seeing which of the women was in the pageant. Maybe all three were?

The bar would still be there in a few. He followed the next group through the sliding doors and settled into a seat in the crowded auditorium.

THE WEEK after they cleaned out the apartment passed in a blur. Veneris night rolled around to find Nedra and Merle escorting Rajeen to the local community center for the District Nine Pageant weekend.

They entered a hallway packed with people and bubbling with excitement.

"How many of these are contestants?" asked Rajeen.

"At a guess, I'd say fifty to sixty," Nedra estimated.

They'd dressed Rajeen in simple black tailored trousers, a teal blouse, high heels and the lightest of makeup. Her hair swung loose about her shoulders. After a brief wait in line, they faced their first pageant officials.

Subtle lines of tension eased on all three as the new creds from Hopper passed without comment from the registrar. The woman handed them name badges and an e-reader. Another official swabbed Rajeen's mouth for the pageant-required DNA scan. Then they went to find seats at the back of the community center auditorium.

Soon after, a slight man with blond hair and a neat beard took to the stage. He wore a black suit with graphic display panels crossing his body on a diagonal. The words "Miss Imperium 2537" scrolled across his clothing. He tuned his microphone into an amplifier hovering overhead. His voice poured over the sound system like honey.

"Good evening, everyone. My name's Daren Cobb. Please join me in our salute to the Emperor." He turned to face a large screen that showed the handsome visage of Maximus II. An Imperial flag with its red disk of the planet framed by archaic earth eagles hung from the screen's base. "All Hail Maximus the Second!"

Knowing what was expected of them, the audience stood and put right hands over their hearts. "All Hail Maximus the Second!"

After the audience sat, the emcee continued. "Welcome to the District Nine Miss Imperium Pageant preliminaries. Tonight, we'll cover the ground rules, bring all registered contestants on stage to introduce themselves, and meet our volunteer judges. In case you didn't know, each district sends its volunteers to other districts to avoid conflicts of interest. My fellow Masters of Ceremony and I are employees of the Imperial Pageant Department. We're here to make sure all levels of the competition are conducted fairly."

Seated on either side of Rajeen, Merle and Nedra leaned back to share an eyeroll over that statement. Rajeen sat forward in her seat, outwardly calm except for the tapping of her foot.

Cobb continued to explain the procedures. "The two winners of this district will go on to the Region One competition which includes all of Imperial City. From each region, three candidates will go on to the Imperial level contest with the best candidate being crowned Miss Imperium by a member of the royal family."

As required, the audience applauded any mention of the Imperial Family.

He went on. "Makes me wish I was eligible! Now, contestants and managers, if you have one, follow along on the e-reader as we go over the ground rules. First and foremost, undisclosed genetic mods may result in a contestant being disqualified. Please look over the list of ones that are absolutely not allowed."

Nedra whispered to Rajeen and Merle, "I'm going to scout around and see what I can hear, especially about the judges."

Back at the sign-in desk, she enquired of the bathroom facilities. She popped into the toilet room briefly, but there was no one there gossiping. With a bit of exploring, she found access to the back of the stage.

There she could hear the emcee's voice reading through the dry contest details — as well as a quiet conversation going on behind a stack of sound equipment containers. She kept to the shadows, trying to ease closer to the people talking.

She heard a woman say, "— and that's just to show how friendly we can be. If Malindy gets to go to Regionals, we'll be expressing our gratitude that much again."

A man's voice rumbled, "Much appreciated. Of course, your daughter needs to do a good job, make it feasible. You understand that, right?"

"Of course, but you know how close these competitions can be. We just want to make sure you realize how generous a family we are."

As the conversation ended, Nedra retreated into a dark corner to watch who went through the exit. She observed a middle-aged woman who could once have been a beauty queen herself slip out the door.

After waiting a minute, Nedra assumed the judge had gone a different way. She lingered, but nothing else interesting happened. She headed back to her seat, getting there just as the contestants began signing the contest agreement on the e-readers.

Next, Cobb called the judges, one man and two women, into the spotlight and introduced them.

Nedra leaned over to Merle and whispered, "We'll need to make sure I get a chance to get close to all three of them."

Merle gave her the briefest of nods.

At last, Cobb asked all contestants to join him. Most of the young women rushed to the ramps at either end of the stage.

Merle signaled for Rajeen to wait. When Rajeen did stand, she was the lone figure walking toward the right-hand side of the stage and all eyes were on her — including her fellow contestants.

She walked with head held high, placing her feet in a line, one in front of the other, without rushing. Her elegance and poise captivated the onlookers. She joined the line of fifty women that stretched across the stage, but most eyes were on her.

With a big smile, Cobb walked to her and said, "Let's start down here. Tell us your name and why you've entered the competition. And everyone, please hold applause until we've heard from all the candidates."

Rajeen returned the smile and looked out at the audience. "Hello. My name's Rajeen Cooper. I entered the competition as a way to challenge myself and become more involved in civic life. Normally, I'm a fairly shy person, but with encouragement from friends, I'm here tonight. Thank you."

Merle leaned over to Nedra and whispered, "How does she do it? She seems so sincere, like she really means it."

"She is sincere. It might not have been the whole story, but she's always been one for getting to know people and connecting with them. She knows every street vendor by name."

They monitored all the other women as they spoke, making a list of those they thought might offer serious competition. Then Cobb invited everyone to another room for light refreshments. The judges didn't attend. After an hour, the event wrapped up with the emcee admonishing all of them to go home and get a good night's rest.

BROCK EXPECTED to sleep in on Saturni, but he got an urgent call to fill in for a sick coworker. It was another surveillance crew so at least he got to follow someone other than Tommy Parker. This new target, an older man with sparse gray hair, spent most of the morning sitting at a café drinking coffee and chatting with a steady stream of visitors. Brock wandered in and out of nearby stores, bought some fruit, and stayed nearby ready to follow if the man got up. Finally, the supervisor ordered him to sit at a café table while the other detective took a break. Needing to look occupied, he pulled out his comm and called up some departmental report forms. He could get caught up on some of his job's busy work.

After finishing a few forms, he was going to close the link, when he paused over the tab to start a data request. He ran his hand over the short beard on his chin, thinking. Having sat through the pageant meeting the previous evening, he'd learned the name Rajeen Cooper. Entering her name, he tapped on a variety of reports to generate. As he was almost done, a new prompt popped up on the screen. "DNA sample acquired. Tests pending. Expedite?"

He mused on that for a moment. Probably from the pageant. The tests would be run at some point. What could it hurt to move things along?

His target stood up and stretched as he clicked *yes*. Brock brought his focus back on his job and closed the screen.

AFTER SPENDING the night at the borrowed apartment, the trio gathered up all the makeup, hairstyling gear, and the day's outfits and headed back to the community center. All along their route, they got inquisitive looks.

When they got to the center, Merle led them to their assigned prep space — a multipurpose room on an upper level. As they opened the door, the chatter of voices hit them like a slap in the face. Nine other contestants and their helpers filled the room. Pandemonium reigned.

They entered cautiously. One young lady waved and smiled at Rajeen and pointed to the other half of her table. She yelled, "Rajeen, we talked yesterday evening. I saved you a spot."

The women made their way to the far side of the room. "Thanks, Leona. This is my manager Merle and my stylist Nedra."

They exchanged greetings.

"Where's your crew?" asked Rajeen.

Leona shrugged. "My best friend said she'd help, but she hasn't shown up."

"We'll help you," offered Rajeen. "As soon as Nedra is done torturing my hair."

Leona brightened. "I'd appreciate that." She had short, mostly blonde hair that had been dyed in swirls of blues and purples to match her clothing. She was already dressed in the first of three required outfits, the one for working in zero gee. She had on a red jumpsuit that nipped in tightly at her waist with a single, blue stripe down the outside of the legs. Sleeveless, it showed off her toned arms. Purple work boots covered her feet.

"Someone tried to grab this last clothing rack, but I told them off and put it next to mine." Leona pushed the rack toward their end of the table.

"Thanks," Merle said. "All the more reason to lend you a hand. But we better get Rajeen started." They hung up the garment bags and unpacked makeup and styling tools.

It seemed like no time before an official started giving them time calls. Soon they would be heading down to the auditorium's backstage. Nedra finished arranging the last of the many thin braids woven with delicate wires to hold Rajeen's hair in a sculpture floating out behind her head.

Leona sat on a chair watching. "That's amazing. I love it."

"Thanks," Rajeen told her. "I'm finally ready. Is there anything we can do for you?"

"Just check me over. Do I look put together?"

All three of them took a moment to inspect her. Nedra came over and unsealed the front of Leona's jumpsuit another seven centimeters. "There. And a little more powder on the nose. You look great."

They heard the call to line up. Leona quickly dabbed her nose and they were off.

———

IT TOOK a good portion of the morning to complete the first part of the competition. As each contestant walked across the stage, Cobb read a description of her outfit. Mid-stage, each woman got a minute to tell more about herself.

People packed the auditorium. Tiny drone cameras buzzed around recording both contestants and audience. After some editing, the show would be broadcast to District Nine screens.

Rajeen's time on stage elicited *oohs* and *aahs* of appreciation and hearty applause. She wore a jumpsuit made of stretchy, midnight-blue fabric covered in small bursts of shimmering crystals meant to mimic twinkling stars. It had full-length pants and sleeves but left little to the imagination. Rajeen appeared to glide across the stage in special socks made to look like work boots. Her hair sculpture added to the illusion of floating.

Rajeen's brief description of herself had been the most difficult part of the whole round. The three of them had slaved over a believable backstory that Hopper could insert into the interwebs. After her parents died, she'd been raised by a kind uncle and her cousins. She worked in an electronics store and hoped to someday go to university to study medicine. In her spare time, she made music on a family-heirloom guitar and worked on her yoga poses.

Hopper had insisted on raising his percentage to six when they asked to use his storefront for Rajeen's employment history. Merle hadn't much choice but to agree.

Lunchtime arrived. Contestants changed back into their street clothes and had a catered meal. Merle kept an eye on their stuff. Nedra ducked into a bathroom to don a blonde wig and went off in search of judges.

She found them in a crush of spectators and relatives of contestants. Backtracking to the now unattended registration desk, she found one of the official pageant worker jackets to borrow. Putting it on, she returned to the judges and announced, "Sorry, everyone, the judges need to eat, too. They need to keep up their strength. Please clear a path."

Leading the two women and one man down a hallway toward the catered lunch, she managed to stumble and fall against the male. As he caught her shoulders, she deftly slid a hand into his pocket. It was full of bribes he'd taken. She limited herself to palming a couple in hopes that he wouldn't miss them.

"Sorry, I'm so clumsy." She righted herself. "Just keep going down this hall. It's the last door on the left."

He gave her an appraising look but kept going. As the last woman started to pass her, Nedra reached out to take her hand. One of the stolen crypto coins was now sandwiched between their palms. She whispered, "For Rajeen."

The woman paused and gave a brief nod before following the others.

Nedra decided she'd tackle the other female judge later in the lunch break — without the wig and in a different outfit. For now, she hustled away before the judges found out they probably weren't supposed to be in the lunch with the contestants.

After lunch, the pageant entered the second of three stages. The entrants had to answer a thought-provoking question while wearing clothing that represented their personal style. The judges would have time to deliberate and then select the top ten finalists.

Nedra returned as Merle helped Rajeen into a comfortable yoga outfit. They'd found an online class to give Rajeen some idea of what yoga was all about. She wore a sleek pair of form-fitting pants, a sleeveless top, and a bolero-style sweater jacket. The pants and top were dark purple while the sweater was a light lavender. Nedra styled her hair into two French-braids tied with purple bows.

"Remember, when you answer your question, put some heart into it. Try to mention some emotional experience in your answer," Merle reminded her.

"Got it," Rajeen nodded. "I hope they don't ask me anything too difficult. This is the part I'm most worried about."

Leona linked arms with her and told her, "It's the thing that frightens all of us the most. Come on, time to line up. Good luck!"

As the contestants headed backstage, Merle had a moment alone with Nedra. "Did you deal with the judges?"

Nedra assured her it was all taken care of. Whether it was enough was another matter.

Standing backstage in the dark, Merle and Nedra waited impatiently for Rajeen's turn on stage. A bank of monitors allowed them to watch the multiple views of the proceedings. The time dragged as fifty contestants worked their way through fifty questions. The questions ranged from "Describe the ideal diet for space travel." to "What are the pros and cons of the newly proposed Martian calendar?".

Nedra paid close attention as Malindy got her turn. She wore a short, slinky gold dress covered in sparkly bits. Turning to Merle she whispered, "That outfit screams sex worker. Do you think that's what she was going for?"

Merle snorted and shushed her sister.

Then Cobb gave Malindy one of the easiest questions they'd

heard all afternoon. "What would you recommend a visitor do on his first trip to the Imperial City?"

Merle groaned softly. "Jupiter! What an easy question. People might be bribing Cobb, too." They listened as Malindy rattled off several cultural institutions, threw in some restaurant recommendations, and finished by mentioning how moving it could be to visit the first emperor's tomb. "I'll bet she knew the question in advance. That was smooth."

"Look, Rajeen's next."

She moved gracefully across the stage and struck a yoga pose before stopping next to the host. "Rajeen, here's your question. How does a person know if he or she is in love?"

There were chuckles from the audience. Rajeen looked out at them with a blank face and swallowed.

"Well," she began softly, "I'm not sure I'm the best person to answer this question. I don't think I've been in love yet."

There were some sounds of *aahs* from the listeners.

"But I have a good friend who's in love. So based on things she's said, I assume love makes you feel all tingly inside — like you're getting too much oxygen. You have a hard time staying focused. When you think about that special person, you get kind of day-dreamy. If that person's not around, you feel a yearning. And when a person is in love, there's something about the eyes — her eyes look full of stars."

There was silence for several seconds.

Rajeen's pageant smile started to falter at what she took for disappointment. Then the audience woke from their trance and gave her hearty applause.

Cobb, correctly gauging the mood, gave her some applause as well.

"Thank you, Rajeen. You may not have been in love yet, but there are twenty men in the audience who are ready to propose! Next contestant."

The afternoon wore on until finally all the young women had

finished the second round. They headed backstage while the judges compared notes, discussed performances, and entered final scores into their computers.

Rajeen came to find Merle and Nedra.

Nedra welcomed her with a big hug. "Well done. You made that emotional connection."

Merle just gave her an angry glare. "Are you saying I'm not focused since I got back together with Tommy?"

Caught off guard, Rajeen looked at Nedra for help. Nedra held her hands up and said, "Don't look at me."

Rajeen shrugged. "I mean, sometimes I find you staring off into space. I've had to ask you questions two or three times to get your attention. You keep misplacing your comm."

A chime saved her. "We have to line up again. We all go on stage for the announcement of finalists." She whirled away.

"Do you want to watch from back here or go out into the auditorium," asked Nedra.

Merle answered by turning and heading for an exit. Nedra followed. They walked quickly through the corridors and made their way into the back of the auditorium, where it was standing room only.

The contestants trooped out onto the stage in one long line. Cobb followed. Screens placed around the room came to life. "I'd like to start by asking you to give these smart, brave, beautiful young women another round of applause." When the clapping died down, he continued. "The judges have scored the contestants and the computer has compiled the results. Let's find out who's going on to the finalist round. If your name is called, come stand in one of the ten lighted circles." Small golden circles appeared on the stage.

Cobb paused dramatically. "Computer, show us the finalists at thirty second intervals."

A melodious computer-generated voice started the list with Malindy Urban. Malindy squealed with joy and feigned humble surprise as she stepped forward. Four more names were called. Nedra and Merle looked at each other nervously. Then Leona's name was called.

"The seventh contestant to become a finalist is Rajeen Cooper."

Nedra and Merle both let out huge sighs of relief and started clapping. They didn't even hear the last three names they were so excited.

Cobb let the applause linger for a minute then calmed the audience down. "Congratulations to our finalists and a big thank you to everyone for competing. We'll continue with the third and final round tomorrow afternoon. There we'll get to see each of our finalists display a talent and learn who is going on to the Region One competition."

Turning to smile at her sister, she discovered Merle gone. Nedra met up with Rajeen in the dressing area. Although they waited, Merle never showed and finally the two of them went back to the loaned apartment to rest.

On Solis, Brock got some extra sleep, went to his favorite restaurant for a meal. During his meal, he'd checked for the reports he requested. Nothing looked out of the ordinary for this Rajeen Cooper. It annoyed him, as he was sure something wasn't right. He thought about visiting his mother, but without any conscious decision on his part, his feet took him by the community center.

The marquee above the doors announced it was the final day of the pageant. A list of ten finalist names scrolled across. Rajeen's was there. No surprise. She was easily the most beautiful woman he'd ever seen.

His curiosity wouldn't leave him alone. Cursing himself

silently, he entered the center. He'd check in with his mother later in the day. Maybe take her out for dinner. She'd like that.

———

Late the next morning, as Nedra worked on Rajeen's hair, Merle slunk into the dressing room. The three exchanged looks.

Eventually Merle capitulated. "Sorry I got angry at you yesterday, Rajeen. I guess we're all under a lot of stress."

Rajeen smiled. "It's okay. I'm glad you're here now." She reached out a hand.

Merle clasped it in her own. "You did great yesterday. Keep it up and I'm sure you'll go on to Regionals."

"Thanks." Rajeen bounced a little from nerves.

"Hold still!" commanded Nedra. "I know I make this look easy, but it isn't!" She was creating an elegant concoction of curls spiraling down from a knot of hair high on the crown of Rajeen's head.

With fewer contestants, they had a table to themselves. Leona came over from hers. Today her friend had come and helped her get ready.

"Wow, Leona. That's beautiful on you." Rajeen complimented her outfit.

Leona twirled around in a purple and blue concoction made up of multiple layers of filmy fabric that matched the colors in her sleeked-back hair. "I like it. I just wish I had somewhere in real life to wear it."

"Yeah, I don't know where I'd go in this either." Rajeen gestured to her emerald green ensemble. The outfit had a floor-length, velvet overcoat with a high collar and low neckline that emphasized her figure. Under the coat she wore a lacy bustier and sleek satin pants. "But it makes me feel like royalty."

"It makes you look like royalty," gushed Leona. "It's

gorgeous — just like you. Good luck today. It would be stellar if we both made it to Regionals!"

"It would. Good luck, too!"

A pageant official stuck her head in the door and gave them a ten-minute time call. Leona and her friend headed out. Merle retrieved the guitar case from under the table and offered to carry it. "I would feel better keeping an eye on it until it's time for you to play."

Nedra finished the hairdo and the three made their way through the congested hallways to the lower level. They were almost to the backstage entrance when a dozen bodies barreled through the area. Young people with faces hidden and carrying portable strobe lights formed a flicker mob rushing through the overcrowded area. These mobs loved to create fear, confusion, and maybe grab a poorly-guarded possession.

Even though the mob shoved everyone in their path, Rajeen got extra attention. She fell to the floor with a cry. Merle almost lost hold of the guitar case as hands reached out to grab it. Merle stomped on the assailant's feet and aimed a kick at a kneecap.

The greedy hands gave up and retreated.

Before either sister could get to Rajeen, a man came to stand near her protectively. He used his comm to take images of the retreating hooligans. Then he crouched down and asked Rajeen, "Are you alright? Can you stand or do you need help?"

Trembling, Rajeen stared into his eyes. The suddenness of the attack left her dazed and unable to answer his questions. This stranger offered her an anchor. She reached out and grasped his free hand. She studied his face intently.

His lips parted in the beginnings of a smile. He repeated the questions. "Can you stand? Or do you need help?" He had his other hand under her elbow now.

That's when Nedra interrupted him. "Thanks for your concern. We'll take it from here." She pushed herself between the man and Rajeen.

"By the icy moons of Uranus, what the hell just happened?" demanded Merle, glaring at a couple of pageant staffers who had approached.

"We don't know," they protested. "You know how those flicker mobs like to disrupt life for Imperial citizens."

"More likely they were paid to sabotage a popular competitor," declared Merle loud enough for everyone to hear. That raised some eyebrows.

"Are you okay?" Nedra asked as they got Rajeen to her feet.

"I think so." Rajeen straightened up and winced. "I've probably got some bruises, but they won't show." She looked around for the kind stranger, but he was gone.

Nedra opened the bag on her shoulder. "Your hair needs work. Come over here for a minute. Keep your head still."

The two staffers were trying to get all the contestants through the backstage doors. One came toward Rajeen.

"We need a minute," snapped Nedra. Then she deftly tightened the knot at the top, rearranged the curls, and sprayed it all again with a holding mist. "Okay, let's go."

Merle and Nedra guided Rajeen through the doors and to her spot in the line with the other contestants just as Cobb called them on stage.

"We better stay nearby. Things are only going to get more cut-throat from here," commented Merle. She kept a tight grip on the guitar case.

BROCK RETREATED. What made him do that? He knew better than to draw attention to himself in a situation like this. He wasn't going to be able to follow these women or Parker without major changes to his appearance. Jupiter! What was wrong with him? He'd have to report this to his supervisor during his next shift.

He was debating whether he should leave now and not

chance running into them again when his comm buzzed. There were still people waiting to get into the auditorium so he went out on the concourse to take the call.

"Perez here."

"Detective Perez, this is Commander Roiko of the Imperial Palace Guard." The gruff voice was insistent and demanding. "You flagged a DNA sample for expedited analysis. Tell me, is the subject someone you've been following? Are you in contact with the woman?"

"Commander, she's someone I encountered while investigating a person of interest in a criminal matter." Brock's voice waivered for a moment but he went on. "I… I do know where she is at the moment. The District Nine Miss Imperium pageant."

"Thank Jupiter! These are your new orders, do not let that woman out of your sight! Do you understand? Do whatever it takes to keep her there. Can you do that, Detective?"

"I think so, sir. She's competing in the pageant. They are about to do the talent show and crown the finalists."

"Good job, Perez. Don't lose track of her. Help is on the way."

The call cut off.

Perez was starting to wonder what alternative universe he'd been sucked into. Shaking his head, he went to find a seat in the auditorium.

ON STAGE, each of the contestants sat on a cushioned stool. One at a time, Cobb called them up to show off their outfits. Following the brief fashion show, they moved on to perform for the audience.

Several of the women sang the Martian Anthem, including Malindy who had trouble hitting the high notes. Two played portable, modern-day instruments in well-known contemporary pieces. Three played an electronic keyboard that was rolled on stage, but they all chose centuries-old classical songs from Earth. Leona did an interpretive dance routine to a popular song that looked lovely in her long, flowing skirts. They went in order of their selection the previous day.

Finally, Rajeen's turn came.

Merle took the guitar out of the case and handed it to a staffer right at the edge of the stage, keeping her eyes on it the whole time. The guitar made its way safely into Rajeen's hands.

The antique instrument fascinated people. Cobb asked her to say a few words about it before starting her song.

"This acoustic guitar belonged to my uncle. He taught me how to play the instrument and helped me learn to appreciate our older songs. This one's in his honor."

She slung the strap over her shoulder and settled onto the stool they placed center stage. Rajeen plucked a string to check the tuning. She tightened several keys and strummed a chord.

A few of the older people in the audience recognized the opening notes and responded with murmurs of appreciation. In her warm, melodic voice Rajeen launched into the ballad. The song lamented the hardships of asteroid miners and the lovers they left behind on Mars. It told the tale of the miner who died an icy death when his ship — hit by meteors — was beyond all reach of help. In the last stanza, Rajeen sang of the man's final transmission. He asked his lover to carry on and raise the child she carried to remember his name.

As Rajeen stroked the final chord and the last plaintive refrain of '*remember my name*' died away, many eyes glistened with unshed tears.

She took a small bow to thunderous applause.

"I didn't know she was planning to perform that one," Nedra commented to Merle.

"Me, neither. She's got hidden depths, that one. Now she's

got them totally entranced. Regionals, here we come!" She hugged Nedra in excitement.

The final three contestants performed and Cobb announced there would be a short pause while the judges finished deliberating. "Don't leave your seats, ladies and gentlemen, this won't take long!"

The ten contestants remained seated in the glare of spotlights, continuing to smile at the audience.

In short order, one of the judges waved at Cobb and he turned back to the crowd. "The time has come to learn who will be representing District Nine in the Region One competition."

Cobb paused dramatically. "Contestants, please stand. Remember, we'll be naming two finalists and two runners-up. If your name is called, come stand by me." Behind Cobb a group of assistants had arrived with bouquets and sashes.

"Computer, announce our finalists and runners-up in one-minute intervals."

"Our first finalist is Malindy Urban."

A handful of enthusiastic family members cheered and Malindy came forward to receive a bouquet of flowers and a sash.

"Our second finalist is Clarine Van Dale." Up stepped a dark-haired beauty with a lovely singing voice. More weak applause followed that announcement followed by a few scattered boos.

"Shit," whispered Nedra letting out a disgusted sigh. She put her arm around a shocked-looking Merle. "I think her grandfather manages one of the gambling clubs."

The boos continued to grow in volume and number.

"Our first runner-up is Leona McCoy."

The boos intensified as Leona stepped up trying to look pleased. She received flowers, but no sash.

"Our second runner-up is Rajeen Cooper."

Rajeen's forward motion slowed as half the auditorium erupted in shouts and yells. Someone started the chant "We want

Rajeen. We want Rajeen. We want Rajeen…" Other voices took it up filling the hall with mob energy. Many in the audience left their seats to converge on the stage.

All three judges bolted, barely hanging on to their dignity as they rushed to an exit. Cobb, edging his way to the side of the stage, tried to calm everyone.

"Ladies and Gentlemen, please stay in your seats. I assure you, everything has been done as fairly and honestly as possible. This is no way to show your disappointment. Go back to your seats. Let me finish the ceremony."

"We want Rajeen! We want Rajeen!"

The back doors of the auditorium flew open.

Police in riot gear flooded in first followed by a squad of special forces in battle armor.

That's when the screaming started.

Merle and Nedra hadn't been sure what to do about the chanting. But seeing police helped them decide. Time to cut and run.

Merle, who was again holding the guitar, ran on stage and grabbed Rajeen's hand. "Let's go."

"All citizens are to freeze!" boomed an amplified voice. "Silence! The center is surrounded. No one is to leave without permission!"

"Freeze! Silence!" repeated over and over on the auditorium's sound system.

Highly exposed on the stage, Merle and Rajeen did as commanded. Faced with armed "vests", the crowd's anger withered, turning to fearful submission.

Merle whispered to Rajeen, "That was a damn fast response. Were they waiting outside?"

"Freeze! Silence!"

With laser pistols at the ready, the riot police spread out and *politely* insisted everyone sit down. The special forces team and their commander ran forward and leaped to the stage. Half the soldiers moved toward Rajeen and Merle while the remainder pushed the other finalists to the back of the stage.

As the special forces team surrounded the two women, their leader came forward, saluted with his fist to his chest. Pointing to Merle, he ordered, "Remove your hand."

"Why should I? We're family."

"I think not," sneered the man. "Step aside." With weapons trained upon her, Merle released Rajeen's arm and moved back a meter.

"Merle," protested Rajeen, "what's going on?"

"You will come with us," the man said to Rajeen in a respectful tone. "We are here to escort you safely back to your real family."

"She *is* my family! I don't know any of you. What family are you talking about?"

Merle had a sinking feeling in her gut.

"Rajeen, you know Uncle just showed up with you one day. He never shared many details. Said it was too painful. To enter the contest, you had to submit a DNA sample to prove you didn't have any illegal gen mods. Maybe someone's been looking for you…"

Rajeen turned to Merle with glistening eyes. "You and Nedra are my family. I don't want to go."

"Somebody has a lot of clout to mount this kind of response. I think you better find out what this is all about." She offered a wan smile. "You know how to find us." She patted the guitar. "I'll keep this safe for you."

Rajeen nodded her thanks. With lips pressed together, she looked out over the sea of rapt faces. She closed her eyes and inclined her head to acknowledge their enthusiastic support. The hot tears she'd been holding back spilled down her cheeks. With eyes open again, she stared at the man who had saluted her and said, "Let's get on with it."

The hushed audience watched in silence as the armored

soldiers formed up with Rajeen in the center and escorted her from the hall. The riot police kept everyone in place until a signal was sent. Then they dismissed the crowd row by row, keeping a watch that no further violence got started.

While all eyes were on Rajeen's exit, Merle eased off stage. She and Nedra slipped into a darkened corner backstage, watching for an opportunity to leave without garnering further scrutiny. They made a quick sweep of the dressing room and took separate routes back to the hideout. There they finally let themselves mourn the failed attempt to free Uncle Bellamy and the loss of a person as dear as any flesh and blood could be.

BROCK RETURNED to his apartment that evening still trying to process what he'd witnessed. Rajeen Cooper taken… what? Not exactly into custody. But not left a choice of whether to go with the Imperial Guard Battle Troops either. Where had they taken her? How could he find out? How did his expediting the DNA analysis play a role?

He had a hard time understanding his feelings about the situation. Something had happened when he looked into her eyes after the flicker mob bowled her over. He already knew she was a beautiful young woman. But her eyes seemed to see into his soul and not flinch. He'd sat spellbound through her whole performance with the old instrument. He was ready to riot with the rest of the crowd when she didn't win outright. He wanted more time with her, to find out who she really was and what had sparked that connection between them. He was sure she felt it too.

Who was he kidding? She was probably just concussed.

He sat on a chair with his head in his hands. Jupiter, he was such a fool. Following hunches. Ignoring orders. Suspecting young women of crazy schemes. Developing… feelings for a total stranger.

He needed to put the whole episode behind him. Forget about Rajeen. For all he knew she was some criminal mastermind who was now going to rot in detention for the rest of her life.

He'd go to work tomorrow and focus on the job he'd been assigned. Hope nobody called him to task for sticking his nose into something that didn't concern him.

He tried. By Jupiter, he tried.

But at work the next morning his boss immediately called him into a conference room and closed the door. He paced for a minute before facing Brock and saying, "I'm sorry for the misunderstanding. No hard feelings, I hope? I didn't realize you were following a lead for the Imperial Family. Your promotion and transfer orders have come through and I hope you'll put in a good word for all us here on the Crime Control Task Force." The man handed over a message wafer.

Trying not to reveal his own confusion, Brock plugged it into his comm and learned he'd been promoted to captain and was now part of the Imperial House Guards.

Life just got stranger and stranger.

Days went by. Nedra and Merle watched and listened, hoping to find out something… anything… through standard news sources. The District was full of rumors that the young woman had been a runaway or a spy or even a visitor from Earth who had been *slumming* with the locals.

A week after the pageant, a highly-edited version of the competition came out. The show ended very abruptly as Clarine's name was called and had nothing about runners-up in it. By then, the regional contest had taken place, where things got more intense. Someone tripped Malindy and she broke a tooth. Neither District Nine woman went on to the Imperial level.

Life in general went from bad to worse. Without Rajeen, it was harder to run some of the grifts they had relied on. Hopper sent messages wanting to know when he was going to see his cut of their long con. Merle got in a fight with Tommy and broke things off again.

The two women sat moping in their hideout one evening when they heard the faint tapping of the code to signal someone wanted to come in. Looking at each other with fragile hope, Merle went to the door and knocked twice. Their visitor gave the return sign. Nedra dimmed their lights. Merle took a moment to undo the locking mechanism — her fingers suddenly clumsy — then she pushed the panel back.

A short, hunched figure waited in front of them in the darkness.

Certainly not Rajeen.

Nedra recognized him first. "Uncle?"

Giving them a weary smile, a man no taller than Merle stepped toward them with open arms. Merle and Nedra rushed to embrace him, neither one holding back tears.

"I can't believe you're free," whispered Merle.

"*How* can you be free? Everything else has gone to Pluto lately!" exclaimed Nedra.

"Lovely nieces, if you'll stop smothering me and let me in, all will be explained," Bellamy offered in gentle reproof. Since last they had seen him, his outward appearance had changed. His unruly gray hair was now shaved close to the head. He'd lost weight but wore nice looking street clothing that fit him well. Prison did not appear to have dimmed his sense of humor, but his shoulders were bowed.

They each took an arm and guided him to a chair at the table. Merle closed and relocked the door. Nedra returned the lighting to normal. Each covertly wiped away her tears.

"I've a long tale to tell, so water would be appreciated."

Merle got him a drink and both women stood shaking their heads in disbelief.

"Both of you, sit down. You'll give me a sore neck to sit here looking up at the pair of you. My, how you've grown in the last two years. Both of you look beautiful and strong."

Merle and Nedra sat but neither looked happy to hear his compliments.

Nedra was first to say, "We screwed up, Uncle. We've lost Rajeen."

Merle was quick to follow with, "It was my fault."

"We both thought it was a great idea," countered Nedra.

He raised an eyebrow. "Lost her? No, I know right where she is and you will soon as well."

They gaped at him.

"Is she okay?" squeaked Merle.

Bellamy held them in suspense with a heavy sigh before he smiled. "She's a bit more than okay. Let me start at the beginning.

"Twenty years ago, the Underground had a more radical wing. People who were tired of singing protest songs, laser-etching rude pictures of the imperial family, and dumping shit on the steps of public buildings in the night. Sad to say, I was one of them. We wanted bloody revolution.

"We began a covert plan to get members hired as servants at the palace. Eventually, a few people got jobs as cleaning staff and one older woman, Kara, was employed in the Imperial family nursery. At the time, the nursery held three young ones of His Imperial Majesty Maximus the Second as well as several more children of his siblings.

"The original plan involved trying to poison all the adults and take the children hostage. Time after time we failed to get anyone onto the kitchen staff. Kara grew impatient and saw an opportunity one night. She smuggled a sleeping baby out of the palace and headed to a safehouse — confident the kidnapping wouldn't be discovered until morning.

"There were three of us at the safehouse that night. We lost precious time arguing about what to do next. Kara wanted to stay with the baby as she was quite fond of the little girl. I convinced her we needed to move the baby again as quickly and quietly as possible. Kara would slow us down and be more recognizable.

"In the end, I alone took the baby to another location.

"The three people still at the safehouse were Kara and your mother and father. The Imperial Guard uncovered the kidnapping much earlier than any of us expected. They used every surveillance drone in the city to track those who had left the palace. Before dawn, the safehouse was surrounded."

He paused to clasp hands with each of his nieces. "Rather than be taken prisoner and face torture and thus expose the entire Underground network, all three of them committed suicide."

Merle shook her head. "You told us they died in an accident."

"You were too young to know the truth. It was safer for everyone if you believed that."

"The baby was Rajeen, wasn't she?" demanded Nedra.

"Yes. I was in this very room the next day when I got word about the safehouse and what had happened. It shook me. Made me renounce violence. There is more than one way to create change. But what I wanted to do took a different kind of strength. It may not have been the kindest decision, but I kept the baby and raised her to see the concerns of those opposed to the Imperial government.

"I didn't reveal to anyone the baby's true identity. I told others in the Underground that I was helping out an old friend from another city. Rajeen grew up as part of our family. A week after her disappearance, the palace issued a news story that the young princess had died from a previously undisclosed birth defect."

"They gave up on her that easily?" Nedra was incredulous. "Why didn't they tear the city apart?"

"My guess is they were embarrassed that someone succeeded in taking her. They didn't want that knowledge to encourage other attempts. After all, they had two male heirs. Yet someone kept looking. As you've now realized, any new female DNA samples were scanned, hoping someday there would be a match."

"So, she's back with them. Did she get you out?" asked Merle.

"Yes. Rajeen, also known as Princess Adaria, is third in line for the throne. I was not taken to see her, but they gave me two messages. Mine informed me that she had insisted they give me a full pardon and a certain amount of credits. It was one of her conditions for returning to the family and agreeing to do so gracefully. Here is her note to both of you."

Merle took the message wafer and eagerly plugged it into her comm.

Rajeen's face appeared above the unit and began speaking. "I told you entering a beauty contest was a bad idea. But here we are. Rather here I am and there you are — with Uncle if you're hearing this. Her Imperial Highness — my mother — was thrilled to find me again after all these years. But father has been a bit distant. He's not sure what to make of my upbringing. They're all embarrassed by faking my death and are trying to decide how to 'correct course' was the phrase I heard.

"Anyway, I think you'd be proud of me. I'm throwing my weight around and making all kinds of demands. I'm telling my parents and brothers things they might not enjoy hearing — about how the general public views them and their Imperial policies. I'm hoping to be a positive influence on them. Someday, I hope to hear from Uncle how he came to make me part of his family. Until then, know that I think of you all often."

She paused.

"By the way, they tell me I need a couple of ladies in waiting, if you know anyone who might be interested in the job."

Rajeen held up her thumb to the camera. "Don't make me call out the guards to come find you!"

THE REAPER'S DUE: A FATHER'S VENGEANCE

HONORABLE MENTION

MH WOODWORTH

I DRIFTED into the house just like I had done countless times. The house was just like the ones I had entered before. Furniture was overturned. Next to a shattered coffee table, a woman of around thirty-six years of age lay on the floor in a pool of blood.

From the looks of her, she had been stabbed several times and was badly beaten. She had put up one hell of a fight. But in the end, whoever did this had won. She was at death's door.

I glided past pictures of her family on the wall… and approached her. Her aura was clean; it shone white and angelic — Heaven. It was an easy reaping.

I knelt beside her, reached out, and touched her forehead. A sharp pain crashed through my body. In an instant, I was no longer in the afterlife but now knelt in the mortal world.

Sounds and smells I hadn't felt in years slammed into me all at once. Distant sirens wailed, the copper tang of blood filled my nose, and the world pressed in with a weight I had almost forgotten. These unfamiliar sensations shocked me to my core; it dragged me back into the real world I thought I had left behind.

The woman sensed my hand on her forehead, looked into my eyes, and whispered, "Brad?"

I paused for a moment, a faint memory invaded my mind, "Elizabeth?"

"He told me you would come, but I told him that was impossible because you were dead," she coughed. A little bit of blood stained her teeth. I grasped her hands in mine. They were already cold from the loss of blood. In one of her hands, she held something. I could feel its power and wanted to pull away, but before I could, she slipped it onto my finger.

"He told me to give this to you."

The room spun. Visions flashed through my mind.

I looked into my mother's eyes; her face smiled down at me.

The scene shifted. In college, I sat across the table from a young woman in the library. She smiled beautifully, reached out across the table, and shook my hand.

"*My name is Elizabeth.*"

I was back in the room. I looked at the once beautiful woman before me and whispered, "What? How? Who did this to you?"

The vision faded again. I stood at the top of a staircase; I looked toward the back of the church. The double doors opened, the wedding march played, and Elizabeth, dressed in a beautiful white gown, walked down the aisle.

I was back in the room once more. Elizabeth coughed, her breath ragged and shallow. She still held my hand. Tears streamed down my face.

Crying? I thought. Was I really crying? I *had not felt a human emotion in many years. How was this possible? What was happening to me?*

The vision shifted one last time. In a hospital room, a nurse walked toward me with a blanket wrapped around a baby. She smiled and said, "*Would you like to see your new baby girl?*"

I looked down into the face of the most precious little girl and heard myself say, "*Nice to meet you, Sarah. I am your Daddy.*"

I was back in the house again. Elizabeth's eyes locked on mine; realization flooded me in a torrent of emotions.

"Elizabeth… where is Sarah?"

"Sarah?" Her voice was weak; her mind too far gone to understand. I pried her hands loose from mine and leapt to my feet. I rushed through the living room and down the hall, and surprised by my own strength, tore the door off the hinges of my little girl's room.

The room was empty. I flipped the bed and searched the closet. Nothing. I ran from the room, and shouted her name, but I already knew she was gone.

I knelt beside Elizabeth. She barely recognized me.

"Elizabeth… who took our little girl?"

Her lips moved, but no sound reached me. I leaned closer, strained to hear. At last, I caught the faintest whisper: she was singing a child's nursery rhyme.

"The itsy-bitsy spider climbed up the waterspout…"

It was time for her to pass on. I reached down and touched her forehead. Would my powers still work, here in the mortal world?

I concentrated, called on my powers given to me by Heaven, and her memories flowed into me: innocence, love, sadness, fear, finally pain, and the last thing she saw — a black spider tattoo on the forearm of the man who stabbed her.

I searched for a memory to cleanse her passing. I found the perfect memory: the day Sarah was born. She was so peaceful and serene, not a care in the world, just unconditional love. Elizabeth lay on the hospital bed and gazed into her newborn daughter's eyes.

I placed that memory gently back into her mind. A smile crossed her face.

Now to ensure she ascended to Heaven properly. I reached for the ring on my finger. It would not budge. I pulled again.

Nothing. Pulled again, harder this time. The ring would not come off.

I tried once more and the pain was absolutely agonizing. Fire raced through my veins and burned me from the inside out. The ring clung tighter, as if it were fused with my very soul. I let go of the ring and the pain went away. I looked down. Elizabeth was dead.

I roared in frustration. I could not join her in the afterlife. I could not see her one last time. I closed my eyes and knelt beside her and sobbed.

Slowly, my grief hardened into rage. My body shook with fury.

Who did this to my wife? Where's Sarah? Who has my little girl?

I rose to my feet, determined to find her.

"Stop! Do not move!"

The sudden unfamiliar voice broke the silence of the room.

"Let's do this easy. Hands behind your back, don't try to reach for that sword. Nice and slow."

I turned around and kept my hands at my sides.

Sword? Then I remembered the sword used to reap souls to Hell. I could feel its weight against my back; apparently it had made it through the transition from afterlife to mortal world.

A man stood before me, pistol raised and aimed directly at my chest. He was lean, his jaw tight; his shirt sleeves were rolled up, the beginnings of tattoos hidden just beneath the rolls of his sleeves. His badge hung around his neck, but his aura was black as night and gave off evil — this told me he was not a good person. He was a predator who hid behind the law.

"Now I want you to slowly reach behind your back, remove the sword, and drop it onto the floor at your feet."

I stared at the man and a smile crept across my face.

"You're not really a detective? And if you are, you're corrupt. You've done some very evil things in your life. And I know you are going to kill me anyway because there can't be any witnesses. Right?"

Before he could answer, I lunged.

He pulled the trigger.

Had I made a mistake? Would this be the end of me? What about Sarah? Too late now!

The sound of the gun was deafening in the enclosed space. I felt the bullets impact, yet I knew that I should have felt pain. There was none. He emptied the gun into me as I advanced, his bullets useless.

So, bullets can't harm me?

Before he realized it, I grabbed him by the throat, lifted him into the air with one arm, and used his body to close the front door, the sound of the door echoed through the room as it slammed shut.

He tried to speak, but my grip had closed off his airway. All that escaped was a hushed whisper: "Who are you?"

I looked into his eyes, the fear evident, and answered, "Not who, but what am I!"

I lowered him to the floor, relaxed my grip just enough for him to breathe.

He coughed violently as air returned to his lungs and tried to double over, but I held him upright.

"Where is my little girl?" I looked at his badge and read the last name etched on it aloud. "Detective Malone."

"I talk, my family dies." I squeezed his throat just a little bit. I watched as his eyes bulged out of their sockets.

"I don't know where your kid is; I swear on my life!" He could barely force the words out.

I thought of an idea. I began to concentrate and used my powers given to me by Hell, and his memories flowed into me.

Maybe, just maybe, I could see what he knew about Sarah or Elizabeth.

I searched, but every time I thought I had something a wall

would go up, and I could not access that memory. I gave up and found the memory to show Malone what I was capable of. I just let him feel a partial part of it, his victim's memory through his eyes, all the emotion and fear. His eyes rolled back for just a moment, and he looked back at me, absolute terror carved across his face.

"You remember, don't you? The undercover cop, Detective Rojas, your friend from the Academy. He begged you to help him, but you handed him over to those men anyway. You knew what they would do to him. You watched them drag him away, kicking and screaming. You heard the shredder roar, and you heard his primal screams as they fed him in. You did nothing."

"How… How the hell do you know about Rojas?"

"Because I can see it. I can feel it. And now you know I can take every secret you've ever buried. So, tell me where my little girl is, before I make you relive that night again and again. Next time, it will be worse."

His resolve shattered. "John… Sam… there's a house. I only know about it from a case I saw. I am just the cleanup man. They will kill my family, and you saw what they do to cops!"

"You should have thought about that before you took the money or whatever else they offered you. Give me the address of the house."

Every moment I spent getting the information I needed was another minute I lost searching for Sarah.

I fed him a new memory, this one of Rojas as he stared down into the teeth of a giant industrial shredder, nothing he could do to keep himself from being thrown in, helpless.

I watched Malone's eyes roll back and he began to convulse. I pulled the memory back.

He slowly returned to normal; his face turned pale, "Fuck this! The address is 3456 Walnut St. That's everything. I swear! You're going to let me go, right? I have told you everything I know."

I smiled an evil smile. "Detective Malone, you see that woman lying over there on the floor. That was my wife Elizabeth, and you were about to cover up the fact that she was murdered by the people you work for. What is even worse is that you were not going to report that my daughter Sarah was missing. What I would normally do is kill you and send you to Hell where you belong, but I have a better idea."

I fed the whole memory of Detective Rojas's death into his mind. Unlike Elizabeth's memory of peace, this was a memory of torture — raw, jagged, and endless.

He began to wail, and I let him fall to the floor. He grasped his face in his hands and clawed at his eyes and began to roll about as the memory played over and over in his head. He would stay that way for the rest of his life.

A voice in my mind spoke, "*You are violating the rules.*"

"I don't care; they will face my wrath till I cleanse the mortal world of their very existence."

I turned back and looked at Elizabeth one last time, pushed the detective aside, opened the door, and walked out into the mortal world.

I WALKED out of the front door of 3456 Walnut Street, the stench of death clung to me, and reminded me of what I had just done. The Reaper side would have been ashamed, but my human side did not care. Someone had to pay for what happened to my wife.

When they finally came back here to see why nobody was answering the phone, they would find the message that I had left on the dining room table.

I had not hesitated when I arrived. Anger and rage overcame me, and I drew my sword, uncertain what this instrument of the afterlife would do in the mortal world.

I kicked in the door. My foot punched through the wood, and

for a moment I was almost stuck — a ridiculous pause in the middle of my fury. Then my strength tore the door from its frame, and I stepped inside.

One man sat on a couch in front of me; another sat in a recliner to my left. They had no chance. The first man lunged, but with a single slash I cut him in two. The blade, forged in hellfire, cauterized the wound as it passed. His halves fell apart; the smell of burnt flesh filled the room. His face was frozen in shock — his death too swift for fear.

I did not even feel any resistance. The blade went through cleanly, not even bone stopped its progress. No blood even spilled.

The second man faltered, as he saw what had just happened to his friend; his hesitation cost him everything. I swung again, and his head left his body. The sword sealed the wound; it left no blood — only silence.

I stared at what I had done. *I had just ended two men's lives in seconds. I had not even checked their auras. Where had all this anger come from?*

A sudden realization overcame me.

Had I just killed the only two men who knew where my little girl was? Had I sealed her fate with my own hands?

A sudden noise to my right startled me. A man stumbled in from the hallway, half-dressed, gun in his right hand, woken by the chaos of my entrance. He tried to comprehend what he saw. "What the fuck?" was all he managed before I severed the hand that held the weapon.

He crashed to the floor and shrieked. He clutched the stump of his arm. I sheathed my sword. I did not let him stay there long. I grabbed him by his half-buttoned shirt and hauled him to his feet.

"What is your name?"

"Mal… Malcom."

"Malcom, who is on the floor over there?" I nodded toward the living room.

"That's John by the chair. And the other… oh my God, what did you do to him?" Malcom's face turned green. "That… or whatever is left of him… is Sam." He began to dry-heave.

I felt a chill as I realized I had just killed both of the men the detective had mentioned. I reached out and forced his face toward mine.

"If you do not tell me what I need to know, I will do things to you that make what happened to them look merciful. I'll only ask once. How much do you know about the Boss? Where can I find him? And where did they take my little girl after they killed my wife?"

I turned his head toward the living room to remind him. Malcom's eyes widened. He knew hesitation wasn't an option.

"I will tell you everything I know."

Malcom told me everything and more — names I had never heard, places I had never seen, a desperate attempt to save himself. He provided me with enough information to send a message to anyone left in the organization: they were finished. More importantly, he told me how to find the Boss.

When he was done, I forced him to his knees; he begged for forgiveness. I ignored his pleas. His aura showed me he was destined for Hell — that was all I needed. One swift strike ended his life; another soul added to Hell.

Death is not going to like what you have done.

I will deal with Death later. I need to find Sarah.

I stepped out into the yard. Turning left, I knew I had one more stop to make — unfinished business that had to be settled.

My blade had stopped two inches from his skull; only my superhuman strength could have stopped the slice so precisely.

The young man who sat there couldn't have been more than eighteen years old. His aura showed he was clean.

What was I doing? I had almost killed an innocent person. Where had all this anger been coming from?

Malcom's information had led me here, one last stop to end the organization once and for all. Without an heir, the business couldn't continue. Four men had guarded him; they were now all in Hell. Their bodies lay strewn across two stories of the house. The rage had consumed me once again.

He hadn't seen me come in. His back was turned, headphones on, lost in a video game. My mind was clouded, focused only on his death. The sword rose high, ready to strike. As it arced downward, something in my mind said, *Look at his aura.* It was clean.

I pulled the blade back and stood behind him as he played on, unaware of how close he had come to death.

For some reason, he paused his game, swiveled in his chair, and saw me there. His eyes widened.

"Marco! Help, someone is in my room!"

"Eddie, right? Marco is not coming to help, and neither is anyone else in this house."

"How do you know my name… Why would they not come help me?"

"Because I killed them all."

Eddie looked at me incredulously, shock on his face.

"Why… Why would you do that? They were my friends; they were like family to me. I mean Marco, Felix, all of them are dead?"

"Yes, Eddie, all of them."

"You're not going to kill me… are you?" he glanced uneasily at the sword.

"No, I was not going to kill you. If I were, we would not be talking right now."

He relaxed a little bit, but he was still apprehensive.

"Eddie, I am going to show you something and then I am going to sheath my sword, and we are going to talk. I want you to watch."

There was a small table next to him with a plastic Solo cup and an empty paper plate sitting there. I reached out with the sword and let the blade rest on the tabletop. The blade began to cut through the table without any force. The wood began to smoke and within seconds the six-inch tabletop split in two and the table fell into two pieces. He stared at what the sword had done to the table.

"What are you?"

I sheathed my sword and sat down on the bed.

"Eddie, do you believe in a Heaven and a Hell?"

He thought about it for a moment. "I believe so. We go to church every Sunday; well, I do and Marco." His eyes teared up at the mention of Marco.

"I was a Reaper. My job was to help people who are good transition to Heaven and those that are evil transition to Hell when they were dying or had died."

"I did this by checking what we call auras. They show Reapers where the person is headed. Whatever aura we saw determined how we treated that person."

I saw no harm in telling him this — no one would ever believe him.

"So, I take it Marco, and the rest did not have good auras?"

"No, their auras were evil and because of this when they died, they went to Hell."

Eddie sat up in his chair. "Wait a minute, you said when they were dying or died. Marco was not dying."

"You were right, Marco and the rest were not dying. Eddie, this next part is going to be hard for you to hear… your dad is evil. I am here to make sure that this evil does not continue. That being said, you were his only child; killing you would have hopefully ended that evil. I was not prepared to find out that your aura was clean."

"Clean?"

"Yes, clean. You have not done anything yet in your life to change your aura. His shoulders dropped, and he sat there for a moment.

"So, my dad is evil… I knew sooner or later what he did would catch up to him, but I never thought it would be like this. I thought it would be a bullet or prison not a Reaper."

"You knew your dad was a bad person?"

"I am eighteen, not five. Of course, I know what my dad does. I made a promise to my mother that I would never get into the family business; it was her dying wish. My mom died of cancer when I was twelve. My dad has honored that wish ever since." This time the tears did fall as he remembered his mom's death.

I stood up and looked at Eddie, and I felt sorry for him. He did not choose this life or his family, but it was the hand fate had dealt him.

"You mean, like Sarah and Elizabeth".

"No, this is different."

"Keep telling yourself that; this is no different than what happened to Eddie."

"You have no feelings or emotions. You would not understand."

"Eddie, I want you to look at me and understand this."

"Your aura is pure for now; that does not mean it will stay that way. If you decide to take over the family business, it will change. You have a good heart and a lot to live for."

I turned to leave.

I had spent way too much time here. Sarah was out there somewhere.

Eddie just sat there lost in thought.

"I have one more question. Are you going to kill my dad?"

I thought about the answer long and hard.

"It will truly depend on what his aura showed. One last thing. I wouldn't leave this room just yet. Call the police and tell them there has been a break-in and let them escort you out. You do not want to see what I have done."

With those final words I turned and left the room.

Why was I chosen to reap my own wife? Had I been chosen on purpose? Elizabeth said that "he" gave her the ring to pass on to me. Who was "he"? I had no time to dwell on that now.

Three days had passed since I killed the three people at the Walnut Street house. They must have discovered my handiwork, as they had waited before they finally came out of the shadows. My patience paid off as they showed up to have lunch outside Sal's Calzones; they sat together like kings of the neighborhood, and they believed they were untouchable. That was when I saw the tattoo, the same one Elizabeth had seen.

I watched them until their driver arrived. When the Suburban pulled up to take them away, I was able to follow them to a warehouse in the middle of an abandoned industrial complex. The faded sign above the corrugated doors read Harborview Recycling Center.

I watched as the driver stepped out and moved to the passenger-side rear door. He opened it, and a short, overweight man in a nice suit climbed out, the Boss.

I felt an instant surge of anger.

"He is right there — what are you waiting for?"

I resisted the urge to just draw my sword and end his life once and for all.

"Patience!"

From the front passenger seat, the man with the tattoo emerged, broad-shouldered and muscular.

The anger and rage swelled to an unbearable level.

"You know what that man did! Finish him!"

"It was not our job to judge souls."

Then the rear door behind the driver swung open and a tall, skinny man unfolded himself from the vehicle.

They gathered at the back of the Suburban; all their auras were black as night. The driver pressed a button on the key fob, and the liftgate rose slowly. All of them stood and waited, except for the muscular man. He reached inside and dragged out a bound and gagged prisoner, and forced him to his feet. The prisoner's aura glowed clean.

The rage overtook me. No more innocent blood would be spilled.

Their backs were turned; except for the muscular man, he was preoccupied with the prisoner.

It wouldn't matter anyway.

Now was my time to strike. Their guard was lowered, and they were convinced they were safe. The muscular man glanced up and saw me advance, sword in hand. For a heartbeat he froze, unable to believe what he saw. That hesitation was all I needed. The driver stood in the middle. I concentrated all of my rage and hate on him.

I raised the blade high and, when I was within reach, brought it down. The steel struck the crown of his head and slid through him as if he were made of butter. The supernatural edge burned and cauterized his flesh as it split him into two.

The muscular man had already shoved the prisoner aside and reached for his gun, but I was too fast.

I moved forward and threw my shoulder into him.

He was hurled backward, and he collided with the rear of the vehicle with a crunch, then crumpled to the ground.

I stopped. Snapped my right elbow into the Boss's face. Teeth flew. He dropped, unconscious.

The tall, skinny man had already drawn his gun. Shots

cracked through the night. I closed the distance. Smashed my fist into his face. He collapsed, incapacitated.

In less time than it takes to blink twice, I had taken out all four of them. I did not want these three dead yet. The prisoner lay on the ground still bound and gagged. I reached down and pulled him to his feet and removed the gag.

"Please don't kill me!"

"I am not going to kill you." I reached behind his back and snapped his restraints with my bare hands.

"Now get out of here."

He took off at a run. I turned back to see if I could use anything in the back of the vehicle. I found some black hoods and zip-ties. I looked down at the Boss, blood flowed out of his mouth; and I spoke to his unconscious form, "Now let's see what you can tell me."

I STARED at the panel that controlled the industrial shredder, and I looked at the green start button with the words above it: HOLD FOR 2-3 SECONDS TO START. I pushed the green button and held it. The massive electric motors growled to life. I stood there for just a moment, and the person who held all the answers waited for me above.

A warning alarm that the machine had reached full speed ripped me from my trance.

I turned and climbed the stairs next to the machine that led to the platform over the shredder.

At the top, I paused and looked down into the machine. The shredder filled the warehouse floor, forty feet of yellow-painted steel. Two counter-rotating shafts, thick as telephone poles, bristled with hooked teeth the size of a man's forearm. The teeth turned slowly, relentlessly. Dried blood and scraps of clothing clung to the teeth and littered the entrance, grim reminders of what had already been fed to it.

I turned back to the platform. The Boss sat in the middle, next to him on each side sat the skinny man and the muscular man. They were all hooded and zip-tied to chairs.

"Everyone comfy?" I yelled, to be heard over the shredder.

"Do you know who the fuck I am? You will regret this!" the Boss shouted.

I leaned in so the Boss could hear me. "I know who you are. You ordered my wife killed and my little girl taken."

I stepped back, "So who's going to tell me where my daughter is?"

"Fuck you! We are not going to tell you anything," the muscular man spoke first."

I was so hoping you would speak first.

I could feel the rage take over again.

I went over and yanked the hood off his head and reached down and clamped my hands onto his shoulders — my hands like vice grips. An audible crack came as I snapped both of his collar bones like dried branches. His eyes bulged wide, flooded with tears, and he let out a guttural, involuntary scream mixed with a harsh exhale; his body went rigid as he fought against the wave of agony that ripped through his shoulders and neck. He was tough, clenching his jaw to stifle the cries, but sweat poured down his face, and every shallow breath made him shudder.

"Frank, are you okay?" the Boss asked, concern in his voice.

"Frank, is it?" I reached down and yanked up his sleeve, exposing a black spider tattoo.

"When I found my wife, she was almost dead. She kept singing "Itsy Bitsy Spider" over and over. I didn't know what it meant until I saw you outside Sal's Calzones, that black spider tattoo on your forearm. The last thing my wife saw as you plunged your knife into her. You killed Elizabeth! You took Sarah! Where is she? I will not ask again!"

"He doesn't know anything, and he'd never tell you if he did!" the Boss shouted.

The rage surged like white hot steel, spreading throughout my whole body. I welcomed it.

Without a second thought I grabbed the handles of his chair. I lifted him, chair and all, into the air. He bellowed and thrashed against the zip-ties.

"What is happening?" the Boss shouted.

I met Frank's eyes one last time. "This is for Elizabeth!"

I hurled him and the chair directly into the teeth of the shredder below.

He screamed all the way down.

One of the teeth grabbed one of his legs and snapped it like a twig, another grabbed the arm with the tattoo and ripped the arm completely off. The shredder groaned but continued to chew him up slowly till his screams stopped.

I smiled down as I watched the last of him disappear.

"Frank? Frank?" the skinny man cried out.

Calm down, or you will never find out where your daughter is. I felt the rage start to subside.

I went over and ripped the hood off the Boss and the skinny man. "Sorry, I forgot to take off your hoods so you could watch." Both men stared at me in horror.

The Boss looked at me in disgust. "What did you do that for? I told you he didn't know anything!"

"Did you not hear what I said? He killed my wife and kidnapped my daughter. I had different plans for him, but this will do. Besides, that was nothing compared to what Hell has waiting for him!"

My voice went cold. "I do not see why someone being tossed into this shredder bothers you. Have you not done this multiple times before, like when you tossed Detective Rojas in there? You were getting ready to do it again earlier, had I not interfered."

The Boss stammered. "What? How would you know about that?"

"I learned that from your clean-up man, Detective Malone — or he used to be."

I stepped in front of the skinny man and looked at the Boss. "So, tell me what I want to know, or he is going in there next."

The skinny man looked at me, fear in his eyes, and he began to shake. Then he spoke. "Fuck this! I'm not dying like that. Let me go, and I'll tell you everything you need to know!"

"Shut up, Louie! He's not going to let us go, no matter what we tell him!"

I lied.

"I might, for the right information."

I reached down and snapped the zip-ties that held Louie to the chair and hauled him to his feet. I picked him up by the front of his shirt and turned and held him over the pit. He began to kick and yell.

"So now, Louie, this is where we test your loyalty. Do you tell me everything I want to know, or do I throw you in there like I just did Frank?" I felt the rage start to flare back up again.

"Drop him, he doesn't know anything!"

"What if he does?"

"Drop him!"

"I will talk… Oh God I will talk! Please… Please put me back down."

I turned and placed him on the platform. I felt his knees buckle, but I held him upright. I made sure to squeeze his arm enough for him to realize he was not going anywhere.

"I'll tell you everything you want to know… just please do not throw me in there!"

"You fucking traitor!" the Boss snarled and struggled against his restraints. "I will kill you if he doesn't!"

"Tell me where my little girl is?"

"When was she taken?"

"About five days ago."

"Lenny and Jeb have your daughter at one of our safe houses. I don't know which one but he will know," he gestured toward the Boss.

"They were supposed to sell her and the other girls this morning, but we have not heard from the client yet. He is never on time, so your daughter is probably still nearby."

Other girls?

"Louie, I swear to God if I get loose from these straps, I am going to fucking throw you..."

I interrupted his tirade. "Sell her... other girls?" My anger flared, and Louie saw the change in my demeanor, instinctively tried to take a step back.

"Yeah, sell her. My Boss is one of the biggest child traffickers in the state. He gets hundreds of thousands per child depending on the age."

I stood there in disbelief as Louie explained how their operation worked. They targeted single parents; if a child went missing it would take longer for them to be discovered, especially if the only parent was dead. I turned toward the Boss.

"Let me get this straight. You traffic in children although you have a son yourself?"

That had gotten his attention.

The Boss's eyes widened. "Wait, what? How do you know I have a son?"

"I paid him a visit, along with the four guys you had guarding him. He didn't know anything. Neither did your goons. You should have done a better job of hiding him!"

Panic flickered across the Boss's face. "What did you do to my son? Where is he?

"What the fuck did you do to my son?" Spittle flew from his lips.

His anger, sudden and uncontrolled, gave him a boost of adrenaline; this gave him almost superhuman strength; and he snapped one of the ties that held one of his arms to the chair. He strained against the rest desperate to break free.

The rage he felt mirrored my own, the same fury that consumed me when I learned my little girl had been taken.

I moved to stop the Boss, but Louie seized the moment. He shoved me backward with all his strength in one last desperate attempt to escape.

I had let my guard down, just enough. The sudden violence caught me off balance, and I felt myself falling backward toward the open maw of the shredder, its teeth waiting to devour me as they had Frank.

But Louie had forgotten about the fact that I had a hold of his arm. I wasn't an ordinary human whose grip he would have been able to escape. I tightened my grip. I could feel bones snap under my hand. The look on his face was one of horror as he realized… he was not going to pull loose and that he had sealed his own fate. I dragged him with me.

We slid down the sides of the pit; Louie clawed desperately for a hold, but the slick metal offered nothing. We hit the teeth together. Louie let out a guttural cry as the machine tore into him, flesh and bone shredded. I did not make a sound as one tooth snapped my left leg in half and another ripped my left arm off.

I looked up at the Boss, who stared back in disbelief and wondered why I was silent, and had not screamed as the flesh was torn from my body. I met his eyes, smiled, and shouted, "I will be seeing you real soon!"

Louie's scream cut off abruptly. At that instant, the teeth ripped the ring from my finger. Agony, unlike anything I had ever known, surged through me as the power released its grip. A flash filled my mind, and then there was silence.

I WAS BACK in the afterlife. Louie was there too, bewildered; he had not yet realized he was dead. He turned to me, then recoiled when he saw my true form. I was no longer Brad. I was Brax, the Reaper.

His voice trembled.

"Where am I?"

"Purgatory, where souls go to be judged."

"Purgatory… I am dead?" he stammered.

"Yes, very much so. Be prepared to be judged."

I reached for my sword, but it was gone. My stomach lurched as I realized what that meant. Another Reaper appeared, silent, swift, and methodical. Before Louie could comprehend what had happened, the Reaper struck him down and sent his soul to Hell.

A familiar pull seized me, cold and absolute. In an instant, I stood in a vast chamber. I immediately dropped to one knee and bowed. I had been summoned by Death himself.

"My Lord!"

"Brax, where did you get this ring? Look at me!" His voice shook the chamber and chilled me to my bones.

I looked up at Death. He sat upon a throne of skulls, his cloak so dark that it pulled the light into it. His red eyes looked at me, and I could tell he stared into my soul. He held my ring in his left hand.

No need to lie.

"My Lord, it was given to me by my wife Elizabeth when I was reaping her soul."

"Your wife? Your memories were taken the day you agreed to become a Reaper. Explain."

"I am not sure, my Lord. When she placed the ring on my finger some of my memories returned. I do not remember everything yet… my memory has slowly been coming back to me."

"That is not why I summoned you! Why, have you been sending souls to Hell before their time? You know this is not allowed! You are interfering with their fate." His voice rose and shook the very walls of the chamber.

"My Lord, they murdered my wife. Took my daughter Sarah. What was I supposed to do? What would you have me do, just allow them to go unpunished?" My voice rose in anger as well.

"Brax! Do not forget who I am! I can snap my fingers and throw you into the pits of Hell if I want! It is not your job to punish mortals! That is what Hell is for! I gave you this job because you requested it; your heroism interested me, and I do not often give mortals a job as one of my Reapers. I am beginning to regret my decision."

"I apologize, my Lord. I could not allow their sins to continue. Send me back. I've got to get to Sarah." I pleaded.

"You have broken the rules, but the ring is what twisted you. It is interfering between your mortality and your immortal self, causing you to act irrationally. It hungers for violence, and I am not sure why it was given to you. Perhaps because now that you have your memories back, this is allowing you to survive the ring's power. Your soul was pure at the time of your death, and your self-sacrifice is keeping the ring's corruption and the need for violence at bay.

Self-sacrifice?

"I have no choice but to send you back. You have worn this ring, and it is now bound to you forever. As I hold it, it seeks you so that you may be joined as one once again."

Is the ring a curse? I am bound to it?

"You will be sent back but know this: While the ring is bound to your flesh, your gift of memory is dulled. It will not show you what you seek."

Could this explain why when I searched the memories of Malone and Malcom, I could not find Sarah?

A sudden pressure gripped my skull, and a sharp, intense pain almost made me fall over. "That pain will remind you of who you still serve. When it comes, you will not kill. You are forbidden."

He released his grip on my mind.

"Once this task is done, you will walk in the mortal world as a rogue. You will not die, and you will not join your wife in Heaven. You will not interfere in your daughter's life. If you do, I will cast you into Hell for eternity."

No interaction with my daughter? Never see my wife again? Was I willing to do this just to save my daughter?

"Do you accept these conditions?"

I thought about his proposal. *But what life would Sarah have if I gave up now?* I shuddered at the thought of her being sold to some evil person and what that meant for her. *I made up my mind. I owed it to Sarah to at least try.*

"I accept."

"So be it. One last thing: know every time you travel to this world you will lose a small bit of your immortality, so be very careful how you use the ring's power."

Every time I travel to this realm? How am I supposed to do that? I can't get it off my finger.

I could not dwell on these thoughts for long, as suddenly I felt an unusual presence. The ring appeared back on my hand, and then an excruciating pain tore through me. I reappeared in the mortal world, right in the bottom of the industrial shredder.

As a Reaper scenes of death and carnage were routine, but even for me the bottom of that industrial shredder was disgusting. It contained the remains of Frank and Louie, a mix of body parts and organs. I pulled myself from the remains, climbed out of the bin, and stood on my feet. As soon as I stood up, my vision faded,

I was a soldier. I found myself in some unknown town in a

desert somewhere. It felt familiar but unknown all at the same time. I held a rifle in my hands. There was a soldier to my left and a soldier to my right.

A grenade rolled onto the ground in front of us. Instinct took over. I shoved both men aside and shouted, *"Grenade!"* I dove onto it covering it with my body.

The blast tore through me. In an instant, the desert was gone, and I was back in the warehouse.

So that's what Death meant by self-sacrifice. I had thrown myself on a grenade. My life for theirs.

I shook the memory away and unsheathed my sword. One last thing remained. I leapt up the stairs to the platform.

The Boss still struggled to free himself from the chair. I must have returned only moments after I fell into the shredder. He sensed me first, then looked up. Horror filled his face. Blood covered me from head to toe, sword at the ready. I probably looked like something from the bowels of Hell.

If he only knew.

He opened his mouth to speak. I gave him no chance.

I brought the blade down. One clean stroke. His free arm tore away at the shoulder. The smell of burnt flesh filled the air.

That felt good.

He screamed. Long. Primal.

I leaned close enough for him to see the hatred and anger in my eyes.

"Sarah — my little girl — where is she?"

Rage surged.

"Who are you?"

I ignored his question. He must die for what he did to my wife and daughter!

I sheathed my sword. The ring fed my fury. I picked him up, chair and all, just like I had done with Frank. I held him over the pit. The shredder teeth waited. A whisper cut through the rage: *"If you drop him, you will never know where your daughter is".*

I stopped and held him suspended over the pit.

The Boss pleaded, tears rolled down his face. "Please God! Do not drop me! I will tell you anything you want to know!"

I stared at him. This was the man who watched others thrown into this shredder — who had ignored their cries — who had never cared what kind of impact it would have on their families. This was the man who sold children to the highest bidders. Now he was reduced to a pathetic shell of a man.

"Please let me go. I promise you will never see me again. I will just disappear."

"If you want me to let you go, tell me where my daughter is."

He stopped blubbering, eyes locked on mine. "You will really let me go if I tell you?"

"I promise."

"Your daughter is being held in a house over on 3rd Street. 2738. Can I ask you something before you let me go?"

"You can ask me anything you would like."

"Did you kill my son?"

I stared back into his eyes one last time and smiled. "You will never know where you are going."

I dropped him into the waiting teeth of the shredder below. His screams rose above the sound of the machine as the teeth devoured him.

I spoke to what was left as he disappeared. "I promised I would let you go."

The Boss was gone. I finally knew where my daughter was. I glanced at the ring. *You almost cost me everything.*

For the first time, I studied it closely. Gold band. A strange symbol at its center. Jewels circled it. Diamonds, rubies. At the top, one stone stood taller than the rest, a blue sapphire. It looked as though it was about to fall out. I pressed it.

The symbol in the middle lit up and a pain ripped through me. Light flashed, and I was back in the afterlife, the ring still bound to my finger.

Pressing it again brought the same pain, the same flash, and I returned to the mortal realm.

So that was what Death meant; that when you travel to the afterlife, I could not reap souls anymore. I could travel at will, *but hadn't he said there would be a price every time? I wondered what that price would be?* My vision faded,

I was standing next to a Ford pickup truck. My wife and daughter were crying. There was a green military duffle bag at my feet. MARINES stitched above my left pocket.

Sarah was around three years old, and she ran from her mother's side and ran toward me. I held out my arms, and she jumped up into them, crying, *"Don't go, Daddy!"* My wife walked over and she placed her arms around us both; and whispered in my ear, tears rolling down her face, *"Come home safe. We love you."*

I was back in the warehouse.

That's it? A memory flashback every time I return. I can handle that.

Do you think something with that much power would have the only punishment for its use be a memory flashback?

I took a step and my chest began to pound, and I felt something drip down my skin — blood. I looked down and my torso was covered in bullet wounds for when I had been shot. My breath became ragged and I staggered, but as soon as they appeared they went away and my breath returned to normal. The bullet holes gone.

That sucked.

I glanced down again and my clothing was normal again. Blood and gore clung to every inch of my body. I could not go back out into public like this. A sign caught my eye: EYE WASH STATION: PULL CORD TO ACTIVATE.

I walked over and pulled the cord; I did not expect anything to happen. Cold, fresh water poured down. I stepped beneath the stream and began to wash away the filth. The water felt amazing.

I could feel the cold, the wetness. Reapers were not supposed

to feel or have emotion. Why had I ever chosen this life? What had my other choice been?

I stepped out from under the water and headed toward the exit, my goal in sight.

THE BOSS HAD NOT LIED. I found the house in a secluded neighborhood, the kind of place where the streetlights no longer worked and nobody cared. I used the ring; I felt the reward outweighed the risk. Maybe I could find Sarah from the afterlife. But that was a lost cause. The ring wouldn't let me see through walls, wouldn't let me pass through them no matter how hard I tried. When we were on reaping duties, we were assigned souls; we did not get to pick them. If I wanted to find Sarah, it would have to be in the mortal world. I now stood behind a wiry man who looked to be around twenty-three or twenty-four years old, his attempt at a goatee barely showed on his chin. He sat in a beat-up old recliner and tried his best to work on a crossword puzzle.

He spoke aloud and sounded the words out slowly: "Five… uh… five across. Who was the most powerful mob boss in Chicago during Prohibition?"

He scratched his head. "Lucky Luciano? No — Capone! Yeah, that's it."

Wait... what? I could hear what he was saying. In the after-life you could never hear sound or listen to what was being said.

A knock at the door interrupted his crossword puzzle. Three knocks, followed by two more knocks and then three more.

They must have some agreed-upon sequence of knocks to ensure that whoever was at the door was legit. Little did he know that the person he needed to worry about most was already in the house.

The man got up from the chair and crossed the room. I

watched as he looked through the peephole and then reached in and unsnapped the retaining clip on his pistol. *Still being extra careful; word of my exploits must have been passed down to him.* The knocks came again before he could open the door.

A voice from down the hall yelled: "Lenny, would you get the fucking door! I am trying to take a nap! It's probably the delivery guy with our food!"

"What the hell do you think I'm doin'? I'm gettin' the damn door!"

He removed the security chain, unlocked two deadbolts, and opened the door.

"Sal's Calzones, we make them fresh for you!" said a young man.

"Yeah, yeah, I know the fuckin' slogan! How much I gotta pay?"

The delivery man had not answered. He had seen me materialize behind Lenny. The boy dropped the food and ran. Lenny sensed something was wrong, reached for his gun, but it was too late. I wrenched his arm up behind his back. The audible pop from his shoulder meant I wrenched it a little too hard. I did not care.

I whispered into his ear, "If you even think of grabbing the pistol in your shoulder holster, I will snap your arm in half. Now close the door and lock it."

I felt something start to happen and I kept my composure as another punishment from the ring shot through my body. I must have broken several ribs when I collided with Frank earlier. My breath hitched for a brief second, but then the pain was gone.

Lenny had not noticed my discomfort and did as he was told.

"Now remove your pistol and hand it to me."

He carefully pulled the pistol from his holster and gave it to me. The weapon seemed familiar in my hand. I cocked the hammer back — the click in his ear sounded louder than it was

— and pressed the pistol against the side of his head. His knees began to shake.

"Don't worry, Lenny. I am not going to kill you yet. Call for Jeb."

"Jeb, food's here!"

"I'm trying to sleep. I will eat later!" Jeb shouted back.

I leaned closer. "You better think of something fast to convince him to come here, or I will blow your brains all over that far wall and then just speak with Jeb instead."

"The food gonna get cold! You know you hate cold food!"

"Fine, I will be right there!"

A door down the hall opened, and floorboards creaked as though someone very large approached.

Jeb entered the room. He was heavy set, early forties; he had a deep scar down the side of his left cheek. "Lenny, this food better be the best food on the fucking planet; if not I am going to break your fucking legs…" His voice trailed off when he saw me, gun pressed to Lenny's head. He reached for his pistol, but I shot him in the leg. Jeb collapsed and cried out as he grabbed the leg I had shot.

"Motherfucker, you shot me!"

I shoved Lenny toward him; pistol aimed at them both.

"Lenny, you might want to do something to stop Jeb from bleeding out."

Lenny ripped off his belt and cinched it around Jeb's leg.

I ignored Jeb's cries, "Lenny, go grab me two chairs from the dining room table."

Lenny moved toward the dining room. Jeb could handle pain better than I thought. I took my eyes off of him for only a second, but Jeb was fast. He pulled a snub-nose pistol that was hidden in an ankle holster and emptied it into my chest.

"Die, Motherfucker! That is what you get for shooting me!"

Five holes appeared in my chest; I felt each impact and pain. Not horrible pain but some pain.

Pain? That was new. So, add another consequence of using the ring.

I ignored it and smiled at Jeb. "It is impossible to kill something that is already dead."

Lenny froze, mouth open.

"Lenny, my patience is wearing very thin. Bring those chairs now."

He brought them over.

"Now take Jeb's guns and help him into a chair."

Lenny went over, and took his guns away; dragged him to a chair, and zip-tied him down.

"Now sit in the other chair."

Lenny sat, defeated. I tied him down and stepped back.

"Everyone comfy? Depending on how this goes, you can die slowly or quickly. Where is my daughter? Or have you already sold her?"

"Fuck you! I'm not telling you anything!" Jeb spat on the floor in disgust.

Lenny looked at me. "How you ain't dead? Jeb shot you five times in the chest. You s'sposed to be layin' on the floor. I'll tell ya what I know, but you gotta let me go."

I could see his aura. I was not going to let him go.

I reached back and pulled the sword from its scabbard. The light in the room seemed to bend toward it as soon as it was clear.

Recognition crossed Lenny's face. "It's you! You the one killed Malcom, John and Sam — put their heads on the kitchen table!"

So, you saw the message I left at the Walnut house.

I smiled. "Yes, it was me! Tell me where my daughter is!" my voice rose.

"Who the fuck are you?" Jeb demanded.

"You want to know who I am? Let me show you."

I reached out with the blade of the sword. Jeb tried to shrink back. I pressed the flat of the sword against his bullet wound. His flesh began to sear; the stench filled the air.

Jeb screamed; spit flew from his mouth.

I pulled the sword away. The wound sealed.

Can't have you bleeding to death before I get the chance to kill you.

Lenny had seen enough. "If it's info you want, Jeb knows it all. I'm just one of the grunts. I won't tell nobody. I'll just disappear."

"Lenny, you son of a bitch!"

"I will tell you what. Lenny, If I touch your forehead and if you don't react, I'll let you go. Deal?"

Lenny thought about it for a minute, "All you do is touch my forehead… Deal."

I placed my hand against his forehead and concentrated. I began my search for Sarah, but a wall immediately went up. I abandoned my search and pulled his victims' memories to me. I found one of him and Jeb. They had tortured a man to get him to give up the name who stole money from the Boss. They had used some extremely sadistic methods and when they were done Lenny shot him as he begged for his life.

"This is not the way this is supposed to work."

"I have not felt any pain in my head, so I will continue."

I pushed that memory into his mind from the start of the torture to the end. Lenny's eyes widened. He gasped and convulsed; his arms and legs tried to move but couldn't due to the zip-ties.

Jeb recoiled, horrified. "What did you do to him?"

I ignored the question. I let Jeb watch Lenny for a few more moments. Then I ended it. My blade arced, and severed Lenny's head. The wound sealed instantly.

Jeb gagged at the smell. Then he screamed.

"Jeb look at me!"

He began to hyperventilate.

"Jeb, look at me now!" I slapped him. He stopped.

"I grow tired of games. Tell me where my daughter is!"

I placed the tip of the sword blade right over Jeb's heart. It began to burn through his clothing and then it began to sear his skin. Jeb began to thrash in the chair.

"Tell me or the blade moves again."

Tears filled his eyes. "I can't. The Boss will kill me and then my family!"

I began to slowly push the blade into his body. The blade burned his flesh as it moved.

"Please stop! Please… I beg you make it stop!"

"Jeb the Boss can't hurt you or your family anymore. He is dead. I killed him. How do you think I found you? Now where is my daughter?"

"The Boss is dead?"

"Yes, I threw him in the shredder at the warehouse."

This revelation changed everything.

Defeated, he sighed. "She is with the other girls in the cellar. The door is padlocked. The key is in Lenny's pocket."

What? Sarah is in the house? She has been here the whole time.

I stared at him. "Why didn't you tell me that first? Before I did all of this to you and Lenny?"

"I was afraid of the Boss. I have seen what he has done to people who betray him and their families."

The Boss's power over them was terrifying.

"Jeb, in my job."

What used to be your job. I reminded myself.

"I am required to make you suffer like Lenny did, I will spare you that agony."

"I started to move the sword forward swiftly to finish him off when a pain shot through my head. A harsh reminder of who was actually in charge. I withdrew my blade and stared at Jeb.

"What — you are not going to kill me?"

"You are in luck, for now. You get to live." I sheathed the sword.

"I need one last thing from you before I leave. Who were you going to sell the girls to?" He hesitated, then gave me the name. I hurried out of the room.

I moved quickly down the hall to the door with the padlock. I did not need a key. I ripped the padlock off, opened the door, and found a switch on the wall. Light came on above the stairs and below. Whimpers rose from the cellar. I took the steps to the bottom two at a time.

At the bottom, I turned the corner. Three girls were chained by their legs to poles, gags across their mouths. I recognized Sarah immediately, though she was now eight years old.

I approached her; all the anger and rage left my body. She backed away, I could only imagine what I looked like to her.

"Sarah?"

Recognition crossed her face. "Daddy?"

"Yes, baby, it's your Daddy."

She began to cry and rushed into my arms. I could feel her. I had found her at last. Tears began to flow from my eyes.

Her voice muffled, "Daddy, Mommy told me you were an angel. Why do you have blood on you? Angels aren't supposed to have blood on them. Where is Mommy?"

The realization that her mother was gone broke me. I began to sob.

We released our embrace. I turned to the other girls. They saw I meant them no harm; so, they let me remove their gags. I broke the chains that held them all.

"Come on, girls. Let me get you out of here."

I lifted Sarah into my arms. Together we climbed the stairs, out of the cellar, and into the night.

We arrived outside Elizabeth's parents' house around 5:00 p.m., two days later. The other two girls I had taken to the nearest police station, along with a note that listed the addresses of the houses and the warehouse, and information on the death of Detective Rojas. He was still listed as missing, and I wanted his family to have closure. I stayed long enough to ensure the girls were cared for and safe before I left.

I took some clothes from a nearby laundromat, and since we had no money to stay in a motel, I found a shelter where we could shower and spend the night. The sword was hidden away so as not to draw attention. Sarah asked about her mommy again, and I finally had to tell her that mommy was an angel now. She cried in my arms and eventually fell asleep exhausted. I cried with her.

We headed out the next morning, on what would be my last day with her.

We stood together, stared at the front door. Only I understood what was about to happen.

"Sarah, you know your daddy and mommy love you."

"I know Daddy. Mommy told me that all the time you were gone."

My heart broke. *Why would Death make me agree to something so horrible? I could not interfere in her life. Did that mean I could not even keep an eye on her?*

"Sarah, Daddy has to leave, and I will not be back. Your Grandma and Grandpa will take care of you."

"No, Daddy don't leave me again. Please!"

"I don't want to, baby, but I have no choice."

"Are you going to go be with mommy?"

"Yes, sweetheart, I am going to go be with mommy. We will be watching over you."

She hugged me tight, tears in her eyes. I almost broke down again, but I had to be strong for her.

"Now, Sarah, I need you to go up there and ring the doorbell for me."

I gave her one last hug not wanting to let her go. She turned and rang the doorbell. As soon as she looked away, I activated the ring and watched from the afterlife.

The front door opened. Elizabeth's mother looked down at her granddaughter.

"Sarah… Oh my God Sarah! She looked around nervously, "Where did you come from? How… did you get here?"

Sarah looked back, but I was gone. "Daddy brought me here." She started to cry.

"Oh, sweetheart. I know you miss him so much. Kevin! Call the police!"

"What?" came a voice from the other room.

"Call the police. I have Sarah."

A few seconds later Sarah's Grandfather appeared in the doorway, talking on his cell phone.

"Yes, send a police car. My missing granddaughter Sarah has just shown up at our door."

"Carrie, how did she get here?"

"She said her daddy brought her here."

I stood and watched. Her grandparents surrounded her with their arms shielding her. I knew Sarah was in good hands. The television was on, a reporter speaking as information scrolled across the screen.

"We have two stories to report this morning. The two girls who had been missing for two weeks and walked into a local police station two days ago are now reunited with their families. We have breaking news: police announced this morning that they have discovered an extensive child trafficking ring within the city limits led by this man Mr. Steven Trulio known in the criminal underworld as the 'Boss.' Police have been trying for years to charge him for crimes committed by his organization. He is suspected in the disappearance of Detective David Rojas, who

went undercover two years and has not been seen since. Police also announced the arrest of Jebediah Cross, one of Mr. Trulio's known associates. Officials have refused to comment on Mr. Trulio's whereabouts or on any possible arrest."

Good, the girls were back with their families. The Boss's organization was finished. Now all that was left was the buyer. Sarah was safe and I had all the time in the world. I would make sure that whoever this buyer was would never be able to do this to another family again. The ring's power yearned to be released as I watched Elizabeth's parents carry Sarah inside and close the door.

THE RETURN from the afterlife had been one of the most brutal. There had been no flashback this time. The anguish from being shot five times by Jeb radiated through my body. The pain and wounds took a lot longer to subside, but in the end, I returned to normal.

I now stood outside two giant wooden doors on the third floor of a three-story office building.

"Alright, Death, on the other side of this door is one of the most vile and sick human beings there is. The man who was going to purchase my daughter. I am going to go through this door, and I am going to make sure he suffers and after that I am going to leave and that will be the end of it."

I waited for pain to shoot through my head, but there was nothing.

"OK, I am going to count that as I have your permission."

I had killed every one of his security detail except for one, his aura was clean; him, I had knocked unconscious.

I reached out with both hands and shoved violently at the two doors. They splintered inward and I unsheathed my sword and walked into a large office.

Expensive paintings lined the walls.

At the back of the room; two men waited. They both stared at me as I entered. One sat behind a desk in front of a wide window; the city's skyline glowed behind him. The other one stood to one side of the desk.

Both of their auras were black as night. They exuded evil.

I crossed the room.

The man on his feet stepped forward to block me and reached inside his jacket. A handgun appeared in his hand. He raised it and pointed it at me.

I walked toward him until the barrel pressed against my forehead.

"Do not come another step closer."

I smiled. "I am going to give you a choice. Put your gun away and walk, or I can send you to Hell where…"

He pulled the trigger. I fell to the ground. He shot me three more times in the chest.

I watched him holster his gun and turn back toward his boss.

"What a dumbass bringing a sword to a gun…"

He never finished his sentence. I interrupted him this time. I had stood up while he was talking, his boss in disbelief, unable to warn him until it was too late. I had placed my sword in the middle of his back and shoved it through. The blade instantly incinerated his heart.

"Fight… is that what you were trying to say?"

I withdrew the blade. The man fell to the floor. I turned to the man who sat at the desk.

His eyes were wide, big as saucers.

"I can pay you whatever you want… I am a very rich man."

"I know you are, Mr. Victor Langford. CEO of Metals Trading and Scrap Export."

I paused, and a big evil smile crossed my face. The ring's power pushed me.

"But money is not why I'm here. I am here to make sure you

are never able to do to someone's family what you did to mine! Of all the families in all the world your seller, Steven Trulio, chose the wrong one. He murdered my wife and kidnapped my daughter, all so she could be sold to you!"

My sword arced out and I cut his left arm off. "That is for Elizabeth!"

He screamed.

My sword arced out again and I cut off his right arm. "That is for Sarah!"

I set my sword on the desk. My hands clamped down on his wounds. He screamed again.

I slammed him into the window. Safety glass shattered into thousands of pieces.

I held him suspended three floors above the ground.

I concentrated. Memories from all of his victims flowed into me and then with brute force I slammed them into his mind.

He convulsed, a raw cry tore from his throat. All those memories of those he had harmed repeated in his mind one after another.

I held him there so he could feel their pain and suffering.

Then I tossed him out the window.

"That is for me!"

He fell and crashed onto a BMW below. The roof caved, windows exploded.

Sirens could be heard in the distance. Red and blue lights flashed as police cars turned onto the road which led to the building.

The man I thought I had knocked unconscious staggered into the parking lot.

So much for getting away without using the ring.

I pressed the sapphire. In an instant I was in the afterlife. I watched as the police cars arrived.

A few seconds later that unmistakable pull gripped me.

In an instant, I no longer stood in the office.

Death had summoned me once again.

I dropped to one knee and bowed. This time, I looked at Death directly.

"Brax, I see you found your daughter."

"I did, my Lord. She is safe. Thank you for allowing me to dispose of that filthy piece of trash just now."

I hesitated.

I had to ask as this might be my last chance.

"My Lord, who gave me the ring?"

Death ignored both my gratitude and my question.

"You have found your daughter. My promise is fulfilled. This will be the last time you kneel before me. If you violate our agreement, I will cast you into the heart of Hell. Do you understand?"

"I understand, my Lord. I will not violate our agreement."

"Good. Then be gone. You have caused enough problems. Do not return to my realm unless it is necessary."

"Goodbye, my Lord!"

I bowed once more and left the chamber.

The ring heavy on my finger.

He'd come for me eventually. But not today.

There were still evil souls out there that begged for my blade.

STARDRAKES AND SCRUTINY

HONORABLE MENTION

RUTH CLARA

"FIRST," I said over the sound of an entire enemy base burning to the ground, "objective. Steal that ship." I pointed across the cratered courtyard to a battered hulk whose engine was somehow still glowing.

"That's suicide, Grip," Dav protested.

"Second," I continued, ignoring her, "strategy. Use the flames for cover where we can — a couple singed scales won't kill us."

"Says *you,*" she muttered.

"Third, contingency. There is none. We do this or we die."

"That's what I like to hear." Pax hefted his blaster, outfitted within an inch of its life with every widget he'd ever scrounged from a battlefield we weren't supposed to take anything from.

"Pax, I want you to trail behind a little. If anyone starts shooting at us, you pick them off."

He grinned, showing a jumbled mouthful of needle-pointed teeth. "Can do."

"*And they raced ever onward, onward,*" the final member of my quattuor warbled.

"Ven," I said, "you stick with me. Good work today, brothers. Now we just have to get out of it alive. Ready?"

Two nods. Dav rolled her eyes, which was her way of saying yes.

"Okay. Let's move."

"Congratulations, sergeant," I said, but the words sounded about as hollow as I felt.

Sergeant Volkan Karatay gave me a tight smile and said nothing.

I inwardly kicked myself. Didn't the man deserve a sincere congratulation? He'd been through hell for this. It was my stupid fault anyway.

After all those years keeping our heads down, my quattuor just *had* to get put in a do-or-die situation and come out guns blazing. Competence kept you alive, but too much of it attracted attention, and attention from the Rienzi higher-ups was always dangerous. Not that I would have just laid down and died, even if I'd known the outcome. I was no prophet, no Krol or Wybran. I was just a corporal.

I tried again. "No one deserves it more than you." It sounded a little more genuine that time. A very little more.

"Thanks, Grip." He didn't look grateful, though, just… tired. "Go round up the others and get them ready for inspection."

"It's just a formality, brother," I pleaded. I was tired too — dead tired.

Karatay gave me a warning look. "There are no formalities for the Stardrakes, Grip," he said.

So that was that.

Supposedly some empires' militaries were completely separate from the populace, but on our base, it was hard to tell where Bastion Isaros ended and the tiny but bustling Settlement Isaros began. I danced my way through the gathering crowd of merchants and workmen, all of them gathering at the rising light of the second star of Isaros like moths to a flame.

Most were Rienzi, like me — though many were subjects rather than citizens, so their transformations hadn't advanced beyond a few patches of scales and maybe slightly sharper fingernails than usual. The odd Isoldi or Braut tradesman wove through the crowd, trying not to attract notice.

Who knew, there might've even been a couple of Vurmen blending in with their soft, completely untransformed bodies.

But it wasn't my job to pick out trespassers. I left that to the bastion's Officers and kept walking. Navigating the base was a lot easier when your transformation left you head-and-shoulders above the average.

"Corporal Mazal." A familiar voice rang out as I crossed the yard, clear as a bell, produced by a person's throat and yet totally impersonal in sound. I turned to see Captain Verveda.

"Heard," I said with a salute. "You are my brother and my master."

Before his promotion Arend Verveda had looked ordinary, and for the most part he still did, unless you looked too close — close enough to see that his blue irises were too bright, had no pupils, looked almost faceted; that the veins under his skin had turned to a brilliant red and seemed to glow; that he moved wrong, more like a bird or a lizard than a person, especially when something surprised him. Also, there was a look in his eyes these days that I couldn't quite place, but which seemed absolutely unnatural.

Other than that, he was totally normal.

"Three days ago, our sister base took a Vurmen woman into custody from a suspected heretic ship," Verveda began, rotely and without preamble. "She appeared in some distress and continually asked about the man she had been travelling with, though they did not recover anyone else from the wreckage.

Yesterday she disappeared from that base, along with Officer Jurgen Boeks of Civilian Enforcement."

"Brother," I responded automatically, not knowing what else to say.

"It is suspected that she may investigate nearby bases in search of this man."

I blinked. "You're sure?"

"Why would she take an officer with her, except to ensure her access to other bases? I have no doubt that she will attempt to free this man."

"He's her husband, brother?"

"Worse," Verveda hissed. His teeth showed and his eyes narrowed. That unnatural look brightened in his eyes. "Much worse, Corporal. He is the heretics' Krol, a man called Yosef."

"The heretics'…? I thought they didn't believe there *was* a Krol."

"Clearly their doctrine is not so ironclad as we thought," he said sharply.

"Understood, brother."

"Tell your quattuor, and be alert."

"You are my brother and my master." I bowed my head in rote respect. "Uh, Captain, Sergeant Karatay is set to be promoted, so we'll be getting ready for the inspection —"

He waved an impatient hand. "Very well, then. Focus on the inspection."

In a flash I realized what the look in his eyes was — or at least what it seemed closest to. It was an expression of acute pain. On impulse I asked, "Can I get you anything, master? Tea?" Verveda had been an infamous tea fiend in his non-commissioned days.

He looked at me like I'd said something unbelievably stupid. "I require only the Impeccable Wine of the Stardrakes."

"Of course, brother," I mumbled.

"Good news, brothers," I said, ducking into the tiny hole the Drakes had the nerve to call a barracks room. "Sarge has been promoted."

Two pairs of eyes and one impenetrable void turned toward me. "And how exactly is that good news, Grip?" Dav asked.

Pax turned back to scrubbing nonexistent grime off his disassembled blaster. "Don't be stupid," he said, though he didn't sound all that enthusiastic himself. "It was only a matter of time — Sergeant Karatay is the best there is."

She glared at him. "Don't you ever stop fondling that thing?"

He worked a brush between two microscopic gears. "Nope."

"You should get yours disassembled and cleaned, too," I told her. "Sarge wants us ready for the inspection."

Dav shuddered. "Right. If there's one thing we need, it's some scaly red hood basta —"

"Easy," I warned. Pax rolled his eyes and went back to the phaser, apparently above it all.

"Still," Dav resumed, "our sergeant. How can they do that?"

"He'll still be on base," I said evasively.

"It won't be him, you know that."

"He wouldn't be the first."

Her jaw clenched. "It's different when it's us."

The three of us enlisted with Volkan straight out of majority, and through our unique blend of luck, wit, and idiocy, we'd managed to stay together. I was the only pessimist of the group, and it would have been a lie to say I didn't get some sick joy out of being proven right.

"It was only a matter of time before the Higher Prophets honored him," Pax said in that same flat, measured voice.

"Honor, my — they just want another pawn to push around and they figure he's strong enough to survive the process."

"Could you quit blaspheming already, Dav?" I snapped, sharper than I should have. I was tired, all right?

"Who says it's blasphemy?" she shot back.

I glanced at the only person in the room who hadn't voiced an opinion yet. "What do you think, Venerat?"

The mass of darkness shifted under its uniform and hooded cloak, and Nescio's deep, warped, singsong voice replied, "*'Who can resist the call of the Eternal Song of the Great Ones of the Stars?' the Singer asked. And the people answered him, 'No one, no one.'*"

"Thanks, Nescio, that's really helpful," said Dav.

The hood dipped as if its wearer had inclined his head, but I knew perfectly well that he had no head to incline. Nomen Nescio had never actually been ordained as a monk, but we called him Venerat, or Ven, nonetheless.

"They don't just look for good officers, though," she continued as Pax slid the grip of his blaster back together with a sharp *click.* "Don't they also look for devout Travelers? That ain't exactly our Sarge."

I shrugged, hoping she'd drop the subject.

"Maybe they're running out of devout Travelers," she suggested acerbically.

"*Davenport,*" I pleaded.

"*In times of confusion the man with few counselors does well; a man may be killed by a single wound,*" Nescio said suddenly.

We looked at him for a minute. "Where is that even from?" said Dav.

"The Sayings of the Wise, Path… Five? I think?" I pinched the bridge of my nose, hard. Sometimes I wonder if maybe I should have gone into seminary after all, but my parents would've gone ballistic. "No idea what he means by it, though."

"So are they gonna make you the new sergeant?" she asked.

I snorted. "Not a chance. They'll bring in some new

starched-coat from a hub system because anyone promoted from within the ranks won't receive the respect of his men. According to the Vassals, anyway."

"Yeah, I wonder where they got that idea," she said.

Pax slammed the lower receiver of his phaser to the floor, whipped his head around to glare at the rest of us, and said, "There's something you all seem to be missing."

"We should stop talking and get ready for the red-hoods?" I guessed.

"Corporal Mazal, my brother, my master, *we can fail the inspection.*"

"*Up came the Krol, and there before him the Gate stood open...*"

I sat quietly, swaying to the gold-hoods' impeccable song.

All commissioned officers were required to attend, and non-coms like myself were *strongly encouraged* to. I didn't mind listening; the songs had fascinated me even as a child.

I glanced down at my hands, now clawed and heavily plated. Had they really been so soft once, flecked only with tiny, pliable scales?

"*Up came the Krol, and looked into the Keeper's eyes, and behold, he was changed...*"

The Keeper — the Great Drake of the Rienzi Gate.

I hadn't seen It, not even for my transformation. The red-hoods handled all that. Even so, it took much more of an interest in Its system than the Keepers of the other systems. Transformation wasn't passive on any Rienzi planet, not like the Isoldi or Braut systems — it was doled out based on merit.

That had seemed like a great system until it turned its eyes on my quattuor's sergeant.

"Up came the Krol, and the Wybran stood beside him as a witness."

"Praise, praise to the Krol," I mumbled with the rest of the attendees. Sergeant Karatay sat across the room from me, but I couldn't read his expression.

"Down came the Wybran, and red was his sword."

"Hail, hail the Wybran." The current Krol didn't have the traditional red right hand, but he'd been acknowledged as Krol less than ten years before, so I supposed allowances could be made.

"They drank of the Impeccable Wine of the Stardrakes, and their followers attuned to the Song."

"The Song, the Song, the Song," we concluded. The goldhoods closed the book, and I stood to leave.

"Heard the Sergeant's getting promoted," someone said, elbowing me in the side. I looked down to see Corporal Rusnak. He was most of a head shorter than me, but tenacious and built like a brick. He led the First Quattuor of our cohort, I the Ninth. We didn't get many flowers, but it kept us out of trouble.

"I heard that too," I said.

"Anything to do with your heroics on Avernum?"

"You'd have to ask Verveda." I shouldered past him and walked out.

I had a meeting to attend.

"First off," I said, slapping my open logbook down on the table, "objective. Fail the Vassals' inspection."

"Secondary objective: get executed," said Dav, propping her chin up with one fist as she stared skeptically at the points I'd outlined.

"Second," I continued without making eye contact, "strategy."

"*But behold, against the wisdom of the Great Ones, all strategy came to nothing.*" Nescio's voice echoed from the shadows behind me without warning.

"Light of our Lady," I swore, suppressing the urge to smack him as I jumped away in surprise. Dav stifled a giggle. "For the last time, Nescio, just walk up like a normal person!"

"*Forgotten, forgotten, all was forgotten,*" Nescio quoted from the Tome of Laments. He sounded apologetic, or at least I thought he did. When a guy only speaks in quotes from the holy texts of the Elder Drakes — like the baby of our quattuor does, as a random example — it can be hard to tell what he means.

"Sure, man," I sighed as his form coalesced out of the shadows — sans uniform this time. Fortunately, his outline is fuzzy at the best of times, so I wasn't seeing anything I shouldn't have, if you know what I mean. "Listen, we're getting inspected in a couple of days, so I need you to remember for a while."

He gave me a crisp salute with a hand that fuzzed in and out of visibility. "*'To hear is to obey,' the Hero replied.*"

"Great. Perfect." I hesitated, thinking of what he had said initially. "Ven, when you mentioned strategy just now — were you trying to say we shouldn't follow through on this?"

He straightened, looking startled — but, again, that's just a guess — and shook his head.

"How come *his* opinion matters?" Dav complained.

"Because he might turn us in if he thinks this goes against the teachings of the Elder Drakes."

Now it was her turn to look startled. "Would you?" she asked Nescio.

He shook his head again.

"See? We're fine."

"Are you sure, Ven?" said Pax. "I mean, we *are* planning to lie to the Stardrakes' Vassals when they come."

"*A truthful man always knows a mistruth, but a lie to a liar is no lie at all.*"

"Sure, that clears it up," Pax mumbled.

"Back to business," I said firmly. "Strategy."

THE RED HOODS arrived two mornings later — sort of. The assembly bell rang out just a couple hours after we went to bed.

I jumped up from the floor, trying not to drag my feet. My body ached. We'd done nothing but drill since the announcement of Karatay's promotion, and I for one was sick of it.

"Big day," Dav said from the darkness.

"*The King rose early on the day of battle,*" Nescio quoted.

"Thanks, Ven, but I'm just a corporal," I said.

Half an hour later we stood at attention with the rest of the base while three red hoods strode up and down, examining.

"We have the sergeant to thank for this, huh?" someone in the quattuor next to mine muttered out of the side of his mouth.

"No," I replied as evenly as I could. "You have the invincible wisdom of the Stardrakes."

I knew I had bigger fish to fry, but I couldn't shake the memory of my conversation with Captain Verveda. There was something important about it, I thought. The Krol was the Stardrakes' ruler, the latest in a long line of chosen kings. Supposedly. I'd never seen him, but they said he lived in the capital city in one of Rienzi's hub systems.

We'd been taught that the heretics believed there was no Krol, and therefore that ours was a false prophet — hence the war. But if they'd chosen a Krol of their own, what did that mean for our dispute?

See, I thought, *I'd understand this a lot better if I'd gone to seminary.*

We performed a number of drills as Captain Verveda called them out, and just as the first star was rising, they sent us "back to your regular duties."

"What's that supposed to mean?" Pax grumbled as the rest of the base dispersed around us. "Our *regular* duties right now would be sleeping for another half hour and then getting breakfast."

"I guess we have an extra half hour for breakfast, then," I said. "Cheer up, would you? We're waiting on an inspection, not a funeral."

"It could be both," Dav moaned.

I ignored her and started off toward the food stalls, still thinking.

"Say, Grip," Pax said, trotting up next to me, "I've been thinking."

"Never a good habit to get into," I said offhandedly.

"Yeah, thanks. But don't you think the red hoods'll be a little leery of old Venerat Nescio over there?"

I glanced back at Nescio. "Why?"

"He's not Rienzi." He spoke quietly, as if embarrassed by the admission.

"Really? I hadn't noticed."

He rolled his eyes. "Don't get smart with me, Grip, you're not suited to it. But don't you think that might put a wrench in things?"

I shrugged. "Not really. He was training to be a monk before he joined us, and they're much stricter about who they let in. If the priests were okay with Nescio I doubt it'll be a problem for the red hoods."

"Fair enough," he grunted, but he still looked doubtful. I kept walking and said nothing, hoping he'd drop it.

Most people on Isaros go to the mess hall for their food, but given that we had an inspection and some extra time I decided to splurge that morning. To say nothing of any ulterior motives. I got a packet of buns stuffed with some kind of synthetic protein and pulled Nescio aside, since he didn't eat. Pax and Dav stood back, hotly debating the merits of seemingly every food under the stars.

"What do the Books say about the Krol?" I asked quietly.

He cocked his head — or anyway, whatever he had instead of a head. "*Knowledge is as a fire,*" he said quietly. "*Too much of it burns a man.*"

"I didn't ask you for a lecture, Ven. What do the Books say?"

"*So the scribe opened the inspired tome,*" he said resignedly, but I thought there was a hint of a smile in his voice. He paused as if running through the text in his mind. "*The Krol, the Krol, who loves all the Rienzi as a man loves his wife or a father his tender son, the man who slays the darkness and leads all systems toward peace.*"

"Why don't the insurrectionists believe in the Krol?"

Nescio shifted uncomfortably and said nothing.

"What was that?" Dav asked as she and Pax joined us. They'd both gotten the same as usual, but they always argued about it first.

"Nothing," I said. "Captain Verveda said there was an insurrectionist near here looking for their Krol."

She frowned. "I thought they didn't have a Krol."

"Exactly."

"Isn't that a little above our pay grade?" said Pax.

"Yes, it is," I said, feeling vaguely foolish. "Verveda said to keep an eye out, that's all."

"When should we be ready for the inspection?" Dav asked with her mouth full.

"They have a ceremony to begin the inspection proper when Isaros's stars align." I glanced up at their slow march. "So we still have a couple of hours before —"

"*Even within your own lifetime there will be those who say 'This man is the Krol' or 'This man is not the Krol.' But you will know him, for he will come from among the True Drakes with a song upon his lips,*" Nescio interrupted.

"Could you lighten up?" Dav snapped.

"*He will not be as ordinary men,*" he continued insistently, "*and will have no father to teach him. The king, the king, he will serve the Heralds and the Eternal Song.*"

"Venerat," I said, trying not to snap at him, "I asked why the heretics *don't* believe in the Krol, not why we *do.* I know he was one of the Higher Drakes before his Ascension and that his father disowned him."

"What's all that scrap about singing?" Dav scoffed.

"It's used as a metaphor for wisdom in a lot of the texts," I said. "It's not literal. Our Krol was the only person ever to answer every question correctly at the Higher Drakes Academy on Rienzi."

"What do you mean, *our* Krol?" Pax frowned at me. "You meant *the* Krol, eh?"

"Undoubtedly," I said.

"'Cause you know what those red hoods might do to us if they catch you talking like that."

"You are my brother and my master," I said. "Yes, I know."

"*I* am? You're in charge here, pal."

"Doesn't feel like it sometimes." I couldn't help a wry smile. "But you're right. You all remember the plan?"

"Brother, master, all that," Dav muttered around another mouthful of breakfast.

Pax nodded.

Nescio said, "*Take care that you hail no man as Krol except for the man who sings.*"

"That's enough of that," I said irritably. "I get it, Ven, okay?"

He nodded, but something told me he was unhappy.

"You see that?" Dav asked suddenly, pointing upward. I squinted, trying to follow her finger, and picked out a distant, tiny, twisting golden shape, surrounded by frills of starlight.

"A Lindvurm?" Pax said, baffled. "What's it doing this close?"

"I mean, it's not *that* close."

"Shut up, Dav."

"Do you think there are Vurmen on it?" I asked idly. Unlike the people in the systems, the people who lived on the backs of the Lindvurms didn't show any signs of transformation.

"They usually keep their Vurmen away from us," Pax reminded me.

"Smart of 'em," said Dav.

A few years back we'd been sent to pick over a Lindvurm, after the battle had been won and the red hoods had had their way with it. The memory came to me, suddenly, unbidden, in vivisected flashes: limp hands — bare, dry organs — toothless mouths — faces frozen in fear, pain, fury, humiliation — slick, red skulls without faces. None of us knew what the red hoods had wanted. None of us wanted to know.

"I'm going a little farther into the Settlement," I said. "You guys stay here."

They looked at me for a minute. "What's up?" Dav asked.

"Nothing. I'll just be a minute."

I shouldn't have been so bothered. Why did I walk away through the crowd of largely untransformed subjects and citizens without making eye contact or returning their hesitant, friendly smiles, without even a clear idea of where I was going? Whatever the red hoods had done was for the glory of the Rienzi Empire and the good of its citizens.

And, besides, what did I think I could do to change anything? My quattuor might be a real terror for the middle-managers of the system, but when things got serious, we played the perfect part of Rienzi's lap dogs. There was nothing we could do to change that.

So shut up about it, I told myself sternly.

"Sir," a voice rang out over the crowd.

But a split second before I heard it, I *felt* something. It's hard to describe; I've never experienced anything like it before or since.. It felt kind of like being tapped on the shoulder, or like hearing your name through a hubbub of irrelevant voices. But mostly it felt like someone had reached through my back, grabbed my organs, and yanked.

I spun around, disoriented and irritable, and scanned the people around me. I didn't quite understand why I was so certain the person was talking to *me,* nor did I recognize the voice. After a second my eyes landed on someone politely but firmly pushing his way through the crowd towards me.

He was a year or two younger than me, I thought, and tall — at least for someone with no visible Rienzi transformation. I took him for a subject, albeit an unusually well-fed one, rather than a citizen.

"Can I help you?" I tried not to growl the words, with limited success.

"Sir," he said, dipping his head in greeting. "It's an honor to finally meet you. I know so little about you, but —"

"What?" I said, baffled. Isaros has its share of lunatics for sure.

"Of course — you don't know me." He stuck out a hand. "I look forward to working with you."

"You're a contractor?" The fog seemed to clear. Maybe that explained —

"No."

"Ah," I said, baffled once again.

"I've been looking for you for a good long while." He had a strange accent, I realized, something I hadn't heard on Isaros before. Was he a merchant from some other system? Then why did he look so much like an untransformed Rienzi subject? "What's your name, sir?"

Why did he keep calling me *sir?* It was an archaic word, long discontinued in favor of the more enlightened *brother* and *master.* And hot on the heels of that question came another: if he'd been looking for me for so long, why didn't he know my name?

I was saved from having to answer either by a sudden, enraged scream from back the way I'd come. I didn't recognize the voice, but shoved my way toward it nonetheless. The initial scream died off, succeeded by a lot of yelling, most of it curses.

The crowd had cleared back in a rough circle, giving its occupants a generous berth, and I wasn't a bit surprised to see Dav inside it. She was pacing back and forth, and Pax — bless him — kept pace with her step for step, staying between her and the circle's other two occupants, a man and a woman.

The man was Rienzi, though pretty low-class going by the sparseness of scales on his hands and face. His companion I wasn't sure about. He had her around the waist to keep her from hurling herself at my quattuor-mates. Her face, a bizarre pale green, was completely suffused with fury.

All four of them were shouting, which didn't bode well for any attempt to separate them, but I strode into the middle of the circle nonetheless.

"Dav," I barked, turning toward her first. "*Davenport!*"

She whirled, seeming as ready to fight me as she was the other woman, but recognized me and hesitated. She also stopped yelling, which made Pax stop yelling, which made the other Rienzi man stop yelling, leaving only the green-skinned woman.

"*— and if you will not recant your words, it will be my pleasure to ram them down your throat!*"

"Ma'am," I began, not in the mood to arbitrate a dispute I knew nothing about.

"Dav started it," said Pax.

"Real cute, Hematti," Dav snarled at him. "I didn't do anything, Grip, I —"

"Then what do you call —"

"— delivering an offense so vile, to me, to my —"

"— you could have *tried* to apologize —"

"All of you!" I snarled at the top of my voice. That quieted them down again. I let out a deep sigh and turned to Pax. "What happened? Davenport, don't interrupt."

She scowled.

"Maybe *you* started it, my brother," Pax said as if reconsidering. "All that talk about the Krol. Anyway, Dav said something about how stupid the heretics have to be to think ours isn't —"

"That's not what I said," Dav snapped.

"Daven —"

"I would be more than happy to relate to you *exactly* what she said," the green-skinned woman interrupted me maliciously. The man with her still hadn't spoken since he stopped yelling. He wasn't holding her anymore, but still had a hand on her shoulder as if to ensure she didn't make any sudden moves.

"Go ahead," I said reluctantly, with a warning glance at Dav.

"She said, 'I don't love our Krol, but you've got to be some kind of inbred backsystem moron to think the real Krol is someone else.'" The woman adopted a lower voice and attempted to imitate Dav's accent.

"Anything else?" I asked. "Be *quiet,* Dav."

"There would have been, had I not silenced her foul mouth."

Dav hadn't seemed all that *silenced* when I came up, but I kept that thought to myself. "Is that what you said?" I asked her.

She scowled. "More or less."

"Word-for-word," Pax clarified.

I pinched the bridge of my nose firmly. "We'll talk about that later. Wipe that grin off your face, Hematti."

Pax sniffed.

"My brother," the Rienzi man began diffidently, "this woman is not completely in her right mind."

I took another look at him. Tall, decently well-built, sort of plain. He wore no uniform, but he looked like he was used to wearing one — something about his posture and the directness of his gaze. "What's she doing here?" I asked.

"Transfer point. I'm taking her to one of the convents on Javonao."

"What's her name?"

He twitched a little — I was almost sure of it — like he was nervous. "Jade," he said. "Jade Azekh."

I made a mental note to check for that name in the system and make sure there was actually supposed to be a mental patient named Jade Azekh passing through today. You know, in my copious spare time.

"I'm sorry for the trouble," he went on. "We'll be going now — unless there's anything else you need from me?"

He played the part of a convent orderly well enough, but I wasn't anywhere near convinced. "Go ahead," I said anyway. "No harm done."

"Grip," Dav protested. I glared at her, and she got the idea and shut up. The two strangers didn't need any more encouragement to clear out, and the crowd followed suit, a little disappointed that they hadn't gotten a better show. Try as I might, Davenport had a bit of a reputation as a roughhouser.

"*Truth and heresy will always come to blows,*" Nescio said, suddenly at my elbow. I jumped, biting back a curse.

"Where have you been this whole time?" I snapped, not so much because he could have done anything to help as because he'd startled me and I was still feeling off-balance from talking to that bizarre subject.

Nescio shrugged.

"Fair enough."

"I can't believe you just let her go," Dav moaned. I rounded on her as a much more deserving outlet for my frustration.

"And *I* can't believe you were talking heresy *out loud, in public, on the day of our inspection!*" I hissed. "You kept whining about how we were going to get executed, well, here's your chance."

"Come on, we talk like that all the —"

"When there aren't red hoods on Isaros, sure, but not right now! Are there any brains in your head whatsoever, or are you an inbred backsystem moron too?"

She looked at me, blinking, her mouth open.

"Leave off, Grip," Pax almost wheedled. "She gets it, okay?"

"As long as she does," I grumbled. "I don't know why I still put up with this."

"You are my brother and my master, and you wouldn't know what to do without us," Pax said.

"You've got that right." I drew in a long breath and let it out. "Everybody ready for our inspection?"

THERE HAD BEEN seven or so red hoods at the general inspection of Bastion Isaros, but only three of them were present at the Inspection for Heresy — the first of three tests for our quattuor. They also had me stand off to one side — they didn't say why — which gave me an excellent view of my quattuor's failure.

"Private Freya Davenport," one of them began in the strangled, hissing voice of a fully transformed — though not ascended — Rienzi. I couldn't tell which of them it was; they all sounded the same.

"You are my brother and my master," Dav replied, looking a little nervous.

"Private Freya Davenport, who is the Krol?"

"Uh… he's our ruler."

"And?"

"And… the future ruler of all the systems?"

"By right or via conquest?"

I'd skimmed enough seminary entry tests to recognize a trick question when I heard one, and Dav sailed merrily straight into it. "Via conquest," she said, the picture of confidence. "Otherwise, what are the Bastions for?"

"Thank you," the red hood hissed, scratching something down.

Pax's interview was much the same.

"By right or via conquest, Private Kaveh Hematti?" the red hood asked.

"By right," he said, neatly evading the trap Dav had fallen into. Then he doubled back into it by adding, "Otherwise we'd be fighting a lot harder, wouldn't we?"

"And the Krol's Wybran?"

"Not important, or else ours would have one."

"Indeed," the red hood whispered, scribbling again.

Nescio was the only one I was really worried about. I didn't know whether he would — or even could — go along with our plan. But we'd explained it to him, and he seemed to be willing to go along with us. He was a strange one. As far as I could tell the only authority he recognized was that of the Travelers' Krol. So why was he going along with our scheme?

Or had he simply been lying?

"Private Nomen Nescio," the red hood began. "You are the member of the quattuor from the Svaera Monastery, discovered by their esteemed Elder. Is that correct?"

He nodded, but they must not have accepted that as an answer.

"*Is that correct,* Private Nomen Nescio? Answer, or you will be held in contempt."

Nescio's void-filled hood swiveled toward me. "That's right," I said. "He… has trouble speaking. He only quotes the Texts."

"Is that so," the red hood murmured, writing something. "Private Nomen Nescio, who is the Krol?"

"*The Krol, the Krol, who loves all the Rienzi,*" Nescio replied, but instead of finishing the full quote he'd given me yesterday he left it at that.

There was a pause while they waited for him to continue. "And?" one of them prompted.

"*...and leads all systems toward peace,*" Nescio said falteringly.

And on it went. Like Dav and Pax, he gave simplistic answers, sometimes only half-correct. Nothing heretical, of course — just enough to give the red hoods pause before promoting our commanding officer as a bastion of the faith.

Then it was my turn. I barely remember what I said, but my interview was no more stimulating than theirs had been.

NEXT CAME the Inspection for Leadership, where they interviewed us again, this time about Sergeant Karatay's performance record. Our plan here required a little more precision.

"Oh yeah," Dav chattered enthusiastically. "Best officer I ever had. He knows the difference between on and off, y'know? Not too good to spend an evening with his inferiors once in a while. We still call him brother and master over drinks, though, don't you worry about that. We know our place and so does he. But he's never proud. That's what we love about him."

"Private Freya Davenport," one of the red hoods said. "The question was regarding your mission six main-system degrees ago, on —"

"Oh, of course, I'm sorry, I remember now. That was a great mission! Sarge — sorry, Sergeant Karatay — is so good at planning, but what he's really best at is coming up with a new plan when the old one goes to — well, you know what I mean. And our plans never work out how he wants them to," she laughed. "But we always get there in the end."

"Private Freya Davenport, if you could direct your attention to the particulars..."

I almost felt sorry for them. They attempted to interview Dav for an hour or so, then called in Pax, but he was no better. He was more than happy to regale them with stories about his own competence and bravery, but any mention of Karatay was an afterthought, and usually a vaguely unflattering one.

They didn't bother interviewing Nescio for this part of the inspection, so after Pax it was my turn.

"I love the guy," I told them. "Lets me do my job, you know? Very hands-off. He does his job, too, but I don't know much about it. He keeps his duties to his world and I take care of mine. I do a lot of administrative work for him so he has more time for… uh, the important stuff, I guess."

The red hoods didn't seem too cheered by my input.

THE THIRD AND final round of their inspection was the Inspection for Weakness — an all-around physical fitness test. Dav and Nescio were the most agile members of our team, I formed the brawn, and Pax was the best shot I'd ever met.

Not one of us performed more than one standard deviation from average. We scored better than an ordinary quattuor, but "better than ordinary" wasn't exactly what the red hoods were looking for.

They took their records with them, saying they'd confer and respond within a week. I wasn't optimistic about that time frame.

"Do you think we made it?" Dav asked frankly a day or two later. "Failing the test without putting our lives at risk, I mean."

"We'll have to see." I poked at my tray of indeterminable slop and wished with all my heart that Rienzi would pay us enough to eat at the food stalls more than a couple times a month. But the poor food quality wasn't the real reason for my lack of appetite.

"I thought we did okay," she pressed.

"So did I. But what *we* think doesn't matter all that much, now does it?"

She joined me in my glum silence.

A FEW DAYS later the Sarge pulled me aside while the others were busy on the range. "I need to talk to you, Grip," he said.

"You are my brother and my master," I responded automatically. "What's up?"

"We've heard back from the red hoods."

I blinked and told my heart to stop trying to beat its way out of my chest. "Already? What did they say?"

He pulled an official-looking document out of his jacket pocket and read, "*After deliberation, the Assembly of Stardrakes has determined that, while Sergeant Volkan Karatay's recommendations are as excellent as expected, certain details have complicated his promotion process. We initially proposed to find another candidate, but having re-reviewed the material obtained during the full investigation, we believe we have already found one.*" Karatay looked at me expectantly.

"You are my brother and my master and I don't know what you just said," I told him, but my heart sank. Whatever this missive meant, it wasn't what we'd been trying to accomplish.

Karatay sighed. "You're replacing me," he said.

I stared at him for a second with my jaw hanging open. Finally I worked out how to talk again. "I… you…" I said intelligently. "You're joking, right?"

"You're funny," he replied, though there was no humor in his smile. "They decided that your accounts of me implied a different situation than the one they'd been given to believe. They think the quattuor's success is thanks to you, and I was just an incompetent figurehead."

There was an impressive lack of bitterness in his tone, but I still felt like something he'd found on the bottom of his shoe. "Sarge," I managed, "I…"

"Careful," he warned me. "The Stardrakes might not like what you have to say."

"I don't think you would like it much either."

He gave me a sharp look. "Grip… you didn't do anything stupid, did you? During the investigation, I mean?"

"Depends how you define stupid," I mumbled.

"You *idiots,*" he said, but he almost sounded impressed. "You really tried it, didn't you? Even knowing what could happen to you if you got found out."

"Brother, master, I disavow everything," I said, fighting not to grin at him.

"Well, enjoy your new position, *Sergeant* Ivo Mazal," he said. "They'll hold the official ceremony in a week."

Just like that, my grin vanished. And my stomach felt like it had dropped into space. "Ah," I said. "Right."

THAT NIGHT I TOOK A WALK. Soldiers weren't supposed to venture out into the Settlement proper after curfew, but I knew a way in that didn't go through any of the gates. As long as you were quiet about it, they tended to let it slide.

The Settlement was almost as quiet as the Bastion had been — the Legion was just as strict with subjects as it was with soldiers when it came to curfew. They'd sent my quattuor out once or twice to "quiet" the inhabitants. Not my favorite task, but you couldn't have everything.

I stared aimlessly out into the distant stars. That Lindvurm still twisted in the far, far distance. I was surprised they hadn't sent a group out from Bastion Isaros to chase it away yet, but they could be a lot to take on without adequate planning. Some of them got bigger than ships.

“You,” a voice rang out, startling me from my reverie. I turned to see the woman Dav had gotten into that scrap with by the food stalls, her face set in anger. She held a blaster, which I recognized as a standard-issue officer’s weapon. Who knew where she’d gotten it, but she probably could have had her pick of young recruits with more hormones than brains. *Blast it* — I’d forgotten to look her up. In my defense, I’d had a lot on my mind.

“Can I help you?” I asked, for lack of anything else to say.

“That depends.” She stepped closer, and I saw that her face was locked into the same rictus of anger she’d worn the first time I met her. “Can you explain to me why I have not found my Krol, although your people claim he is here?”

I just stared at her, dumbfounded. “Come again?”

“I do not understand what you mean by that.”

“I mean I don’t know what you just said. Also —” I wasn’t sure why I said this “— you should be careful saying things like that. You could get into a lot of trouble with the Stardrakes. They only acknowledge one Krol.”

“As do I. We simply disagree on which is the true king of our generation.”

“You really are crazy.” I almost had to admire her. “Maybe that’ll keep your head attached. But I don’t know what you’re talking about — there’s no Krol here.” Then, like lightning striking, my numb skull finally made the connection. “You’re the woman who kidnapped Officer Boeks, aren’t you? But you’re not Vurmen.”

She let out an enraged, guttural hiss. “You should not speak of that which you do not understand,” she spat.

I sighed, shaking my head. I didn’t like having that blaster trained on me, but my scales would provide some protection, and she held it like a civilian; she couldn’t hit me enough times to take me down before I reached her, I hoped. “That was Boeks with you in the marketplace, wasn’t it? Where is he now?”

"You should be more concerned with *me,* you false drake," she sneered.

"Your manners need work," I shot back, "but fine — I'll bite. What do you want?"

"I want you to help me find someone. Officer Boeks is a good man, but he has proven woefully inadequate in this area."

"You're looking for this supposed Krol, aren't you?" I eyed the blaster in her hands, which showed no sign of wavering.

"*Supposed?* He is the first true king we've had in centuries."

"Are you an insurrectionist?"

"I wish only to follow the Krol. If that pits me against this alleged Empire, I will fight it to the death."

I sighed. There's just no talking to some people. "How exactly am I going to help you if Boeks couldn't?"

"The right hand can always find its owner."

I squinted at her, trying to work that one out, but before I could another problem presented itself.

A shadow appeared behind her, wielding a blaster of its own. "Jade," a man's voice said, filled with irritation and relief, "you have to come back with me. Now."

That voice… "Officer Boeks," I said.

He twitched. The barrel of the blaster flicked toward me for a second before he thought better of it and pointed it tentatively back at Jade. Who was standing almost directly between us. I took a couple steps to the side so only Jade's blaster was trained on me.

"If you do not stop moving, I will shoot you on principle," she warned me.

I wasn't *sure* she would do it, but that type of crazy might do just about anything. I stopped moving.

"Officer Boeks," I said urgently, "help me arrest her and I'm sure —"

"Sorry, pal," he interrupted. "I've got my own thing going on."

I ground my teeth. "You went with her willingly? Why?"

"Oh, quite the opposite," Jade said airily. "But I think I've grown on this officer of yours. He will not return so easily to your *Empire.*" She almost spat the word. "He loves me far more than your false king."

"He's pointing a blaster at you," I felt bound to point out.

"Ah." A slow smile spread across her face in the darkness. I thought she looked different than she had in the market, but couldn't pin down why. "He *is* still a red-blooded male, is he not?"

I sighed. "Rienzi blood is green."

She waved the hand that wasn't holding the blaster. "La."

"Boeks. What's in this for you?"

Boeks shook his head sharply. "Just forget you ever saw us," he barked. "Jade, *come on.*"

Jade turned halfway around to stare at him, but not far enough that I thought I could take her by surprise. "Jurgen," she said softly, "are you — are you still loyal?"

"Jade," he said, sort of hopelessly.

"Do not call me Jade. Call me by my true name or call me nothing, *Officer.*"

"What's going on?" I asked.

"Jade, listen to me." Boeks still had the blaster pointed at her, and now he looked like he might actually use it. "Everything I've done is for you. Just trust me. This is the safest way —"

"I know what you want to do to me!" she shrieked. "You want *your* people to twist me into something else, to give me a new form, a new name."

"If we don't find a cure —"

"I *have* found one. But you will not help me look for him."

"If you're going to be at this for a while, can I go?" I interrupted. Jade turned back toward me, her eyes flashing. They were literally glowing, I realized with a start — and, by their light, I saw what was different about her. Her skin was *greener* than it had been, by a long shot. Even the shape of her face seemed different. But it was the same woman — I was sure of it.

"Stay where you are," she hissed.

I raised my hands. "You are my brother and my master. But what *are* you, exactly?"

Her lips formed a warped smile. "The subjects of your Empire, those who first found me, called me Azekhasher'strezymanaia'ikharizan'khelarish."

"The lost girl whose form cannot be contained," I translated. "Is that your true name, then?"

"You know something of the Sages' Tongue," she said.

"I should have gone to seminary. You didn't answer my question."

"Which one?"

"Pick one."

"It is the truest name I have left," she said.

"Right, well, now I just have more questions." I clicked my teeth together a couple of times. "Boeks, I need you to —"

I broke off. My gut had gone all hot, something like it had in the market weeks ago.

I didn't need to hear the voice to know who was approaching in the darkness.

"Azekh?"

A *familiar* voice. It was that not-quite-right-in-the-head subject of the Empire I'd run into in the market — though now I had to wonder if he was either of those.

"Sorry I took so long, I —" He paused, apparently taking in the situation.

"Take your time," I sighed.

"So I've found you again, too, sir." Again with the archaic terms of respect. He inclined his head to me, then turned to Boeks with eyes of iron — itself an archaic material. "I'd advise pointing that somewhere else," he drawled.

Boeks glared back, then shifted his blaster from Jade to the stranger. "You're the one she's been looking for, aren't you?" he said.

It occurred to me once again that this situation was rapidly turning pear-shaped, and also that there was nothing I could do about it. I'd left my blaster in the quattuor's hole in the wall, not expecting that I would need it in the middle of a settlement filled with people half my size. Served me right — they'd spent months drilling into us that a soldier should always, *always* have a weapon. Then again, we'd spent the last several years systematically forgetting our training in favor of what actually worked in the field.

"If you hurt him —" Jade swung her blaster away from me toward Boeks, eyes blazing. I tried not to feel left out. "Did you ever care for me at all, Jurgen?"

"This isn't the time for that question, darling," he replied. His eyes never left the stranger.

"Both of you stand down," the stranger said firmly. "We'll have time to go through all of that later. Right now, I need to talk to this man." He gestured toward me.

"Get in line," I answered, not in the mood for any of what was happening.

He smiled, unbothered by the blaster pointed at him. "But Azekh has already found me. She doesn't need to talk to you. Boeks was also looking for me, not you. So I'm the only one *in* the line, ain't I, sir?"

"Yosef, if you do not do something I may kill this man," Jade warned. Boeks gulped.

The stranger — Yosef — looked at her for a second, then pulled out a blaster of his own and pointed it at her. "How's this?" he asked. "It's the best I can do, under the circumstances."

I reconsidered my assessment. Maybe he *was* touched in the head. "Who is she looking for?" I demanded. "Who are —"

"Please, Yosef," said Jade. "I've waited for so long…"

"Don't move," Boeks snapped to Yosef, then turned to Jade,

his voice meticulously soothing. "Darling, this kid can't help you. We bring him in, I can get you the help you need."

Jade shook her head wildly. "Help? No, your people would not help me — they would destroy me. If you love me, why can't you see that? Why —" The blaster wavered in her hands. I tensed, readying myself in case one of the three lunatics discharged a blast —

"Okay," someone called. "Everybody relax."

And I did — because I recognized *that* voice, too. It was Dav's.

"You are my brother and my master and you shouldn't have left your blaster in the barracks room," Pax added, emerging from the darkness opposite her voice.

"*Beware, beware,*" Nescio said, melting out of the night. Right behind me.

"Ven," I muttered, "*how* many times —"

"You're all going to chill out really fast," said Dav, "or we're going to start shooting. Put those toys away."

"Yosef," Jade whispered.

"I know," he said gently. "Put it down. We'll figure this out."

She did as he said, but there were tears on her face. Yosef dropped his blaster, too, and Boeks quickly did the same.

"All right," Dav continued. "Hands on your heads, nice and easy."

"*Yosef.*" Jade's face contorted, almost involuntarily. "I can't — not much longer. Please. Do something."

"Easy," he said.

I started to think that maybe the lost girl whose form cannot be contained might do something unexpected. "Careful, Dav," I said. "She's… weird."

"You can say that again," Dav snorted. "Step toward me, lady."

Jade glanced around wildly. If she stepped toward Dav she'd be moving away from Yosef, and though I didn't understand why I knew that was the one thing she absolutely didn't want to do.

I squinted at her in the dark. Something was writhing under her robes.

"Davenport…" I said.

"I can't," Jade whispered. "I can't, I can't, I can't…"

"Toward *me!*" Dav commanded.

With a howl of despair, Jade… *erupted* into a fountain of impossible limbs, appendages, at least a dozen different faces — all of them screaming. I jumped back on instinct; my shouted curses lost in the uproar of her transformation.

With my quattuor distracted by whatever *that* was, Yosef sprang across the ground in a flash. He touched a hand to the writhing mass that *had* been Jade and…

I can't tell you exactly what he did. I hesitate to call it singing, because it wasn't, but it was less unlike singing than it was unlike everything else in the universe. When it was over, a pale-skinned woman, who I recognized with a shock as Jade, stood in the place of the abomination she'd erupted into. Yosef stood beside her, looking almost feverish, his eyes bright and his face pale.

"Everybody all right?" he asked, his voice hoarse from —

Some primitive reflex prevented me from finishing that thought.

"Yeah," Dav said shakily. Pax stared.

"Light," Boeks swore at last. "Aw, *blasted* Light of our Lady and all the blasted Heralds, I —" He stared at Yosef. "You…"

A stunned stillness fell. Nescio moved first, striding across the room to kneel in front of Yosef. "*But you will know him,*" he said, his warped voice shaking, "*for he will come from among the True Drakes with a song upon his lips.*"

"*The king, the king,*" I responded automatically, "*he will serve the Heralds and the Eternal Song.*"

Yosef smiled, a totally unselfconscious expression. "Didn't

think I'd be recognized so easily," he said with his typical candor. He looked me straight in the face with those feverish, too-bright eyes. "But I'd expect no less from you, my friend."

I shook my head, frowning. "You don't even know my name."

"No — I know something better. I know your calling. I'm here to give it to you."

I felt my eyebrows climb in absolute disbelief and waited for him to elaborate further. But the next speaker wasn't Yosef — it was Nescio.

"*With the Wybran at his right hand, all worlds are open to the Krol's singing.*"

"Venerat," I muttered. "Don't be stupid."

"He's completely right," Yosef said firmly. "I came here to find you."

"No," I said, shaking my head. "No, that's stupid. I'm not… I can't be…"

"You *are.*"

I shook my head some more. My quattuor stared at me. Boeks and Jade were looking at each other.

"Darling?" Boeks's voice trembled. "You're… better."

"I *told* you he could help me. Why do you never listen?"

"Then he's really…"

Boeks turned his eyes on Yosef in something that was very nearly awe. Personally, I hadn't looked away from him since his bizarre declaration. What had he *done* with Jade just then? He'd fixed her with a song somehow. But singing was for dry services and figurative language. It wasn't — it didn't —

"Ninth Quattuor!" Sergeant — now Corporal — Karatay's voice rang out as he appeared from the darkness. My night's brooding was getting awfully crowded, I thought hopelessly. "There you are! What are you all doing *here?*"

"You are my brother and my master and…" I paused, at a loss. "It's the place to be, I guess."

He stopped, taking it all in. "Who are they?"

"Officer Boeks, the woman who abducted him, and the heretics' Krol," I said. "I think."

"That's right," Yosef said with another smile. "And you're coming with us, mister…?"

"Corp — Sergeant," I corrected him, then myself. "Sergeant Ivo Mazal. And, no, I'm not. I can't —"

"Grip, listen to me," Karatay interrupted. "We just got word from the red hoods. We're being executed."

I just stared at him, my ability to process bizarre information completely shot.

"The embarrassment of a failed promotion," he explained rapidly. "They changed their minds, decided it's better to claim we died on a mission before the promotion could take place."

"Wh… *all* of us? Dav and Pax and Ven, too?"

"The whole quattuor," he confirmed. "But they'll take me to be one of the mute servants in the Svaera Monastery, if I ensure everything goes to plan."

"But you're telling me," I said.

Karatay hesitated. "You… you were willing to risk yourselves for me, with what you did in the investigation. You were the only quattuor that did. I can't just sentence you to death."

My eyes stung, and I blinked hard. "Well, I appreciate that, but I'm not sure there's anything I can do about it."

"There is," Yosef interrupted. "Come with me. Follow your calling. Be my Wybran, the one who opens the world to my song."

Karatay frowned at him, then turned back to me. "You want to explain what's going on?"

I shook my head helplessly. "The crazy kid just helped the crazy girl. She thinks he's our Gate's destined king — and he thinks I'm the chosen one."

"Not *the* chosen one, Ivo Mazal," Yosef put in. "But *a* chosen one, naturally, and *my* chosen one, specifically."

"Grip? *Our* Grip? No way," said Dav. "No offense.

"There is a way," Yosef insisted. "Where the Eternal Song is concerned, there is *always* a way." His eyes bored into mine the same way his song had drilled through my ears. "Will you stay here and die, sir? Or will you come with me and become what you are meant to be?"

"*Meant?*" I snorted. "Meant by what, brother?"

He looked at me levelly and responded to my irony with absolute sincerity. "By the Eternal Song. That which I serve. That which you *must* serve."

Nescio said, "*'Who can resist the call of the Eternal Song of the Great Ones of the Stars?' the Singer asked. And the people answered him, 'No one, no one.'*"

I looked at him sharply. "You really think I'm all that, Ven?"

Once again, he seemed to incline the head he didn't have.

"It's better than being executed," said Pax, still eyeing Jade warily. "Probably."

I should have gone to seminary. I opened my mouth to tell Yosef to jump into open space without a suit — but my squad was watching me. They trusted me — and if I didn't step up, they were going to die because of me.

Destiny felt shaky, but duty? *That* I could do all day.

"Well, then," I said with a deep sigh. "I guess we need a plan, don't we?"

"*And they raced ever onward, onward,*" Ven warbled.

I couldn't help a smile, despite all that had happened. "Ready?"

Three nods from my quattuor — Karatay, Pax, and Nescio.

Three from Yosef's motley crew.

Dav rolled her eyes.

"Okay. Let's move."

Our cluster sprinted across the pavement, Pax lingering behind to pick off anyone who saw us. Karatay went first, badge in hand, slamming it against one of the containment bay doors.

After about ten years it let out a quiet beep. The door opened.

"Go, go, go!" I howled. A childish, idiotic grin erupted across my lips. Karatay dove into the pilot's chair, with Officer Boeks beside him as copilot. Pax rammed his blaster into his shoulder and hit a couple of the base's more enterprising soldiers with blasts set to stun. Served them right for being overly competent.

The ship's engine roared. Everyone except Yosef grabbed one of the handles as we shot away. He stood there like it was level ground.

"*They pursued like howlers on the hunt,*" Nescio warned as a couple of smaller ships peeled off from Bastion Isaros.

"That way." Yosef pointed into the darkness. "Top speed. No limiters."

"We won't last ten minutes," Boeks snapped. Karatay wrenched the ship into a spiral, avoiding a spatter of fire.

"We don't need to. See?"

In the distance, the Lindvurm twisted.

"You're kidding," Karatay groaned.

"No. Do it now."

Pursing his lips in frustration, our former Sarge did as he was told, turning the space around us into gold and silver bars.

"You guys must be crazy to come with me," I muttered.

"You are my brother and my master," Dav said, "and you wouldn't know what to do without us."

Try as I might, I felt a grin spread across my face. "You've got that right."

MORE FROM CANNON PUBLISHING

Join the Crew!

Stay up to date! Sign up for our newsletter at https://www.cannonpublishing.us/_for the latest updates on new releases and more.

Follow our authors at their Amazon Pages!

J.F. Holmes
Shane Gries (Dragon Award Finalist)
Lucas Marcum
Al Hagan

James Copley
Jason Kyle
G. Scott Huggins
Michael Morton
Jon LaForce
Jason Weiser
Kal Spriggs
Brian Gifford
Charli Cox
Dan Kemp
Jonathan Shuerger
J.R. Wise
Steven Vickers
David Hensley
M.L. McIntosh

Great Series from Cannon Publishing

The Fae Wars

An ancient enemy invades Earth, returning to claim their home world. The men and women of the US Military find themselves matching technology against magic as cities burn and armies clash.

Volume One: Onslaught
Volume Two: The Fall
Volume Three: Futures Past
Tales From the Occupation: A Fae Wars Anthology
Volume Five: Insurgent
Volume Six: Ghost
Volume Seven: Northwest Front
Volume Eight: Vendetta
Volume Nine: Relics of Empire
Volume Ten: Harley's War
More Tales From the Occupation

Irregular Scout Team One

In July of 2016 a plague swept the world, and the civilization collapsed and fell. For a lone National Guard sergeant, a veteran of the wars overseas who had settled down to a new life, the nightmare began on a hot summer evening at the barricades. Orders and chaos, gunfire and being overrun, his unit dwindles away in the face of the infected.

Volume 1
Volume 2
Volume 3: Civil War
Volume 4: Bad Company

Volume 5: End of Days

The Line

When the world descends into chaos and anarchy with an unbelievably swift plague, turning victims into ravenous maniacs, the soldiers of America's storied 1st Infantry are asked to hold the line. From the brutal streets of urban combat to the bloodied, desperate defense on the plains of Kansas, they fight a war against an unrelenting enemy who used to be their fellow citizens.

As civilization falls, can they hold the line?

The Thin Dead Line
Dead Storm Rising
The Big Dead One

Fallen Empire

Empires rise, but Empires also fall. The Terran Union has spent five centuries under the control of the alien Grausians, like a barbarian tribe under the thumb of Rome. Now, after almost two decades of civil war and succession struggles, the formerly subject races have settled back in their ancient territories to lick their wounds and re-arm, leaving hundreds of settled planets to exist in a political vacuum. Into that space steps the free companies, mercenary units that fight for gold, honor, power and glory. Veterans who can't get the wars out of their souls, new recruits looking for adventure, corporations with their own agenda. Join us in a 27th Century that echoes history.

The Irish Brigade

Overrun
Silent Violence
Doom Company

Dirty Deeds Trilogy

Sandy Decker had a problem. Well, multiple problems. Some good, some bad. Some pretty bad. The good problem is that she was up a whole bunch of credits and the title to an Azelia class yacht called Vagabond King. That was the good problem. The bad problem was that she was in debt to Daresh An-Jaska, Former Princeps in the Golden Legion, Grausian exile, and the biggest gangster in the sector. Not a money debt but a favor debt, one that she paid principle on doing favors in return. Dirty deeds that never seemed to pay enough, of course. That was until yesterday, when she found a line she couldn't cross.

Vagabonds: A Fallen Empire Novel

Athenaeum, Inc

The Professor has problems, and not just what decades of soldiering did to his back and his knees. His boss just died, leaving him as CEO of the extremely discreet intelligence contractor Athenaeum, Incorporated. His old buddy the Operations Director is a highly skilled Army Ranger veteran but his finance chief is slightly unhinged and spends her money on highly inappropriate work outfits. The surviving old men on the Board of Directors are stuck in the 1970s. Running Athenaeum out of an old Cold War bunker and keeping their roster of experts together is expensive, but the government contracts are drying up or going to bigger, flashier corporate players.

Door Number Three
Doubling Down
Triple Play: The Battle of Cell Tower Hill

Off World

When nuclear war erupts on Earth, the American colony in the Alpha Centauri system is left stranded. As the new day dawns, a furious attack by the native inhabitants threatens to overwhelm the colony's defenses. It's left to the thin red line of the US Army's 9th Regiment to stem the tide and ensure humanity's survival in this harsh new world. From two time Dragon Finalist and author of the best selling series "Irregular Scout Team One" and "Invasion" comes a new tale that tells of the struggle for survival on a brutal planet.

Offworld: Ragnarok
Offworld: Expeditions

Valkyrie

Humanity engages in a desperate struggle with an alien species for this side of the Orion Arm. Space ships die in instantaneous bursts of light and turn into vapor, but on the ground Marines scream and lie wounded in the mud and blood, praying for the Valkyries to come save them. They aren't wishing for death and a Nordic goddess to take them to Valhalla, the wounded are praying for the men and women of the '348th Field Hospital MEDEVAC to dive through fire and hell to come save them. Because they know that ...Valkyries never die!

Valkyrie

Valkyrie: Rebellion
Valkyrie: Attrition

High Caliber Awards

The Cannon High Caliber Awards are an annual contest for new writers. In it we ask them to submit a novella length story of Science Fiction, Military or Fantasy genre to challenge their skills.

2024
2025
2026

The Wishkiller Saga

While on patrol Captain Aethal Paaling discovers evidence that an ancient terror has reached the rich soil of his home: the Lotus, a prolific growth whose addictive leaves devour their victims from within turning their hosts into horrible, terrifyingly violent mockeries of humanity. Created at the dawn of history by the twisted power of a godly relic called the Well, the return of the Lotus may be a harbinger of even more horrors to come.

A Cold and Mortal Spring
War of the Shattered Moon

Hexen

When nine out of ten people in the world have died in a brutal plague, what do those who remain do to pick up the pieces? Does the creed, "Duty, Honor, Country" have a place any more if there's no country left? On his way across the devastated remains of Texas, Marine Corps veteran and survivor Eric Marten rescues a young woman from a vicious attack by men who have turned into savages. As Dani slowly learns to trust him, they try to stay alive in the deathlands that America has become, using all their wits to survive a post-apocalyptic nightmare.

90% Death Rate: A Post Apocalyptic Thriller
Angel of Death: A Post Apocalyptic Thriller
The Bloody Princess: A Post Apocalyptic Thriller
The Devil's Pitchfork
Crescent City Shootout

———

Hell Train

A single train carries what might be the last vestige of civilization through a hellish nightmare.

A few hundred alive out of millions, lights going out all across what was once America as the possessed arose from the dead and murdered the living. A few hundred survivors travel across the country in an armored train, seeking some place to shelter in a fallen world. All that remains is a dystopian nightmare marked by rains of blood, impossible horrors, and portals to Hell opening in the skies.

Hell Train: All Aboard
Hell Train: Green Line

———

Invasion

More than a decade after the Confederated Earth Forces were defeated, their commanding general, a boyhood protegee, lives in exile and disgrace. His life on an isolated farm is forever changed when two strangers show up at his homestead, and the war comes crashing back down on him. The problem though, remains the same. How do you fight an enemy that is technologically superior and holds the high ground?

Invasion: Resistance
Invasion: Day of Battle
Invasion: Total War

Into the Darkness

A darkening tide of barbarism was washing across Britain's shores and the lights of civilization were slowly flickering out into darkness, only kept burning by the legendary Red Dragons cavalry unit. Led by their Tribune, Arthur, who serves no kingdom but goes where the fight is hardest and most crucial, they wage desperate battles to keep back the tide. The Red Dragons ride the length of Britannia to fight the invading Saxons, Scoti and Picts, wherever they show, from across the seas or down from the Highlands.

Beyond the Wall
The Wolves of Caledonia

Semper Die

The dead rose expecting a feast. What they got was a firefight.

Sergeant Alex Slaughter and the Marines of Alpha Squad

were on a routine training exercise near Quantico when everything went silent. No comms. No command. No clue.

What they find when they return to base is worse than anything they trained for: a bioweapon has unleashed a zombie virus that has shattered civilization, and now they must survive the Collapse.

Lock. Load. Semper Fi. Semper Die.

Semper Die
Espirit De Corpse

More Books from Cannon Publishing

Military Sci-Fi/Fantasy Anthology

Path to Freedom: The Path, Book One

The Hundred Worlds

MECHA

Under A Different Sun

Sea of Fire: Demonrise

Hell's Bells: War & Love Downrange

Cannon Fodder: Tales From the Gun Crew

Troll Hunter